Second Chances
at the
Cottage
by the
Sea

BOOKS BY REBECCA ALEXANDER

Rebecca Alexander

Second Chances at the Cottage by the Sea

bookouture

Published by Bookouture in 2024

An imprint of Storyfire Ltd.
Carmelite House
50 Victoria Embankment
London EC4Y 0DZ

www.bookouture.com

ISBN: 978-1-83790-734-2
eBook ISBN: 978-1-83790-733-5

To my son Carey, who has always been my first reader and editor.

PROLOGUE

18 MAY 1953

The pregnant girl twisted from side to side, the oxygen helping a little as she gasped. The midwife pressed her ear trumpet to the side of the labouring mother.

'The baby's heart rate is dropping,' she said, listening to the instrument. 'Is she going to need a caesarean?'

Dorothy patted the girl's forehead with a damp cloth, as the contraction eased off. 'You poor girl,' she soothed. 'As if you haven't had enough troubles in your short life.'

Hector came back into the room, gowned up. 'How is she?' He took the mother's thin wrist in his fingers. 'We can't wait too much longer,' he warned.

'I can – do – it,' the girl ground through her teeth, staring into Dorothy's eyes.

'I believe you can,' Dorothy said. She glanced at the midwife, who nodded. 'It's time to push now, dear,' she said. 'With the next pain.'

It went very swiftly, Dorothy urging the young woman on, the midwife helping turn the small baby, and Hector quick with his stethoscope when the child was born.

'She's tiny,' he said, deftly clearing her airway. A thin cry rose into the air and the mother turned her head away.

The mother looked grey, and Dorothy made sure the gas was flowing. 'Well done,' she said to the girl. 'Very well done. Rest now. She's small but strong.'

'I want her to go to a good home,' the woman whispered.

'She will. I've already been in touch with a lovely adoption agency, and a social worker will be coming over to the island in a couple of days.'

'I want to go home before then,' the girl murmured, muffled by the mask.

'You need a few days to rest, before you do.' Dorothy looked over at Hector. 'I'll have her transferred to the Doctor's House as soon as she's stable. Then we can get her back to the mainland once she's well.'

'I don't want to see the baby,' the girl said, in a strangled whisper. 'Take her away. Just make sure she's all right.'

Dorothy lifted the little scrap of a baby in her arms, looking into the wavering eyes. 'I promise,' she said fiercely. 'We'll make sure she has the very best life.'

1

PRESENT DAY, 4 MARCH

Eleanor Markham's walk from the airport on St Brannock's Island was straightforward. There was just one main high street, and the civic building she was heading to was well signposted.

The shops were small and each one was painted differently. The focus of at least half of them was tourism. Gift shops, sweet shops, ice cream parlours, boutiques and cafés. Most were made of blocks of stone, maybe granite. They looked like they had grown out of the rock sticking up in the fields behind the town. The whole place smelled of the sea, unfamiliar to someone who was brought up on the Sussex Downs with its sheep farms and rolling chalk hills. This was a hard-edged place, the granite in walls and houses, heavy slate roofs on the buildings, small windows against storms off the sea. Spring bulbs glowed from every patch of grass and garden. It felt a million miles from the mainland rather than twenty-eight.

Eleanor checked her pale linen suit with its green-flecked waistcoat, which matched her eyes. Her bleached hair was easy, very short, taper-faded at the sides, but it felt overly smart here. She felt out of place where people seemed to dress in jeans and

T-shirts even early in the spring. She walked into the council offices and was shown to a waiting area.

The building was busy, and noisy. It doubled as an advice centre as well as a library, presently full of pre-schoolers and a couple of teachers.

'They're ready for you now,' the receptionist murmured. 'In the conference room at the top of the stairs.'

It had been a long time since Eleanor had had to interview for anything. Even now, she wasn't sure why she needed to be questioned about the services her company provided running music festivals all over Britain, as well as several around the world. The door was open and a group of people, mostly older women, looked at her.

'Miss Markham? Please come in.' One chair had been left in the centre of the long table.

'Thank you. Please call me Eleanor.'

One person whispered to another, and a man at the end passed a note. She couldn't help smiling as she counted five people. The last festival she had organised had sold forty thousand tickets, and she hadn't had to interview at all. The clients had come to them.

The woman who had spoken cleared her throat. She was tall, flamboyantly dressed in layers of tropical prints, with a mass of white hair caught up in a scruffy bun. She looked between sixty and seventy. 'Welcome. I'm Liz Retallack, the chair of our festival committee. I hope you had a good flight?'

'Very, thank you. It was a beautiful introduction to the Atlantic Islands.'

Eleanor's flight from Exeter had been smooth, barely an hour. She'd flown low enough to enjoy the wonderful scenery in Cornwall; she couldn't remember seeing anything like it before. Her mother had always been drawn north for holidays – Scotland or the Lake District. When the plane reached the rocky coastline, it almost felt as if it had launched off the cliffs to soar over the sea. The Atlantic was mottled with different shades of green from lime to almost black, until low hills ahead proved to be the islands. St Brannock's was the biggest, with a central town along the harbour, but several others had villages or houses dotted around.

'Do you know the islands at all?' asked Liz.

'No,' she answered, looking around. 'But I think one of them cropped up on my family tree.'

That made several of them look up and there was a murmur around the table.

'Well,' said Liz, 'as you know, the islands have received some public funding to develop a music festival. It will be limited by the capacity of the ferry and the space we can allow for camping. We're hoping festivalgoers will also take up rooms in hotels and local bed and breakfasts.'

Eleanor shook her head slowly. 'Most ticket holders will want the whole festival experience; camping is part of that.'

'What about older people?'

Eleanor smiled at her. 'The average age will probably be mid-twenties to thirties. The older visitors sometimes look for glamping options, like tipis or yurts. But you're right, some will want hotel rooms. Cost will be a consideration, of course, as the crossing is already quite expensive and they will have to pay for the festival ticket as well. Most *will* want to camp, and for free as part of the ticket.'

There was a ripple of conversation between them. 'I think,' Liz said slowly, 'you aren't familiar with the ferries. There is a limit to how many people and how much equipment can come across on *Islander III*.'

'I see.'

An older woman with short grey hair laughed. 'I'm Andrea, the treasurer. It seems that we *do* need help. How many visitors were we hoping for, Liz?'

'I suppose,' Liz said, 'several hundred at least.'

Eleanor looked at Liz. 'You're going to need more than that,' she explained. 'You'll need several thousand guests to have a chance to break even. And you need to put some money away to create a self-sustaining annual event.'

Liz smiled, immediately looking younger. 'You must think we're all absolute idiots trying to do this.'

'Not at all, and neither did the grant-making body,' Eleanor said briskly. 'I think it would help if you can give me all the documents you used to make the application. If you are happy to go with Sunlight Festivals, of course. But I think you should consider now whether you still want to run a music festival. It's an oversaturated market.'

'Your company was the only one that answered our call,' Andrea explained. 'I think we're too small for most of them. But we really need the exposure: an amazing percentage of the British public think we're either the Shetlands or the Channel Islands. We were surprised when your company got back to us.'

'That was me,' Eleanor said, blushing a little. 'I'm easing myself back into work after some time off, and I thought a small, new festival might be a great opportunity to set up something unique and charming.'

Again, they turned to look at her. 'Coffee, tea? And we have biscuits,' Andrea said.

'Coffee would be lovely,' Eleanor said, and the group seemed to relax, smiling more. 'What I really need to see is your original argument for the grant. Then we can make sure you fulfil their brief.'

Liz looked up and down the table. 'Is everyone all right with me handing over our grant application? I think we are agreed that we need to discuss this further with Eleanor before we proceed.'

There were nods all round, and a tray of teas and coffees was placed in front of Liz with a jug of milk. It was nothing like a work meeting; it felt more like a Women's Institute gathering.

Liz stared into Eleanor's eyes. 'I'm so sorry to hear you've had time off. I hope it wasn't an illness?'

Eleanor nearly choked on a bite of shortbread. She swallowed it down. 'A bereavement. I lost my mother.'

'Oh. How terrible.' Liz leaned in, fixing Eleanor with an intense blue gaze. 'And is it your mother's family that had a connection to the island?'

'Yes, but—'

'What was her family name? We might know someone who can tell you more about your family tree.'

The last few days of her mother's illness came back to Eleanor in swirling flashes, like a dream. 'I...' Eleanor put her palms down on the table and looked around the room. 'I really came to see if we can help you with your festival, and I think it's possible. I can review the conditions and vision from your grant application, and then perhaps we can talk over feasibility? If you want my firm to help, that is.'

'Have you booked somewhere to stay?'

Eleanor looked down at the details in her bag. 'I'm staying at a bed and breakfast place – the Doctor's House.'

'That's a wonderful choice. I'm sure you will be comfortable there. May I ask one more question?' Liz said. 'We were led to believe you are quite senior in the company. Would *you* be working directly with us, or would you send someone more junior?'

Eleanor could see how earnest she was, how much they all wanted the project to work. 'It would be me, with a few people to work out logistics and legal issues. I've decided to stay away from big ventures this year, work on small grassroots projects. They're quirky and individual.'

And it will give me time to ease back into work after months of looking after Mum...

.   .   .

The bed and breakfast was away from the town, along the high street and down a tiny lane with a couple of cottages in it. The property had a gate which led to a front garden, with spring flowers in bud. The house behind it was a Victorian double-fronted, impressive, with the winter skeleton of a climber over an open wooden porch. The house was painted light blue with white sash windows, several cracked open in the spring sunshine. The porch led to a navy door with a brass knocker in the shape of an anchor. It stood half-open, and the hall inside had a flagstone floor that looked cool and inviting. Eleanor's suitcase seemed to have damaged one of its wheels, and it rattled and bumped as she dragged it down the gravel path.

A woman peered around the door, then opened it fully, breaking into a smile. 'You must be Eleanor!' She was small and slight, grey streaks in her long brown hair, but it was difficult to guess her age. Maybe sixty, maybe more, although her face was barely lined. 'I'm Sally.'

'Yes, I'm Eleanor. What a lovely house.'

'It is. Come in, I'll put the kettle on and show you around. I hope you'll be comfortable,' she said over her shoulder as she led the way across a spacious hall, with several doors off it. 'I've put you in the doctor's old consulting room, it looks over the garden.'

Eleanor followed her into an enormous kitchen, the ceilings soaring overhead and a huge range against the wall putting out warmth into the sunlit room. In the middle was a long table, solid wood, that looked like it must have been constructed there. It had eight, no, ten chairs, mismatched and painted different colours. A back door stood open, blue flowers leaning over as if to get a look at her, daffodils nodding in the breeze.

'Can I get you something?' Sally said.

'I think I just need to unpack,' Eleanor said. Her eyes felt gritty after the long journey; she had left London long before it got light. Sadness had crept in over the day, knowing she was coming back to the island where her mother was born, and having just had her thirty-third birthday without her.

'Then would you like some tea? I have all sorts.' Sally looked so keen to be helpful, Eleanor gave in.

'Thank you. Whatever you're having is fine with me.'

Sally picked up the heavy bag over Eleanor's protests and carried it back across the hall to the opposite room. 'This is my favourite room. You have doors on to the terrace.' She pushed the unlocked door open.

French doors opened on to a garden with mists of bulbs in flower, shrubs covered with buds and a few small trees just breaking into leaf. A table and chairs looked over the garden from under a pergola. Spring had come early to the islands and miniature daffodils sprouted everywhere, even between the slabs of the patio. The old-fashioned bed looked comfortable; the wardrobe and chest of drawers were antique in a light wood. It looked like a room out of a magazine.

'It's beautiful,' Eleanor said, looking through the doors.

'You get yourself settled. Can I suggest something?'

'Please.' Eleanor was a little stunned by the place still. She took in the watercolour paintings of the coast that hung on the walls – she recognised the shape of the island from her aerial view as she'd flown in.

'I think I have just the right herbal tea for you, something to help you relax after your long journey. You look tired. It will be good to put your burdens down for a little while.'

Eleanor's eyes prickled and she dipped her fingers into a bowl of dried flowers, the scent of summer lavender and rose reaching her. 'Thank you. The room is lovely. And tea sounds nice.'

'I'll give you ten minutes to wash off the dust – the bathroom is just over there, in the old dispensary. Then maybe you can come out in the garden for your tea. And tell me your story, because you look like you're carrying one.'

2

FEBRUARY 1943

Dorothy Harding-Rowe sat on a slatted bench off a metal corridor on HMS *Dart*, which was bringing supplies and troops to the Atlantic Islands. She was tired and seasick, clutching her bucket and breathing in a little fresh air, which was pouring in the door as it was opened and shut by a seemingly endless number of young men in uniform. She had never worried much about her appearance, but right now she must look at her worst: pale, probably green about the mouth, and her clothes rumpled after her night on the train.

'We're making good time, ma'am!' someone shouted cheerfully as he walked past. She barely had time to register he was an American before *mal de mer* consumed her again.

'*Doctor*, not ma'am,' she struggled to say, long after he had gone, wiping her mouth on a handkerchief which was certainly going to be thrown away, if not burned. Her luggage had been stowed somewhere, and so she had no chance of getting a fresh one for now.

Fighting the nausea, she closed her eyes and leaned back, breathing as calmly as she could. She jumped when someone spoke to her.

'Ma'am? Do you need medical assistance?'

She looked into the light blue eyes of a tall man crouching in front of her, bracing himself against the wall.

'I *am* medical assistance,' she snapped back. 'I shall be completely restored when this ship is out of rough waters.'

He smiled, a crooked twist of amusement on his rather severe face. He stood up then, up and up, his thin frame making him look even taller than he was. Dorothy suddenly felt short and rather stout, wrapped up and hunched over in her best woollen coat.

'You must be the new doctor, then. Dr Rowe.'

'I am.' She squinted up at him. 'Dr *Harding*-Rowe.'

'I'd choose one name and stick to it,' the man said. 'The islanders are simple people. And this isn't what they would call rough weather, just a little fresh.'

He didn't introduce himself, but touched his cap and disappeared onto the deck, letting in a blast of cold air and even a shaft of sunlight for a few moments. She looked down at herself and sighed at the splatters on her silk scarf. This was not how she liked to present herself to strangers, especially attractive doctors. The ship lurched, and she resorted to the bucket again.

When the spasms subsided, she leaned back with eyes closed, and remembered the interview she had had with the medical board of trustees in Penzance a month ago. She could afford to buy the general practice that was for sale, with all its prior contracts, but would have little to live on. Her father had been adamant that he would not increase her allowance if she was not going to get married, and he didn't see why her brother should have to sustain her in old age.

Surely, a medical practice where there was no alternative doctor must at least cover its costs and provide a simple living? The retiring GP on another island had written to the board, asking for a younger practitioner and one with obstetric and gynaecological expertise, the last locum having been recruited straight into the forces. The islands had been without a full-time family doctor for more than three months.

The board had not seemed encouraged to see her, however. They asked questions about her medical training, certainly, but they seemed most concerned about the fact that she was female.

'We were wondering whether the candidate was considering marriage?' one gentleman had said, with great delicacy.

'I am not,' she had replied. 'I will be completely available for my patients.'

'We find that doctors are greatly supported by their... spouses,' he had answered.

'I will be assisted by staff at the practice,' she had said with more confidence than her dwindling finances could bear.

In the end, the board had to agree to her application as it was the only one.

The allowance from the National Insurance scheme was low, much lower than she had expected, and few families benefited from the scheme. It was dependent on breadwinners earning over a minimum wage, and the islands were known to be areas of want and ill health. The war had already taken the higher earners away, and some would not be returning, leaving many widows relying on small pensions. She had been buoyed by the knowledge that at least she would have plenty of patients, even if payment would be slow or less than she was expecting. Five shillings per appointment and more for visits would soon allow her to invest in good nurses, and perhaps even a trainee doctor.

But now, holding onto her bucket with her eyes closed, her head throbbing, she didn't feel quite so convinced.

'How you doin'?' came the same soft American voice. 'I brought you some water. You should drink.'

'I know I *should*,' she said, without opening her eyes. 'But I doubt it would stay down.'

'Doctor's orders,' he said with more of a snap in his voice.

'I'm a surgeon with the US Army, and I'm giving a medical order.'

She squinted up at him. He was smiling again. 'Indeed?'

'Captain Hector McBride,' he said, his voice softening. 'Drink up.' He disappeared again, leaving her with a bottle of cool water.

Sipping the drink was manageable, and he was right: within a few minutes she did feel less weak. By keeping her eyes shut and feeling the ship pitch and roll less as time went on, she was able to put the bucket down and rest at last. *American doctors*. She hadn't thought much about the other physicians on the islands, although she knew there was a small district hospital supported by a charity. She wondered if Dr McBride was based on the ship or the island, but put the idea out of her mind as the vessel slowed and the rumble of the engine dropped.

Dorothy staggered ashore at St Brannock's quay, her feet finding the ground almost as rocky as the ship, but the fresh air and stone buildings ahead reassured her. She looked around for a taxi, but saw none. Instead, several army lorries were filling up with young soldiers carrying kitbags almost as big as they were. A tall figure advanced towards her.

'Can we drop you somewhere?' Captain McBride asked. 'There don't seem to be a car service here.'

'No, I—' Common sense kicked in. 'Well, I might need help with some of my luggage.'

'I'll leave my car here to help.' He waved over a young man in US army uniform. 'I guess we're going to be colleagues.'

'It might seem so, Dr McBride, although I'm not sure how the hospitals here work.'

'There are far too few medics to do all the work. We help each other when we can. You can call on us if you need us. I'm the chief medical officer at the airbase hospital. Good luck, Dr Rowe.'

He touched the brim of his cap again and hopped into an awaiting lorry. She watched the lorry drive away. The young man sat quietly on the wall, watching as bags and boxes, and even a couple of motorbikes, were unloaded onto the quay.

'That's mine,' she said to several sweating sailors hauling a large steamer trunk ashore. 'Medical equipment,' she explained, blushing at the thought that the driver might have thought she had brought masses of clothes and shoes to this tiny place. 'And those cases, too.'

He started putting bags in the car, and two sailors secured the trunk on the back. 'Is it far?' he asked.

'Actually, I'm not sure,' she said. She walked over to an elderly man sat outside a public house, watching with a grin from a bench and smoking the foulest-smelling pipe tobacco she had ever encountered. 'Excuse me. Do you know where the Doctor's House is?'

'*I* does,' he said, spitting to one side.

'Well, could you give us directions, please?'

He looked past her to the open-topped car. 'You the doctor's wife?'

'No, I'm— Oh, never mind. The house?'

'Down the high street, second road on the right, Springfield Lane. It's the big house at the end with the anchor knocker on the door.'

She fished in her jacket pocket for a shilling, and held it out. He seemed astonished, taking it slowly.

'Thank you,' she said, head held high.

3

After a week of working on the outline of the festival, Eleanor sat in the garden of the Doctor's House under a wisteria creeper dripping with lavender-coloured blossoms. Every now and then the weight of a bumblebee dropped a wilted flower onto her papers.

The application the committee had made was charmingly homemade, little quirks and anecdotes added to give weight to their main point. The six inhabited islands were at the mercy of the whims of tourism; during the pandemic, many of the businesses had come close to failing. The committee seemed to believe that a festival would bring a new generation of tourists to the islands who would return as they aged, replacing the present demographic of visitors that averaged over sixty.

The committee recognised that there were few resources aimed at the younger people living on the islands. They hoped to make the music festival an annual one, along with other annual events like the gig racing, the embroidery exhibition and the poetry gala. Music would be centred on the young. Eleanor noticed that most of the committee appeared to be older, which was often the case. Retirees had the life skills and time to serve on committees, but she needed some young ideas, too.

Sally appeared by the table in a long, floral-print skirt. She didn't wear shoes in the house and it felt like she drifted about like a ghost. 'How's your research going?'

'It's – interesting. Do you know whose idea it was to apply for this grant in the first place? It isn't clear.'

Sally sat on the other garden chair. 'I suppose the first idea was many years ago. It was a retired teacher, Patience Ellis, who thought we needed to invest in something for young people.'

'Who is she?'

'She *was* a very old lady when she helped set up the committee. She was just one of those people who came up with good ideas and could run with them. She died a few years ago, but people took up the idea in her memory. They applied for funding last year.'

'Do you know what her original concept was?'

Sally brushed the lifeless flowers onto the flower bed beside the patio. 'She felt that something in the islands was dying, along with that generation of people who had grown up during the war, or lived through the hardships afterwards when the fishing industry collapsed. She said she could feel the heartbeat of the islands slowing down. The idea resonated with many of us.'

'You were involved?'

'In the beginning. I couldn't cope with all those meetings, though. It's best to leave it up to people who are good at thinking about facilities and bookings and tickets. But I'll go. I love music.'

Eleanor smiled and leaned back in her chair. Close up, Sally looked younger, but her bearing was that of an older woman. 'I hope you don't mind my saying, but I keep trying to work out how old you are,' she said.

'Probably too old to dance at a music festival,' Sally

answered, with a big smile, 'but I'm still going to. I was just about to make some tea. And maybe some sandwiches for lunch. Can I tempt you?'

'You can, but you don't have to look after me.'

'Who else is going to, then?' was Sally's parting shot.

'Me?' Eleanor muttered under her breath, but it was nice to be pampered. Mothered. That's what she had missed. Alone in the garden except for about a thousand bees and bombarded with flowers, she could let a few tears well up. *Mum would have loved this.* Her mother had planned to come here to follow up her family history but was too ill at that point.

By the time Sally returned, Eleanor had finished reading the application and was ready for a break. A pile of sandwiches and slices of cake were accompanied by a teapot that smelled like berries. Usually a coffee drinker, Eleanor had been beguiled by each pot of tea created by Sally, some herbal, some fruity, and some just smelling like the garden itself.

'Can I ask you a question about someone who lived on the island a long time ago?'

'Sure,' Sally mumbled around a bite of sandwich. 'Everyone kind of knows everyone here.'

Eleanor pulled up her mother's family tree research on her laptop. 'My mum Diana was adopted. She was born in 1970, and her birth name was Hecta Allen, which is pretty unusual. She was adopted at two months old through an agency. Mum got her actual birth certificate just before she got ill. We were researching her family tree when she died.'

Sally froze for a moment, then leaned closer to look. 'That's so sad, I'm so sorry for you.' She sounded like the thought had hit her hard. 'There are a couple of Allens still on the islands. They could be your cousins.' Sally wrinkled up her nose. 'What was her mother called? On the certificate.'

'Alys.'

'Hmm, I don't think I've heard of an Alys. Of course, they

could have come from a different island or even the mainland.'
A bee bumbled down to the cake crumbs on the table and they
watched it explore and taste. Sally dripped a little of the cooled
tea onto the wooden table for it to drink. She seemed tense.

'How would I find out more?'

'Well, you've made a good start by asking me. I keep myself
to myself now, but I went to the high school – there's only one –
around that time. I was there in the middle of the sixties. That's
how we all know each other.'

'Could you ask around?'

'I tell you what I'll do. I have friends around the islands, I'll
ask them to have a think, maybe ask among their own families
and friends. If that's OK? The downside is, everyone will want
to know all about you.'

Eleanor hesitated. But how many people could really get
involved? Sally seemed to live a quiet life, even a bit reclusive;
Eleanor hadn't seen anyone visit all week. 'Thank you. That
would be helpful.'

'And the school will have records, I'm certain. Of course,
the building has been replaced but they might still have some of
the papers. It could be worth a visit.'

'I'm planning to talk to the headteacher about getting the
current students involved in the festival as volunteer stewards.
If they ask me to do it, and *if* we can get it off the ground.'

Sally's eyebrows shot up into her long fringe. 'Is there any
doubt? If Liz is in charge, it'll happen.'

Eleanor smiled. 'She does seem to be a force of nature.'

'You should ask *her* about your Hecta and Alys Allen! Her
family know just about everyone on the islands. She's part of
the graveyard project.'

'What's that?'

Sally topped up her floral tea. 'Our churchyard was a bit of
a wilderness corner. Recently, volunteers – led by Andrea, she's
on the committee – have been clearing brambles and recording

the old stones as they restore them. She might know an Allen or two.'

'I was curious about the names Hecta and Alys,' Eleanor said, watching Sally closely for a reaction. She spelled out both. 'Are they local names? They are quite unusual, I've never heard of Hecta before.'

'Alys is an island spelling of the name Alice. Hecta might be something to do with Dr Hector McBride. He helped a lot of people on the islands. A few boys were named after him. I do vaguely remember stories about a Polly Allen, but I think that was much earlier.'

Eleanor shuffled the papers neatly into a stack. 'My mother always felt she didn't know a part of herself. I suppose being adopted might make you feel like that.'

'I suppose so.' Sally was very quiet for a moment. 'You'll hear it from someone, I'm sure, but I was adopted, too.'

'Oh, I didn't realise.'

A mix of emotions skated across Sally's face. 'I was lucky,' she said softly. 'I was taken in by the family that used to live here. I was ill as a baby. People used to be very frightened of seizures, fits. In the end, I was adopted by an older couple. They were very kind to me.'

'I'm glad it worked out for you. My mother was loved and cared for, too, she just said she didn't know who she *was*.'

Sally started to clear up, putting empty cups on the tray. 'I never looked into who had given birth to me. It seemed incidental, because I got the best parents in the world.' Her smile lit up her whole face. 'I was adopted by Dr Dorothy.'

Keen to get a feel for the place, Eleanor spent the afternoon walking the coast path along the back of St Brannock's. The island had a spine of dark rocks, brooding over the upland. All around, grassy fields and low scrub filled the landscape. The beach lined the harbour at low tide, and spread out onto sandy tidal areas at each end. The town hugged the shore, three or four streets deep, the older properties so small they looked miniature from the path as she climbed behind the houses. The path was an easy three-mile circular walk, along a footpath from the top of the town to the distant tip of the island. It was divided into fields, two with sheep and lambs, and the eastern coast had waist-high meadows bordered by low trees. The grass was full of tall plants, splashes of colour like buttercups, clover and other flowers that were new to her. The footpaths ran between scrappy hedges, and she could catch sight of each coast as she stood on a stile.

A bark made her start, and she almost fell off the step. A black and white sheepdog jumped up close, just beyond a rickety wire fence, woofing furiously. She liked dogs, but the collie's sudden appearance left her a bit shaken. In the distance a man whistled, and the dog immediately ran off towards him. Despite the chill in the spring wind, he was in shorts and a ragged old T-shirt. He stopped to stare at her a moment, then patted the fawning dog, turning away as if he'd lost interest.

'I *am* on the public footpath,' she muttered to herself, climbing down, slightly worried the dog would come back. The path was lined with daffodils and primroses and a few stems of large daisies nodded in the breeze.

As she walked, Eleanor couldn't help glancing over at the farmer a few times. He was stocky, not much taller than her, but his strong features were visible even over the distance of a field. The sheepdog was occupied rounding up the rest of the stock and guiding them through an open gate. The man held it open, then closed it behind the last of the lambs. He leaned back to stare at her for a long moment, then turned to walk uphill and away from her. She carried on, a bit flustered. Everyone had been so friendly, so lovely to her, it was odd that he seemed hostile. Or perhaps it was just the dog's reaction that had rattled her.

She finally reached the top of the hill and her breath was snatched away. The whole southern end of the island was before her, the coast on both sides, the sea all around. It was turquoise today, with a few white tops to the waves, the wind catching her by surprise as she left the shelter of the hillside. She caught a deep breath, then another. People would pay to come here, she was sure of it. They would camp on these gentle slopes, and listen to amazing music.

Purple spikes of flowers rambled between umbrellas of white buds. Birds cried overhead – she thought they might be lapwings; she had once had a coaster with a line drawing of a lapwing on it. A nondescript brown bird the size of a sparrow waited for her on a fence post, then launched itself into the air with a string of liquid notes – maybe it was a skylark. She stared at it, shading her eyes against the sun, just a speck in the sky, singing for several minutes as it rose and fell.

She was moved by the lushness, the different greens all around her. She rarely got out of London except to travel to somewhere warm for a holiday – or a festival. It reminded her of the holidays she had had with her mother, when they had thrown a tent in the back of their beaten-up car and driven to a wild campsite. They would cook up something based on beans, lie back on a blanket to watch the stars come out until it got too cold, then make up stories. Two days later, they would get back dirty, tired and sunburned, in time for baths and school and work on Monday. They were precious memories of a woman who had created her biological family with Eleanor, and had made Eleanor feel like she completely belonged to someone.

Now her mother was gone, Eleanor felt rootless, alone. Sally's kindness had comforted something that was injured when the cancer had ripped Diana away.

4

FEBRUARY 1943

The Doctor's House was large, a pair of small windows each side of an imposing door surrounded by a trellis porch, covered in dead foliage. A brown door knocker in the shape of an anchor sat in the middle of it, a rust stain tracking down the wooden panels.

Dorothy rapped, hard. A light came on behind the filthy pane of glass just above the knocker, but no one came to the door. She waited, and after a minute or so, the light went off. She fumbled in her pocket for the key, which was one of a bunch sent to her by the solicitor. By the time she had rattled a couple in the lock to find they didn't fit, someone put the light on and came to the door.

'Who is it?' The voice was strident, and from a woman, a dark shape though the glass.

'The new owner,' Dorothy snapped back, too tired to be polite. 'Please open up, I've been travelling all day.'

The woman opened the door, her dark hair striped with white strands and pulled back from a broad, freckled face, above a dirty floral overall. The woman was much taller than Dorothy and stared down through narrowed eyes.

'Who are you? I didn't know the doctor was married.'

'I *am* the doctor.' Dorothy was annoyed that she had said this so many times already today. 'Will you please let me in? This young man is waiting to help me with my luggage.'

She shouldered past the woman so she could put down the bags she was carrying in each hand and under each arm. The driver started to pull the large trunk off the back of the car but Dorothy shouted in alarm. 'There's delicate equipment in there, wait...' She walked back to help but the box was difficult. 'Will you help?' she puffed in the direction of the woman.

''Spose so,' the woman said. She was strong, and between the three of them they managed to carry it down the path and into the wide hall. There were flagstones on the floor and deep skirting, also ornate plasterwork around the ceiling, all looking stained and dirty in the light of an oil lamp on the wall.

Dorothy tipped the young man, hardly more than a boy, and he thanked her in an American accent she could hardly understand. 'Where are you from?'

'Virginia, ma'am,' he said, grinning and taking a cigarette from behind his ear. 'If you need any more help, you can let Dr McBride know, ma'am. I mean, Doctor.'

She thought about the helpful doctor, his lazy drawl and blue eyes. 'Well, thank you. I may have to do that.'

He walked up the path, leaving Dorothy in the fading dusk with the woman. In addition to looking dirty, she smelled stale, too. Dorothy wondered how fresh she smelled herself. 'I'm sorry. I wasn't expecting anyone to be here,' she said.

'I lives here. Well, I lives in the cottage, but I thought I'd better light the fire in the house every day, keep the damp out.'

She remembered that there was an outbuilding as well as a stable attached to the property. 'You have permission to live here?' She really was too tired to be civil. She sank onto a chair standing against the wall. 'I'm sorry, I don't know your name.'

'I'm Mrs Oppy. I was Dr Lavenham's 'ousekeeper. He needed a lot of help at the end. With his illness.'

'The end?'

'He died 'ere,' Mrs Oppy said with some pleasure. 'I found him upstairs. Of course, the locum doctor, he's already gone off to war.'

Dorothy wasn't superstitious, but standing in the barely lit hall she didn't relish sleeping in the deceased's room. 'Well, we can talk about all of that in the morning, but I probably won't need a housekeeper.' *Or can afford one.* 'But if the stove is already lit, maybe we could put a kettle on?'

'Let me,' the woman said begrudgingly. 'I usually 'as a pot before I go back to the cottage.'

Of course you do, using my coal and probably the late Dr Lavenham's tea.

'Thank you. That would be kind.' She followed Mrs Oppy to the kitchen, to find it a step down and the ceiling beamed and low. It looked like a much older building. In the middle was a large table, covered with odd bits of crockery and pots, as if someone was preparing to sell them.

'I thought I would give it all a clean,' Mrs Oppy said with so much hostility in her voice Dorothy was sure her suspicions were right.

'Very kind of you. You must let me reimburse you for your work,' she offered reluctantly.

She sat at the table as the older woman washed up a bone china cup and saucer and filled a small pot with tea.

'You don't mind if I joins you?' Mrs Oppy said.

'Not at all.' She waited until the tea was poured and a little powdered milk was stirred in.

''Ent got any sugar,' Mrs Oppy said.

'No problem,' Dorothy said, as the warmth from the stove counteracted the draughts coming from the cracked window, through which a mass of plants leaned in, as if appraising their new owner. 'Is there a bed? Not Dr Lavenham's, of course.'

'We 'ad to throw his mattress away,' Mrs Oppy said with relish. 'He'd been dead a few hours when I found him. But there's a small bed in the other doctor's room, and a few sheets in the press on the landing. They 'ent been aired, mind.'

'I'll hang them out for a couple of hours,' Dorothy said. 'And I have dry blankets in the big chest, around my microscope and surgical tools. Thank you for the tea,' she added, formally.

The tea was warm, and welcome. Except for those sips of water given to her by the American doctor, she hadn't kept anything else down all day. As Mrs Oppy got up to leave, showing her where the cottage was down the end of a long garden, she wondered where he was. So far, all the welcome and kindness of her journey had come from Dr McBride.

5

PRESENT DAY, 3 APRIL

Returning to St Brannock's Island three weeks later, Eleanor had answers to a lot of the logistical questions about the festival. The initial specifications in the application were straightforward: more like a village fete with a few musicians booked to entertain. Eleanor knew it was going to be so much more complicated than that. It couldn't break even with less than three thousand ticket holders; four thousand would be better.

The biggest problem was that the ferry came over once a day and carried a maximum of five hundred passengers and crew. Allowing for a hundred on the plane per day and fewer for the helicopter, she couldn't see how she could get everyone, including bands and crew, on the island in less than four days. Even if they allowed free camping before the bands started playing, what was she going to do with all the early birds?

Allowing for maybe a few hundred ticket holders from the neighbouring islands – the whole population of the archipelago was only about three thousand, although that would increase with holidaymakers – it was still going to be difficult. She sat at the kitchen table at Sally's B&B and thought about it. The tourist board were very keen to speak to her. Perhaps the whole week could be promoted as a package? But, looking at the tourist demographics, that would suggest older visitors who would want slightly different music. At least she had lots of questions for the statistics whiz-kid back in the office.

'I'm just going for a walk!' Sally called through the house. 'If you want to come?'

'I'm meeting up with Liz, to look at the Carlin Adventure Centre. Enjoy your walk.'

Sally put her head around the door. 'Ask her about your grandmother's name. Liz knows everyone.'

'I will. Bye, Sally,' Eleanor said, waving.

Liz had dressed for the outdoors in waxed jacket and wellies, and Eleanor felt very underdressed in jeans, jumper and trainers. 'What is this place we're going to see?'

Liz wound a scarf around the white bun on the top of her head. 'It's just at the southern end of the village, less than a mile further along. It's our outside adventure centre. We have a lot of school groups visiting at the moment, doing canoeing and paddleboarding and whatnot.' She strode out along the coast road past the harbour, leaving Eleanor behind her. Several people waved or called out to Liz – everyone seemed to know her.

'It's a lovely place,' Liz said, over her shoulder. 'They do adventure days for seniors, too. I've done abseiling and kayaking there.'

'And you say they can cater for sixty students at a time?'

'Well, they do sometimes. We thought their grounds might be suitable for camping, and we would be able to put up a couple of stages in tents. That's what these festivals do, isn't it?'

Eleanor didn't know where to start explaining festival stages, their construction, lighting, sound, power requirements and safety features. 'It's a bit more complicated than that.

Normally the sets come in large trucks and specialists put them up.'

Liz stopped. 'Well, that would be difficult with the ferry. How big, and how many?'

'There are smaller alternatives. There are yurts and geodesic tents that we can put small, low stages in. But it will be very different to the music festivals you might have seen on tele-vision.' Some of the lighting rigs she'd worked with before filled a large truck and cost half a million pounds each. 'We need to establish this event as something unusual and distinctive. Small, but with a big heart.'

'Distinctive how?'

'Well,' Eleanor said, puffing as she walked up the hill. 'Every event has its own unique selling features. For example, it might be a green festival, solar-powered. Or it might be aimed at families with children, or be like a party.'

'What have we got that would be unique?'

Eleanor stopped and spread out her arms. 'Look at this view!' The grass, dotted with sheep, rolled down to the cluster of low buildings, presumably the activity centre. Beyond lay the sea; the beach was a biscuit-coloured band at the edge, and a hundred or so small boats bobbed on moorings. 'Surely the sea is the unique feature? It's *gorgeous*. People will be able to stand on the beach and listen to the music.' She surprised herself with her passion. 'They will be able to swim and paddleboard. Maybe a surf school or the centre could run sessions?'

'I suppose so,' Liz said, looking around. 'I probably take it for granted, but it is pretty.'

Eleanor could imagine the whole thing. The fields were fairly level from side to side and all led gently down to the Carlin Centre. Camping would be up the hill; the dates would be flexible because it would take time to get the ticket holders here, giving people up to a week to enjoy the camping. The stages could face the sea so people could dance on the beach and enjoy the music, or relax on the wide grassy area. But getting these people to the islands would be difficult. There must be power and water at the centre – perhaps they could use some buildings to act as green rooms and to house all the necessary management. Behind the centre would be food outlets and stalls, creating the festival 'village'.

'We could do it,' she said, staring back up the hill. 'If we put the acts up in the hotels, then put the paying guests on these fields.'

Liz looked around. 'Here? I doubt...' She wrinkled her nose. 'The thing is, the farmer is unlikely to want people camping all over his grass.'

'He'd be paid. Probably much more than he would get from a few sheep. We'd just get him to cut the fields, maybe for hay, and move his animals.'

Liz looked back up the hill. 'I still don't think he'd be interested. He's a bit of a... *character*.'

Eleanor wondered about the man and his barking dog. 'I may have seen him. Not very friendly. But I've persuaded farmers to root up crops and seed with grass ahead of an event. Honestly, it will be a good deal for him, and us.'

'You haven't met Bruno Roskelly.'

Eleanor laughed. 'No, Liz. Mr Roskelly hasn't met *me*.'

As they walked back, Eleanor remembered Sally's advice. She took a deep breath before she opened up the topic of her mother.

'I don't suppose you've ever heard of an Alys Allen, spelled with a Y? She had a baby here in 1970, called Hecta.'

Liz stopped at the top of the hill, catching her breath. 'Is this for your family tree? I can't remember any Allens at school when I was there, and I'm about the right age. Let's walk through the churchyard, it's just there, behind the church. There may be a few Allens mentioned in there.'

The steepest part of the hill was covered with hundreds of slate marker stones, many of them old and leaning. A rusted gate creaked open onto an overgrown path. The churchyard looked down over the patchwork of roofs, and to the sea.

'Do you think there could be some family graves?' Eleanor asked. It made her feel tingly and shivery, the thought of an ancestor – maybe even her mother's birth mother – being tucked away on this hillside.

'I have no idea, but it's Tuesday, so I know someone who will. Our churchwarden is working on a database to record grave markers in the oldest part of the churchyard.'

Eleanor could see that part of the graveyard was tidy and cared for, but the top part was wild with long grasses and nodding flowers, and the new lime-green shoots of nettle. She followed Liz into the porch of the church.

'Andrea? Andrea!'

'I'm in the front, clearing up,' came an echoing call, and they walked towards the nave down uneven flagstones. The church looked much older inside, as if the original small building had been enlarged and modernised. It was beautiful in its plainness.

Andrea, the grey-haired committee member Eleanor had met before, walked forward, holding a bin bag filled with browned flowers.

'Just cleaning up after a wedding,' she said, smiling. 'Hi, Eleanor. Still here? I thought you might have run off after a load of silly old bats told you their plans to join the twenty-first century.'

'Not at all.' Eleanor smiled. 'I'm going back to London in a couple of days, and hopefully we will have an outline for you to discuss with your committee after that.'

'Eleanor was wondering if you'd ever heard of an Alys Allen?' Liz said. 'She had a baby – when was it?'

'Nineteen seventy,' Eleanor said. 'She had a baby, my mother, who was adopted.'

'People didn't talk much about babies born out of wedlock, which I assume was the case?' Andrea put the bag down and stripped off her gloves. 'It seems like such an old-fashioned idea nowadays. But there were Allens over on Morwen, I remember. I think Mr Allen was something to do with the steamship. We used to have a paddle steamer being done up here, all through the sixties. You could ask at the museum, or the library might have someone. Nineteen seventy... You'd think I would have known an Allen – I was at the school in the early seventies. But an Alys? I don't remember that name. Maybe she was older, or from the mainland?'

'I thought you might have found one when you were cleaning up the graves,' Liz said.

Andrea smacked her forehead with her palm. 'Oh, for goodness' sake! We *did* find an Allen last year. It was an old lady, that's why it didn't spring to mind. A Katerina Allen, died in her eighties. A long time ago though, about 1914. It's a delight to see someone who lived so long, back then before the National Health Service and antibiotics. A nice change from young children. Those baby graves are so sad.'

Eleanor felt as if something was squeezing her heart. 'Katerina? So, born about 1830s, 1840s? I can look her up, maybe trace her family name forward.'

'Maybe she's a relative?' Liz said. 'You could probably look them up on the census returns. The 1891 census might even have Katerina's children and grandchildren on it.' Liz pointed back along the hill and spoke to Andrea. 'We were just talking about Bruno's fields. Eleanor thinks they would be perfect for camping.'

Andrea made a face. 'Bruno's not exactly cooperative at

best, and I can't see him letting us use that land. He hates talking or working with anyone, or at least, he does nowadays. He's become quite withdrawn since his wife left.'

Liz made a face. 'He was so happy before, with the baby and the farm. He took over when his dad got older. They all lived together but I'm not sure it suited his wife, Michelle. She was lovely, but I wouldn't have put them together.'

Eleanor smiled at them both. 'I'll make an appointment to visit, see if I can persuade him. We look after all our landlords, and we'll make it worth his while, and it's for the good of the island.'

The two women exchanged glances. 'You could *try*,' Liz said dubiously. 'To be honest, he rarely answers his phone. You'd probably be better just banging on his door.'

Eleanor smiled as they walked away. She hadn't failed to recruit a farmer yet.

6

FEBRUARY 1943

Apart from finding a functional but filthy bathroom – Dorothy hadn't developed a high opinion of the housekeeper's skills – she had been too tired to look around the Doctor's House. She found a small bedroom with a bed in it at the front of the place. She'd needed the blankets she had packed, and had draped her coat over the top as the glass in the window was cracked and missing in places, the February wind whistling in all night.

But the daylight after a few hours' sleep revealed a pretty, if neglected, front garden and a pleasant room faded by the sun. Her hair was a hopeless tangle, her usual yellow curls frizzy. There didn't seem to be any hot water in the antiquated bathroom, so she washed in cold water, and ruthlessly brushed her hair into a bun. Her breath misted in front of her, so she put on an extra jumper. She wore clothes suited to dirty work; the house would need a top-to-bottom scrub before she could see patients.

There were four bedrooms; she had slept in the smallest. A door on the landing led to narrow steps to smaller rooms upstairs, presumably for maids back in more prosperous days. The plaster in the loft rooms was mostly cracked or falling into piles on the floor; she could see the undersides of slates in places and even a little daylight. Damp seemed to have crept in, and a few bunches of sticks and dried grasses indicated that birds had nested under the eaves. Their droppings were everywhere, and stains suggested water was getting in as well.

The main bedroom overlooked the front garden, but extended over the wide hall below, so was airy and light. Even this early in the year and day, sunshine was creeping over the sill. The large bed was made of some ugly dark wood, but the back room, perhaps a wife's or daughter's, had a pleasant enamelled metal bedstead from the last century. It was covered with dustsheets which tore when she moved them, but the mattress was sound and so high off the floor that it should have escaped mouse damage. Unlike the fireside rug, which was chewed to pieces. Mouse droppings lined the edges of the room.

Downstairs she found the stove had gone out and there was almost no coal in the scuttle. She had locked both front and back doors when she went to bed, but both had been hard to turn and she wondered if they were ever used. She needn't have worried about unlocking the front door the day before, she could have just walked straight in, if manners had permitted.

It's my house now, she reminded herself. *It's my somewhat decrepit house that is stuck in the last century.*

She stepped through the door at the back of the hallway, opposite the kitchen. It was a large consulting room, with two windows overlooking the garden, between which were a pair of French doors. Along one wall were glass-fronted cabinets full of books and equipment. A large double-fronted cupboard took up most of the room, with drawers below. It was locked, which might have preserved its contents from Mrs Oppy, so she tried the smallest key she had been sent by the lawyers.

Inside was a museum of old remedies, many of them downright dangerous or displaced by modern alternatives. Cocaine, opium, mercury, arsenic. Mixtures of lotions and balsams and quackery from before she even trained. Below, in shallow drawers, were surgical instruments only useful if you were going to do kitchen-table surgery, whereas now they had a hospital nearby. She turned her attention to an old examination bench, covered with cracked leather, impossible to sterilise. A chair for the patient sat beside an oak desk, which was ink-stained but practical – something she did like. It had two blocks of drawers each side, and a central drawer had scraps of paper and a few notes.

The patient records were by the door in an unlocked chest, and were in chaos. Mice had made ingress and created nests out of important papers. She noticed that not only were the windows cracked, they were so shrouded in spiderwebs and dust that they looked as if they had lace curtains over them. Rubbing away a small area, she saw the garden, green and lush and almost reaching the French doors. There was also a riot of early flowers – pink coltsfoot and yellow celandine stars – dotting the long grass.

Dorothy had grown up with maids and housekeepers but had become used to doing a few things for herself when she was studying medicine. Her landlady had insisted on the young ladies making their own beds and keeping their rooms dusted. This felt like a much bigger job, but presumably Mrs Oppy had some soda, brushes and dishcloths.

Dorothy managed to light the stove with the last of the coal and a few old newspapers and sticks in a basket by the door, so she at least had a kettle warming by the time the housekeeper appeared at the back door.

'I was wondering about my wages,' Mrs Oppy snapped.

'Certainly.' Dorothy set the broom down on the kitchen flagstones. 'For what work, precisely?'

'Well, for 'ousekeeping. And looking after Dr Lavenham. He needed a lot of nursing at the end.'

'I'm afraid you would have to speak to Dr Lavenham's

executors to claim wages back. And by my calculation, that was four months ago.'

'It was. October.'

'So, what "'ousekeeping" have you done since, may I ask?' There was an acidic tone in the air as she spoke, and Mrs Oppy pulled herself up defensively.

'There weren't any work needed doing. I kept the house aired and dry.'

'But not *clean*, Mrs Oppy.' She relented. 'I tell you what, you could help me scrub the house, so it is clean and safe for patients. Then *I* will pay you.' *Out of a diminishing pot of savings.* 'What about the cottage? Do you pay rent on that?'

That got a bigger reaction. 'I've had that cottage for twenty-two years,' she blustered. 'Since I started this job. I don't pay rent, the 'ousekeeper always gets the cottage, and the old doctor didn't think it proper I stayed in the house since he were a widower.'

'Well, let's see how we get on, shall we? If your work is good, perhaps we might talk about your continuing employment.'

The tension in the room collapsed, and Mrs Oppy looked at the kettle, now beginning to hiss. 'I'll make the tea, shall I, missus?'

7

PRESENT DAY, 5 APRIL

With some hesitation, remembering the dog, Eleanor approached the front gate to Bruno's farm, which was chained with a padlock the size of a fist. She had printed off an outline of how it would work for Bruno to rent his field to the festival, and she clutched the papers tightly as she cleared her throat.

'Excuse me, Mr Roskelly? Can I have a word?' she shouted.

Somewhere in the house, behind a concrete yard with farm buildings on either side, a dog started howling.

She waited and counted to a hundred. She repeated the words, more stridently. Before she was halfway through the second hundred, the door opened and the black and white dog charged forward. Eleanor jumped back at the sight of a red mouth and white teeth, but the dog's tail was wagging wildly.

The man she had seen with his sheep marched after the dog, scowling at her. 'What do you want? I'm not buying anything.' He looked angry, his dark eyebrows tight over equally dark eyes, mouth downturned. He was a bit older than her, maybe late thirties, and was dressed in old clothes covered with mud.

'That's good, as I'm not selling anything. I want to talk to you about leasing some of your land, for a few weeks, for a very generous remuneration. It's for the music festival.'

'I'm very busy, I have animals to check,' he barked. 'Shut up, Haze!' The dog's barks subsided. 'Say your piece and push off.'

Eleanor thought he was a bit rude, snapping like that. Her shoulder muscles tightened with anger. She pulled herself up to her full five foot ten, about his height. 'Mr Roskelly, if you don't want to hear anything I have to say, why did you come out to meet me at all?'

'I knew what you wanted. Someone in the village said some bossy woman was trying to organise a festival, telling people what to do. Now, get on with your pitch.'

The 'bossy woman' description amused Eleanor, puncturing her anger. Obviously, the Atlantic Islands were still stuck in the past, possibly the seventies. So, Eleanor took a deep breath and pitched. She talked about the benefits to the island and to the younger generations, the income that would be generated and the substantial payments to the landowner.

'So I would have my pastures flattened by a few thousand townies leaving rubbish everywhere? And what about water? I only have a spring supply. And no electricity up here at all.'

'It's all in the proposal, and we would organise all of that. We will pay to have your land restored to pristine condition and reseeded if needed. We even use metal detectors to check for tent pegs and bottle caps afterwards. Just read this and get back to me with any questions. My mobile phone number is at the top.' She pointed to the first sheet as she passed it to him.

He swiped the papers out of her hand. 'I have to make a living. I have a large flock of sheep with lambs at the moment. What am I supposed to do with them?'

'It's a couple of weeks, Mr Roskelly. Perhaps you have a smaller field they can go into?'

He stared down at the papers. 'It's farming. It's not that easy.' He read the card attached to the top. '*Ms* Markham.'

'Eleanor, please. We've worked with farms before, and we have all sorts of solutions. Dairy herds are much more of a problem than sheep. We know farms need to diversify to raise revenue, so this is one way to do it.'

'Well, Eleanor, I mostly agreed to listen to you because my daughter asked me to. I'll read the papers. Now we're done.'

He turned and stalked away, leaving Eleanor seething. Who on earth did he think he was, the arrogant so-and-so? But at least he took the papers with him.

As she turned to go, she realised she had stepped in sheep dung at the farm gate. She was trying to wipe it off on the long grass when she heard a female voice.

'I like your hair,' a slight girl in her mid-teens said. She had straight blonde hair to her waist and was dressed in jeans and a fleece. She walked from the open doorway to the gate. 'He's my dad. He's a bit grumpy at the moment, but he's a nice guy really.' She had her father's dark brown eyes. 'I'm Ruby.'

'I'm Eleanor. Thank you,' Eleanor said, giving up on the shoes and hoping it would wear off on the way back.

'I persuaded him to see you. I think a music festival would be awesome. All my friends want to go but Dad says I'm too young to camp at a festival.'

'How old are you?' The girl seemed friendly. She was pretty with delicate-looking features.

'I'm fourteen. But I would literally be camping in my own back yard. With all my friends and my dad just there,' she said, waving at the house. 'It's not like I would be hitchhiking to Glastonbury or something.'

'Well, I've left the proposal with him. When I get back, I'll see how he feels then.'

'Great!' the girl said. 'I'll work on him, then maybe he can give you a tour of the farm.'

Eleanor hesitated. She didn't want to be seen as putting any pressure on a child to benefit her own project. 'I suppose it won't hurt if you occasionally say how nice it would be for your age group to listen to live music. But that's up to you.'

Ruby jumped up onto the gate and sat astride it. 'He's just a grump because my mum left. He's all right, really.'

'I'm sure he is. Bye, Ruby,' she said, waving over her shoulder as she walked away.

There was something about Bruno Roskelly that confused Eleanor. He was older than her, heavily tanned and grubby from farm work, and she was pretty sure he smelled like sheep. Not her sort of guy at all, but she found herself thinking about him that evening, anyway.

Sally had started to prepare dinner for them both, to celebrate her last evening on the island. They sat under hundreds of fairy lights in the garden hung around a pergola as the vegetables cooked. Sally's approach to gardening seemed to be to love everything equally. Eleanor was fairly sure some of the plants were carefully tended weeds, but beyond the arbour was a long lawn filled with low trees which backed on to farmland.

'I didn't know your garden went all the way back there,' she said, as Sally took her for a tour in the dusk, to watch the birds launch themselves from the eaves of the Doctor's House into the last of the light.

'It used to be an orchard.' She ran her hands over a stunted, twisted tree, the bark gnarled and split. 'And that pile of ivy is the old stone shed. It was a cottage once. These few apple trees are all that remain. I get someone in each year to prune them to keep them alive. You met him today actually, Bruno.'

'He does that?'

'He does all sorts of jobs around the island. I don't think sheep farming on poor soil is enough income for the two of them. His wife used to bring in a decent wage, but she's gone now, about seven years. She hated living on the islands, she wasn't born here. When her dad got ill, she couldn't go to help him when he needed it, not without going on the boat. If she'd been on the mainland, she could have driven in an hour.'

'But she left Ruby behind?'

'No, she took Ruby with her. But the girl kept running away trying to get back. I think she was only seven or eight the first time. There was a proper manhunt for her, police and all.'

'Does Ruby see her mum now?' Eleanor shook her head, not sure why she was so interested.

'Fairly often. Less since Michelle remarried a few years back. Just a couple of weeks in the holidays, and every other Christmas. Ruby adores her father. I'm not sure she ever got over the divorce. And I'm certain Bruno hasn't, either. He loved Michelle, he didn't really see it coming. To be honest, I think he still grieves for her.' They had wandered to the very end of the garden, a rambling hedge three or four foot high with gaps filled with rusty wire. 'This backs on to his top field. When he lets the young lambs in here, one or two always find their way through. Last year one turned up in my kitchen, bold as brass, wagging his tail at me. I suppose he wanted a bottle but I only had soya milk at the time.'

Eleanor smiled at the image, but Sally was staring across the field to the top of the hillside and the dark sky above, just starting to sparkle with stars.

'What is it?' Eleanor murmured.

'This is where my father died,' Sally answered, her voice soft. 'He was trying to climb through the hedge, to help a sheep that had fallen over. He had a heart attack. He cried out, my mother heard him, but he died here before an ambulance could save him. I was sixteen, it was the worst day of my life.'

It was as if everything at dusk was more raw, richer, and Eleanor's memories floated up to the surface painfully. 'My mother died trying to get out of bed at the hospice. She kept

saying she wanted to go home.' She spoke into the darkness as if
the hillside was listening. 'I suppose she did, then.'

'Go home? I hope that's what death is like,' Sally said, and
linked arms with Eleanor. 'Let's not be sad. All I have to do is
cook the fish for supper. I hope you like bass. I made the fish-
monger fillet and bone it.'

They walked back to the house, carefully over the
hummocky grass, which was up to their knees. 'It's lovely here,'
Eleanor said, almost without thought. 'It's such a great house
and garden. I'd like to make it my base if we come back to do
your festival.'

'I'd like that,' Sally said. 'I'll keep the consulting room free
for you. Come back when you like.'

'Oh, I couldn't ask you to do that! I'm sure you're booked up
in the summer.'

'I only open to people I know now – I don't need the money.
People who travel here for work, like you, or a few trusted old
patrons that feel like family. I don't need much money and I'm
too old to run up and down making beds and cleaning bathrooms all the time.' She half smiled. 'It gives me a sense of
purpose and I enjoy a bit of company.'

Together, they stepped into the kitchen, and Sally put a pan
on the heat. She brushed grass seeds off her long skirt and put
them in the bin, and Eleanor found she was scattered with
them, too. The smell of hot butter filled the kitchen, then the
smell of fish followed, as fresh as if it had just been caught. The
opalescent flesh hit the pan, starting to curl immediately.
Eleanor took new potatoes from the warming oven, glistening
with more butter, and put the bowl on the table.

'You grew up here?' she asked.

'All my life,' Sally answered. 'I was born here, right in this
house.' She brought the pan out, placed it on a folded tea towel
to spare the table. 'It was a home for unwed mothers. It was
quite a secretive place back then. The mothers stayed out here

in the back, drinking plenty of fresh milk to grow strong babies, waiting for their labours to start. There were quite a few discreet visitors, too, adoptive parents or their own families.'

Eleanor's brain started to make connections, even as Sally poured her a glass of wine. 'What was it called back then?'

'Springfield House,' Sally said, the bottle stalled. 'Why? You sound quite alarmed.'

'Not alarmed,' Eleanor said, the garden growing wobbly and misty in front of her as she teared up. 'Wait there.'

She scampered through the house to her bedroom, heart hammering. She grabbed a small folder from her bag with shaking hands. When she brought it back, she held the paper to Sally.

'Is this your mother's birth certificate?'

'Read the bottom, place of birth. This was her *original* birth certificate, before she was adopted and called Diana. Hecta Allen, born 18 May, 1970. Her new parents – my *grandparents* – changed her name to Diana.'

Sally froze for a moment, then took the paper and stared at it for a long time. 'She only got this recently?'

'Three years ago, when she first got her cancer diagnosis,' Eleanor said, swallowing the lump that had formed in her throat. 'We thought she would get better, then. She wanted to find out who she was, maybe meet her birth family.'

'I only have my adoption certificate.' Sally ran a finger along the bottom. 'Eighteenth of May? My goodness. I was terribly ill in hospital around that time, with my epilepsy. This was registered by Dr McBride at Springfield House Maternity Home. They had two or three babies a week being born here.'

'So this is the house was where my mother was born!' Eleanor said, grasping the paper to her chest. She had to brush tears away. 'I couldn't find a full address for it. How on earth did I end up staying in the same place?'

'It's not that surprising,' Sally said, staring at the paper. 'It's the only house on Springfield Lane big enough to be a bed and breakfast. I returned it to its original name: the Doctor's House.'

Eleanor stood up, staring at the walls. 'She was born *here*. I felt a connection when I first got here.'

'Which makes us connected in more ways than one,' Sally said drily, with a smile. 'Because my mother would have been the doctor who delivered her.'

8

FEBRUARY 1943

The cleaning of the Doctor's House took two full days, and Dorothy knew that sorting out all the medical supplies and pharmacy cupboard would take even longer.

Curtains bleached and cracking from sunlight were taken down, and the surviving ones from the north-facing bedrooms were washed and hung in their place. Mrs Oppy's large and sullen son, a man in his thirties, helped move the painted bedstead into the front bedroom – Dorothy had decided to risk the late doctor's ghost. All the cupboards and chests of drawers were empty; presumably the Oppys had found a market for the contents, and Dorothy reasoned it was probably only ignorance that had kept them away from the medical equipment.

The coal bunker was almost empty but the one by the 'cottage', which appeared to have just one room on each floor, had plenty, so Mrs Oppy reluctantly agreed to 'share' before a coal delivery could be organised. The garden was overgrown and neglected, but had two dozen fruit trees in a field beyond, leading to farmland with cattle.

Dorothy was pushing a poker up the consulting room fireplace, which appeared to be completely full of sticks and soot, when the door knocker went and someone opened the front door with a squeak.

'Hello?' she called, while leaning around the doorway into the hall. A young man stood there, supported by an older man, dripping blood onto the flagstones. His clothes were saturated with it down to his boots, and he was gripping his arm.

'It's Bobby Moyle, missus,' Mrs Oppy said briskly, appearing from the kitchen. 'You'd better come in the kitchen, lad.'

Dorothy followed them in. 'You have cut yourself?'

'He got tangled in the winch rope,' the older man said. 'Could have torn his arm off, but I cut the rope. Quarter of a mile of hemp gone.'

'Sorry, Dad,' the boy said. He was white.

'We need to stop the bleeding immediately. Get up on the table and lie down. I'll take a look.' Dorothy went over to the sink, stripped off her sooty apron and started scrubbing her hands and arms with carbolic soap.

'We needs a doctor,' the father said. 'I s'pose you're the new nurse?'

'There is no new nurse.' She dried her hands on a clean tea towel from the dresser drawer. 'I *am* the doctor. Mrs Oppy, pour some boiled water and a good slug of the orange antiseptic on my desk into a clean bowl.'

The wound was partly crushed, fibres of rope in the raw slash, and she would have to clean it carefully before she could have a good look. It was still oozing blood. The boy was stoic, grimacing at the pain.

'I'm afraid I have to debride this wound before I can stitch,' she said, looking carefully at it. 'I must clean out all the hemp fibres. The two ends should heal, it's just this deep cut in the middle that is down to the muscle. You did very well to cut that rope, Mr...?'

'Harry Moyle. He's my youngest,' the man said. He still looked suspicious.

Fortunately, she had previously managed to clean up and sterilise her own instruments on the stove, and they were wrapped in muslin in the desk drawer. 'I ain't heard of no *lady* doctor before,' he said, as she fetched a set.

'Well, there are nearly nine thousand women doctors now, and more in training,' she said, focusing her attention on the wound. The boy's pulse was very high and weak, and more blood was oozing onto the scrubbed table. 'I'm going to give you some morphine, Bobby. It will make you feel better. But cleaning this wound will hurt. Mrs Oppy, a pillow for Bobby, please?'

'It will get dirty,' Mrs Oppy warned.

'Just do it, woman. Like the doctor says.' Mr Moyle turned back to her. 'Should he go up to the hospital?'

Dorothy drew up and injected a little painkiller. 'It would be dangerous to do it before the bleeding stops. Once he's stable, we'll get him there. He would be better monitored in a ward.'

Over the boy's muffled cries and his father's encouragement, she cleaned and stitched the centre of the wound and applied a sterile and antiseptic dressing from her own supplies.

Afterwards, Bobby looked sleepy, but had a little more colour in his cheeks. 'Right, I think I should call the hospital. Mrs Oppy, where is the telephone?'

'We don't have one,' Mrs Oppy said with satisfaction, arms folded. 'Dr Lavenham said we didn't need one.'

'The hospital isn't far. My lads are outside, the rest of the crew. We'll carry him down.'

'Well,' Dorothy said, putting her coat on, 'I'd better come with you.'

. . .

Mrs Oppy reluctantly admitted that one of the neighbours had a car and received a petrol ration for the surgery. The neighbour was both willing and friendly, helping lift the swooning boy into the back of the car and driving the quarter mile slowly. The light was going and the wind was keen. Dorothy's wool coat was warm, but she was still shivering in the passenger seat.

'We always did the driving for the doctor, missus,' the driver explained.

'I wondered if I should get a car myself.' She could also see the benefit of having a local person driving, at least at first. 'How much do I have to pay you?'

'The old doctor got it written down,' he explained. 'My father was the old horseman, when the doctors used a horse and carriage. You still got a trap in the stable up there, if the woodworm dint eat it.'

He pulled up in front of the hospital; just a dim glow of a cross shape under a cover suggested it was open, and under blackout rules.

Dorothy rang the bell. A starched and caped nurse, perhaps about to go home, opened the door.

'I have an urgent case here, Sister,' Dorothy said. 'He needs hospital care.'

'That's for the doctor to decide,' the woman said, but she did open the door for Mr Moyle and the driver to carry the boy in.

'As you can see,' Dorothy said, checking that the dressings were not full of blood, 'he has had a crushing laceration of the forearm. He has lost a lot of blood.'

'Come through to the side room,' the nurse said, and quickly turned down a prepared bed. Bobby's face seemed just a shade darker than the snowy sheets. 'I'll get Doctor.'

Dorothy sat down heavily on a chair next to the boy. It was a relief to get him here; if he started bleeding again, they would certainly be able to respond quickly. She could hear the doctor speaking down the corridor.

'We don't just take them off the streets, they need to be referred by a GP...'

She stood, acutely aware of her thick coat over the old clothes she was wearing for scouring out the stove and clearing the chimney. Only her hands were clean, scrubbed with disinfectant after she had stitched the lad up.

The man swept past all of them, straight to the patient. He felt his pulse, looked in his eyes. 'Someone has administered morphine,' he growled, and turned to look at them. 'On whose orders?'

He didn't seem able to tell from their raggle-taggle bunch which was the doctor.

'Mine.' She stepped forward. 'Dr Dorothy Harding-Rowe, late of the Royal London and Chelsea Women's Hospital.'

He didn't extend a hand, just stared down at her with faded blue eyes under white, short hair.

'Whatever next,' he said, turning back to the patient. 'We're going to need saline, Sister. Prepare the patient, please. He'll need cleaning up, too.'

Dorothy bristled with an anger she hadn't felt before. 'And *you* are, sir?'

'Bristow, consultant. In charge of what the locals like to call "the hospital". It's barely a clinic, but we do our best. You need to phone through next time, if there *is* a next time.' He started poking at the dressing.

'What do you mean, *if* there is a next time?' she snapped to his back.

He looked over his shoulder, eyebrows raised. 'I mean, the other locums have barely lasted a month.'

'I'm not a locum. I'm the new general practitioner, I bought the practice.'

He smiled at that, a twist of his thin lips that wasn't friendly. 'More fool you. I give you three months. Maybe less.'

'The islands *need* a doctor,' she said, forcing the words out.

'Let me explain something, my good woman,' he said, walking uncomfortably close. 'The men won't come to you because you *are* a woman.'

'Then I will start with their wives.'

He looked her up and down, and glanced at her hands. 'The women won't come to you because you are... unmarried. What knowledge can you have of their lives of bearing yearly brats, only to lose them to epidemics and disease?'

She pulled herself up to her full height, to make eye contact with his clavicular notch, under his Adam's apple. 'There are almost nine thousand women doctors in the country, Dr Bristow. The islands will have to get used to the idea.'

'*Mr* Bristow,' he said, denoting his status as a surgeon. 'I suppose, since you have already done emergency treatment on this poor lad, you had better tell me what you *have* done. The rest of you can wait in the hall,' he said over her head.

9

There was a busyness about the London office that Eleanor loved. The festival company owned a whole floor in a building and had a small roof terrace as well. The business had started to recover from the pandemic, where their organisational skills had been called upon to provide vaccination centres and conferences. Now, the bulk of the events were for the arts again. The building was surrounded by little cafés and shops, and laughter and a mix of languages drifted through the open window, muffled by the sound of traffic and car horns. As much as she loved it here, Eleanor found she was missing her early runs along the aerodrome road, along the sea and back through the town on the island.

'Are you really planning to offer only four thousand tickets?' Joey, her right-hand man, asked as he sat down at their shared desk. His floppy blond fringe was dyed pink, and he looked like he belonged on a surf board. Or selling ice creams somewhere, in his beach shorts and grunge band T-shirt.

'It's *exclusive*,' she explained. 'A unique setting for a special festival. We've set aside a thousand tickets for locals as well.'

'I thought it was a typo at first,' Joey said with a grin.

'We did an eight-thousand-ticket event in the Forest of Dean,' she answered, going through the neatly filed stacks of paperwork. 'I remember wild boars rummaging through the bins at dawn. Very picturesque. I was worried someone would get hurt.'

'That was a food festival,' he reminded her. 'It was basically sausages and beer.'

'Yeah, but the sausages were *good*,' she said, grinning at him. 'Especially the wild boar ones.'

'The beer was excellent, too,' he agreed. He glanced at her again. 'But are you OK?'

Eleanor remembered just how awful the weeks after that last festival had been, as her mother suddenly declined.

'I'm still sad,' she admitted. 'I have the odd nightmare, need a bit more sleep. But I couldn't have been better looked after on St Brannock's.'

She told him how motherly and sweet Sally had been, and the connection to her mother's birth certificate.

'I found out loads about the Doctor's House. It's gorgeous, you should see it...' She laughed. 'I think you'd like it. It's all hippy fairy lights and herbal teas, right by the sea. But my mother was born there, possibly in the room I stay in. Can you imagine? I knew nothing about her birth family, and then I was suddenly right where she was born.'

'I was born in the Royal London by C-section,' he announced. 'There isn't even a plaque.' He reached for his tablet and smiled. 'Right, I've been looking at logistics and I've found that the ferry only visits once a day but it *can* do twice a day at a push. There is also a dedicated cargo ship that could accommodate several of our food vendors and the equipment. Festival toilets would be a big issue – we will need a couple of sets of portables.'

'Could we get those nice ones?'

He nodded. 'Already put the call in, reserved two long banks and two disabled.'

'There are also facilities at the outdoor adventure centre. Have you spoken to them?'

'They are totally up for it, but they can't do all the dates.' He showed her the calendar. 'Second week in September jumps out for me. It's still a massive turnaround in less than six months, but August would be more problematic.'

'They've got the funding, and I'd really like to do August if possible. It's more than four months away, and it's a small festival. If we can establish it, and it breaks even, they will be able to run it next year as well. The committee couldn't be more motivated, and they did get public money to start it.'

'Priming the pump, sure. But they need to make a small profit to have a chance of doing it again next year, right?'

'I'll talk to them about the date.' She lined up the papers in front of her. 'And they'll want to do most of the food themselves.'

'Which is why I've only suggested Indian street food stalls and the vegan company with the big tent. The island doesn't have anything like that, but they do a lot of seafood stalls for the other events on the island. Tell me, boss, what's a gig? They do the world championship in gig racing, apparently.'

She brought up one of the pictures she had taken of the harbour, with several colourful long rowing boats drawn up above the quay. 'They bring over two hundred boats on the ferry, to compete with teams of rowers. They come from all over.'

'That's crazy. Why don't they just sail them across?'

'*Row*, Joey. It's nearly thirty miles of very rough seas, that's why. They'd be too tired to compete. Or, they'd capsize and drown.'

'So that's the challenge, getting the visitors over. I see why you're talking about a whole week of camping.'

'The islanders are going to run various events earlier in the week, so there will be lots to do for the early birds. One of the smaller islands, Morwen, has a ceramicist hoping to put an exhibition together in the towns with other local artists. There are several folk and shanty bands, dance groups, a faith music event that hopes to bring the churches together, and there's even a local brewer who wants to sponsor a tent for the whole week.'

Joey pulled out a printed picture. 'Here's my secret weapon. There's this guy. *He* might be a real help.'

She looked at the album cover. 'Case Shot? Who are they? I recognise the name.'

'His name's Mitchell Tate. The band was famous back in the eighties and nineties. He makes musical instruments for some *really* famous people, and he lives on one of the smaller islands. I was wondering how we were going to get brilliant bands to show up for just four thousand people.'

She looked at the list he had written. 'I don't hold out much hope for many of these big names, Joey.'

'I'm telling you, he knows *everyone*. Some of these people have bought guitars from him.' He handed her another list, of local bands. 'He also runs music sessions at a pub on Morwen Island. He knows a lot of the local musicians – they might be able to play during the day.'

'OK.' She shrugged. 'I'll speak to him when I go back in a couple of weeks.'

Joey fell silent, and when she looked up, he was staring at her. 'Are you sure you're all right? I mean, you look tired.'

'I was travelling most of yesterday,' she said. 'But it's getting better. I'm not looking forward to Mum's first anniversary, though. But seeing where she was born, where her life began, makes me feel a little connection to her.'

'If you need me, or anyone else, to travel down and sort things out, you let me know.'

'I will,' she promised. 'But I'm enjoying being right at the birth of this little festival. I knew I would. All the genealogy stuff is just extra value.' She smiled as she looked over the cityscape below. 'But the islands are beautiful, so picturesque and green.'

'You might find your long-lost family and never come back,' he said, smiling. 'Nah. That would never happen. You love us too much.'

Walking home, Eleanor felt invisible. People were pleasant but impersonal, barely making eye contact. On the islands, strangers smiled, said hello, and even stopped for a chat.

Back in her fifth-floor apartment, overlooking the Thames between two blocks, she relaxed on the oversized couch. A previous boyfriend had brought it when he moved in, and she had kept it. He was long gone, and she liked her space now. She thought about when her mother stayed... She blinked back tears.

She had an industry dinner to go to at the end of the week, so she could spend some time talking to the technical experts. There were lots of questions to be asked, like how much water and electricity would be needed and where they would come from. This wasn't going to be a cheap and cheerful excursion with composting toilets and hand sanitiser, and just a few solar lights strung up at night.

She ordered takeaway dinner to be delivered from a local restaurant, and unpacked her travel bag, much of it straight into the washing machine. She hadn't known what to wear on the islands. Next time, she would dress more casual, and more boho. All of which would fit in better at the Doctor's House with Sally, who wore a lot of flowing Indian prints. Too tired to work, she opened her laptop while she waited for the food, and signed up for a genealogy website.

There were three Allen families listed on the Atlantic Islands in the census of 1891. It made a tingle run up and down her spine, so she opened a bottle of wine. One of the families could be an ancestor.

She searched for an Alys with the unusual spelling, finding an Alys Mortain born in 1913, too early for her grandmother. Checking the census in 1921 showed that she was one of two daughters and two sons, born on Morwen Island. She typed in the location to an internet search to see a cute, rocky island with tiny cottages and a long quayside with a couple of fishing boats. *Morwen is the smallest of the inhabited Atlantic Islands...* she read, turning back to the records.

One of the earlier Allen records was from that island. She clicked on the entry to see a whole page of families in a row of houses in The Ope, presumably the name of a street. The Allen family lived in number two, Michael as head of the household and his wife and three children all under ten years old in 1911. Perhaps one of the boys married the girl next door to make her Mrs Allen? Katerina Allen was at number seven; as an old widow, maybe she was the mother of Michael Allen? Could they all be her ancestors?

The idea of blood relations made her yearn for a connection of her own, and a family she might fit into once again...

10

MARCH 1943

After the hostility from the local hospital, Dorothy worked to make the surgery ready for patients. The upstairs bedrooms had been scrubbed, although Mrs Oppy made excuse after excuse not to help. The room at the front of the ground floor was made a waiting room, with four decrepit chairs.

Looking back at the inventory she had been given, Dorothy had made stern representations to the former housekeeper that the entire contents of the Doctor's House had been sold to her by the executors of Dr Lavenham's will. Mrs Oppy argued that 'the old man' told her she could take any furniture she liked. Four mahogany chairs were reluctantly returned from the cottage once the papers had been re-examined, although the old housekeeper barely looked at them. As well as the seats, a children's bed and mattress, a useful side table and a small chest of drawers that Mrs Oppy's son had been 'cleaning' were hastily returned after Dorothy mused whether there was a police station on the island.

She hung handmade posters up in the library, shop windows and around the island on noticeboards, letting people know the new doctor was taking on new patients at board rates.

She had cautiously put her name as only Dr D. Harding-Rowe. She had invoiced young Bobby Moyle's family for ten shillings, much too low a fee but she was worried about overcharging. At least he wouldn't have to pay for the hospital care as it was provided free, and Mr Moyle came by to thank her, paid the ten shillings and gifted her two plaice, and said that the boy was making a good recovery without infection.

'I have *one* satisfied patient,' she said to herself, ready to deep-clean the stained sink in the kitchen. Perhaps he would spread the news to other fishermen.

When the door knocker clattered, she peeled off her gloves and apron and swept her fair curls out of her eyes.

A young girl, probably no more than nine or ten, stood on the threshold. 'Please, missus,' she stammered. 'Mam says she needs the doctor. It's the baby.'

Dorothy slipped into her coat and grabbed her medical bag from where it hung in readiness. 'Where?'

'Silver Street, missus, down the side of the Pilot's Inn. Mrs Allen's.'

Behind the quayside pub was a warren of tiny lanes between adjoining houses, each no wider than one door and a window, maybe ten feet across. She didn't realise she was there until the girl scampered through one of the doors. 'This way!' she called over her shoulder.

Dorothy had worked in free clinics with people at the edge of destitution, streetworkers at the end of their lives with syphilis, starvation or infection. But she had mostly worked out of a modern hospital, with electric light and room to examine and treat, or at least offer comfort. This was dark and steamy, and she could barely see across the tiny room. A fire had been lit, which was smoking so badly it was no surprise she could hear children coughing.

'It's the croup,' a thin young woman said, appearing out of the gloom and holding a towel around a tiny baby. 'We needs some of that special balsam.' She stopped when she saw Dorothy. 'Are you the new nurse?' she asked, head on one side.

'I am Dr Rowe,' Dorothy said firmly. 'Let me have a look at the baby.'

'She's coughing something fearful,' the mother said, handing over a bundle so light it felt like folded laundry. 'She stopped feeding last night.'

The tiny body radiated a fever through the towel, and managed a croaky cough. The smell was vile, and horribly recognisable as dead tissue in her throat.

'How many children do you have?' Dorothy asked, while staring at the baby, making observations about the blue colour around her mouth, the heaving of the tiny ribs. Her pharynx was swollen, and inside, a thick film was covering her tonsils.

'Four girls, Doctor. That's my youngest, she's just three months.'

'I need to see the others. Can you gather them outside in the light so I may examine them? I don't want them to come into more contact with the baby.'

Children filed down stairs so steep they looked like a ladder, and Mrs Allen shooed them outside. Dorothy gave the baby back to their mother and followed them.

The eldest child, Cecy, seemed healthy. The middle two children Branwen and Polly clearly had swollen glands and were warmer than they should have been. Polly, had a cough but neither had the distinctive coating in their throats that could close the airway. Yet.

'I need to speak to the hospital, and the board of health. I'm concerned that this is an outbreak,' she said firmly. 'Where is the nearest telephone?'

'The post office. Just down there, a few doors down from the pub. What do we do now? Outbreak of what? It's just the croup, isn't it?' She sounded desperate.

'My dear, you know this is not just the croup and that the

baby is very seriously ill. I'll make arrangements to take the three sick children into isolation at the hospital.'

Mrs Allen started back as if she'd been slapped. '*Take* my baby? They don't let the mothers stay. If they take her away, I'll never see her again!'

'They will let you look after her because she is still nursing.' Dorothy put her hand on the woman's arm. 'If we can get the right medicine – an antitoxin – then she has a chance. Can you see?' Although she had little hope after seeing the child's pearly skin and blue lips. 'And it's very important the girls don't come into contact with other children, or they will become ill.' She looked at the oldest. 'Have any of your children been vaccinated against diphtheria?'

The mother shrugged. 'I don't know what that is.'

'We must look into it straight away,' Dorothy said. 'Go indoors and keep everyone warm and I'll make the call.'

The local hospital had no space to take in three infectious patients, even though the older girls could share a room. 'You'll have to manage them in their own home,' a harassed-sounding house officer said. 'We've got a serious measles patient and two with whooping cough. We're full.'

'Can you at least take the baby?' She put as much authority into her voice as possible, trying not to beg. 'Without diphtheria antitoxin she doesn't stand a chance. And she's still breastfed, so you need to admit the mother, too. Her name is Mrs Allen, the baby is Bathsheba.'

'I'll try,' he said.

A few minutes later, they called back to accept the baby into the isolation unit as an emergency, with her mother. By the time the ambulance arrived, which looked more like a grocery truck painted white and just had a bench seat in it, Mrs Allen was resigned to going to the hospital with her baby. She seemed terrified at the prospect but Dorothy persuaded her.

'You must feel that you've done everything you can for the baby, my dear,' she said. 'This is her only chance.'

'Only, the nurse gave us that special balsam,' she pleaded. 'It's always worked before...'

'Perhaps it does help with the croup,' she soothed. 'But this is diphtheria, it's quite different. Who is this nurse?'

'Well, it's Mrs Oppy.'

Dorothy felt a surge of rage towards the housekeeper, who had probably been selling quack cures out of the surgery, causing parents to delay seeking medical help.

'Will your family be able to look after the other girls? I'll visit every day, of course, and they will be treated with antitoxin as soon as possible.'

Having made the promise, Dorothy knew that finding the medicine was even more crucial. She resolved to start phoning the medical board and the ministry of health as soon as possible, as well as the London hospitals she had previously worked in.

Someone had to have some, even if she had to buy it herself.

11

PRESENT DAY, 27 APRIL

Two weeks later, Eleanor put her bag down in the hall of the Doctor's House. She was getting used to the front door being unlocked and, on this beautiful April day, standing wide open.

'Sally, I'm home!' she sang out, and her landlady came out of the kitchen and hugged her. The top of her bun just nestled under Eleanor's chin.

'Welcome home!' she said. 'I feel I can say that since your mother was born here. How did you get on with your festival planning?'

'I have made about a hundred enquiries, and am prepared to do a thousand more. But we have posters ready to fill in with the artists' names and have already booked a few bands!'

'Wonderful! How about Bruno's fields?'

Eleanor lifted the heavier of her bags and pushed the bedroom door open. 'I have an interview with Mr Roskelly first thing tomorrow morning. Then I'm talking to Liz about the budget, and after that we need to sort out a firm date so we can confirm all the publicity. I would much rather we did it in August, though, but that will require a lot more compromises from the adventure centre. I'm going to speak to them, too.'

Sally put the smaller bags on the bed. 'And the ferries?'

Eleanor smiled triumphantly. 'I have just confirmed that we have *two* ferries a day for *three* days.'

Sally squealed with excitement and hugged her again. 'This deserves lunch out. I want you to come and eat at Le Petit Bleu. It's run by a friend of mine from Brittany, where they *say* they have the best lobsters in the world.' She shook her head. 'They don't really. I think ours are better, but I must say the food is spectacularly good.'

Eleanor was immediately embarrassed. 'I don't want you to go to any trouble.' *Or enormous expense.*

'Don't worry. I get mates' rates.' She winked at her. 'I used to flirt with his father once, before I knew any better, which helps. Oh, and I left some papers on your bed, about more Allens. Andrea asked the library to research something she found.'

As Eleanor went to get changed, she picked up an envelope with a Post-it on the front: 'Found new grave from 1940s, thought it might deserve a look. Andrea x'.

She opened it and unfolded a photocopied newspaper story.

Sick Child Taken to Hospital with Diphtheria

It was one of those words she was familiar with but didn't know what it meant. In her head, she associated it with polio, and she knew that caused severe illness. She read on.

Three children have been treated on Silver Street, St Brannock's, with suspected diphtheria. Branwen (8), Polly (6) and Bathsheba (3 months) Allen remain under the care of doctors. Local children are being checked daily as the island fears an outbreak.

The date was 1943, the middle of the war. Were there even antibiotics, and did any of the children get better? If Andrea found a grave... It made her eyes prick just to read the words. How on earth did the parents cope with three children with a deadly disease? They could have been her ancestors... Presumably the doctor here would have been involved in their care. She might have seen them in this very room.

For a moment, the ghosts of the past seemed to drift around her, before she shook them off.

The meal at Le Petit Bleu was amazing, and the running banter between the patrons – all of whom seem to know each other – and the kitchen staff was hilarious. The *chef patron*, Erwan, was from an island off Brittany called Ushant, a mirror of St Brannock's sixty miles due north. Sally explained that previous generations of fishing families had intermarried between the islands.

'But we are not *French*,' Erwan said in an outrageous accent. 'Any more than Sally is *Cornish*.'

He served a warm salad of sea vegetables dotted with peach-coloured shrimps, which made her mouth water just from the scent, let alone the oozing butter.

'I'm going to put on pounds just smelling it.'

Sally laughed. 'You're such a skinny thing. You should let your hair grow, you'd look like a model.'

'You are very beautiful,' Erwan said, taking a moment to pick up her hand and kiss it lightly. 'As is Madame Sally.'

Eleanor laughed, before she attacked a lobster claw which had astonishingly sweet meat. She said so – Erwan had been waiting around for just this reaction, and went back into the kitchen with a big smile.

'We should advertise all the local restaurants and produce.'

Eleanor patted butter off her chin with a snowy, starched napkin.

'Well,' Sally said, pushing her empty plate away, 'I hoped you would say that. Erwan does the most incredible Breton street food, too – galettes, buttery buns, fish stews. The food is intense.'

'This has been so helpful,' Eleanor said. 'Do you have any more recommendations?'

'Actually,' Sally admitted, 'I thought we could go somewhere different each visit to check out who wants to have a stall at the festival. If that's the sort of thing you do?'

'It is *exactly* what we do,' Eleanor said. 'I anticipated we would use our favourite partners, but I didn't realise the islands would have so much to offer. Besides locally caught fish and chips, of course,' she added. 'I tasted them last time.'

'We have local breads and cakes, and scones of course. I hate to admit it, but we have Cornish fairings and pasties as well. We have a delightful Sri Lankan restaurant just on the quay, and a Malaysian one on West Island. We have amazing restaurants and food. I think they would all like to do a stall. Even our local cafés would love a go. We'll make sure everyone is fed, and that will make them happy.'

'I've already checked out a few local beers,' Eleanor said. 'And I hear there's a vineyard?'

'Pricey but exceptional,' Sally said. 'We should probably go over and do a tasting.'

'You've been working on this all month,' Eleanor said, narrowing her eyes with a grin.

'It's not that I can't afford to eat out,' Sally admitted. 'But I can't bear to eat alone. When I don't have a guest, I just heat up a ready meal.'

She made it sound so sad, Eleanor was almost fooled, but the smile playing around Sally's eyes made her suspicious. 'How many ready meals do you *actually* eat a month?'

She laughed. 'Well, I usually eat with my visitors in the summer, which gets me through most nights. Or a friend will pop over to keep me company, and we get some fish and chips or a curry.'

'You seem to have a perfect life,' Eleanor said. 'In your beautiful house, surrounded by friends.'

A shadow fell across Sally's expression. 'Sometimes, in the winter... Don't think I'm a sad old woman, but sometimes I can't face going out. The garden dies back, the wind creates draughts at every door and window, and I become a bit of a hermit. It's getting harder each year to spring-clean and open to visitors. I was quite low by the time you appeared last month. But you woke me up.' She beamed.

'I'm glad.' Eleanor smiled at her, a little mistily. 'And now you're getting out more?'

'I like to think I'm doing research for *you*,' Sally said, standing up and shaking off lobster shell crumbs.

'Perhaps I should pay you,' Eleanor said, only half joking.

'You can, by taking me out to see some of these restaurants and cafés,' Sally said. 'And we'll probably get mates' rates at most of them.'

'Why? How do so many people know you?'

Sally shook her head. 'I've been here a *really* long time,' she said, smiling.

They walked home, stopping to greet people who knew Sally and had to be introduced to Eleanor. A young girl was waiting by the front garden of the Doctor's House. She jumped down from the low wall.

'Ruby!' Eleanor said with some surprise.

'I do gardening for Sally after school some days.' She grabbed a rucksack.

Eleanor looked questioningly at Sally, who shrugged.

'I do need help in the garden, and she's brilliant at weeding. Sometimes she digs up the wrong plant, but we just put them back in.'

'She thinks half the weeds are too pretty to take out,' Ruby said, rolling her eyes. 'She makes me *water* them.'

'How have you been?' Eleanor asked, following them into the cool house.

'Exams,' Ruby said shortly. 'But I did win a running race.'

Sally scoffed as she led them into the kitchen and filled the kettle. 'Tell her the truth, Ruby. It was an inter-island race, and you won your age class.'

'I am fast,' Ruby admitted as she sat at the table and took a biscuit from a plate offered by Sally. Eleanor declined – she might not have to eat again for days after that lobster. 'Dad says I have too much energy for a kid, he can't keep up.'

'Farming must be a lot of work,' Eleanor said, thinking back to the brooding and unfriendly man she had encountered. Despite his frowns, there was something about him that had stayed with her these last few weeks.

'Sometimes. Lambing is mad, and haymaking is all day and sometimes half the night. But otherwise, it's not too bad.' She reached for another biscuit.

'I'm coming to see him tomorrow.'

'I know, I told him to clean up. The place is a *tip*.' She picked up the last crumbs and licked them off her fingers, then jumped up. 'Do you want me to start at the big borders, Sal?'

'That would be lovely. The tools are by the back door.'

After Ruby had gone, Sally looked back at Eleanor. 'She's such a great girl. Her dad is lovely, too, once you get to know him. I knew him as a teenager. He was just as bouncy as Ruby.'

'Something's changed, then,' Eleanor said, remembering the taciturn, rude man. But he was interesting, especially as he had somehow created the bubbly Ruby. 'His marriage ending upset him, I suppose.'

'I don't think he's ever got over that. He didn't see it coming, that was the problem. One day he came home and she was gone, and had taken Ruby with her. He never told me what she said, but I know she left a letter.'

That resonated with Eleanor. Her last relationship had ended badly and it had come as a shock. 'Well, I'll stay off the subject of marriage generally. Not that I know much about it.'

Sally stretched out in her kitchen armchair. 'You never got close?'

'Not really. Maybe. The last one...' Eleanor trailed off into memory. His smile when he had just woken up, his kindness, his brilliance with children and animals. Maybe she had started to dream, just a little... 'How about you?'

'Oh, I dabbled with boys when I was young. But I never really wanted to lose my independence.'

'So we're two old maids, living our best lives, free as birds,' Eleanor said, staring at the glints of sunlight reflected on the floor, feeling hollow.

'You can call yourself an old maid if you like,' Sally said, looking up from refilling their cups and smiling broadly. 'But I don't think of myself as *old*.'

12

MARCH 1943

Dorothy soon learned that the 'as soon as possible' life-saving antitoxin would not arrive until the end of the following week, which would be much too late for the Allen girls and any contacts they might have made at school. There was a limited supply at the local hospital, really only enough to look after the critical baby Bathsheba. Denied access to the isolation ward, she spoke to the house officer, who looked like he should still be in school. He turned out to be a third-year medical student, seconded due to a lack of doctors.

'But why aren't all the children *vaccinated*?' she said, exasperated. 'It's free and compulsory. Why hasn't the doctor – or the school nurse – done anything about it?'

'The school nurse is a hundred years old and checks for nits, worms and bedwetting,' he said, leaning against the wall and rubbing his face. 'And the GP was already going senile.'

'Who do I speak to?' She shook his thin shoulder urgently for emphasis. 'To get supplies?'

'Keep trying the board of health, I suppose,' he said glumly. 'You could ask at the American base hospital, they were vaccinating their staff before Christmas, they might have some left over. Now you have to excuse me, I have my last rounds before I can get to bed.'

She let him go with some sympathy, remembering how gruelling forty-eight- and seventy-two-hour shifts were in her own training.

She asked one of the nurses if she could call the airbase hospital, and they put her through to the duty medical officer.

Dorothy put on her most officious voice. 'I'm enquiring for a critical patient with diphtheria. She also has two symptomatic sisters and there's another child who is asymptomatic at the moment. We don't have any antitoxin available to vaccinate local contacts, or treat the patients.'

'Hold on, there,' drawled a vaguely familiar voice. 'Who is this?'

'My name is Dr Harding-Rowe,' she began before she recognised the accent. 'I am the general practitioner.' Her heart skipped a beat and she instantly remembered his smile. 'Is this Dr McBride?'

'It is. We do have diphtheria antitoxin, but not in the volume you would need for mass vaccination.'

'I'd just like to start with the family and school friends,' she explained.

'And who is going to pay for all this?' he asked, and her stomach lurched.

'Can you help now? We can work out remuneration afterwards. The baby probably won't survive, and the mother can't afford to lose all four of her children.'

'I've seen it decimate whole schools,' he said sadly, 'back in my training. Come on up, I'll let the gate know. I can probably let you have an ampoule or two, but the British are going to have to come up with the rest.'

. . .

Standing in a brightly lit reception area, Dorothy felt uncharacteristically nervous. Still in her old clothes, she pulled her coat around herself. She walked through the gates, guarded by two cheerful British soldiers, and was directed to the back of the aerodrome, past hangars and what looked like low barrack buildings. A new brick building had a large sign outside: BASE HOSPITAL 31.

She couldn't help speculating on what Dr McBride would be like. Was he really as tall and handsome as she had remembered? She shook off the thought. Over the last two decades, she'd taught herself to think and act in a manner that would see her accepted as a female doctor. And that included pushing away schoolgirl daydreams about attractive colleagues. Most female doctors she knew did everything they could to establish themselves in the profession – a friend from training had even adopted masculine clothes and manners. Dorothy hadn't taken it quite that far, instead preferring to present as professional, authoritative and knowledgeable. Much like a maiden aunt, she thought. But she did wish she was wearing something nicer than a dress from before the war that she used for painting and digging the garden.

'Welcome,' Dr McBride said warmly, walking through the doors, smiling down at her. 'Come back to my office,' he said, and winked, pushing open a door. A young man sprang up from a chair. 'This is Dr Irwin Peaty, my young colleague. Dr Harding-Rowe.'

She followed him. 'Have you found any antitoxin?'

'Straight and to the point. I normally prefer to be wined and dined before I hand over US Army supplies illegally.' His eyes twinkled with humour.

She was too tired to attempt to flirt, if that was what he was doing. He held open his private office door for her, and on the desk were four glass ampoules, enough for a dozen children each. She had to fight not to snatch them up. 'Can we have them?'

'Ma'am, I mean *Doctor*,' Peaty said. 'Dr McBride thinks these are almost out of date, so not suitable for our forces personnel, ma'am.'

'We have enough that if we used these, our younger stock will then become out of date,' McBride said, still smiling. 'Meanwhile, you have an outbreak on your hands that will impact on *my* hospital. I'm making an executive decision.' When she didn't answer or take her eyes off the precious vials, he elaborated. 'But yes, you can have these.'

She looked up at him. He was looking at her, eyes gleaming. His long nose was a little crooked and his mouth wide, but very attractive. 'Thank you, Dr McBride,' she said. 'Are you fully vaccinated yourself?'

'I am. And you're welcome. How is the new venture going?'

She carefully wrapped the vials up in her handkerchief and slipped them into her coat pocket. 'It's early days.' She turned to leave. 'I have to get these to the family.'

'Not so fast, I'll come with you. I haven't seen a case for several years. I think we've been ahead of you in rolling out vaccination.'

Dr McBride's height made the cottage seem even smaller. The father had done his best to keep the two ill children tucked up in their tiny beds in the attic, while the older girl would stay downstairs. Dorothy examined both sick girls, carefully inspecting their sore and swollen glands. The father turned to McBride instinctively.

'Will they get better, Doctor?'

Dorothy bit her lip. Before she could answer, he spoke up for her.

'I don't know. You should ask Dr Rowe, she's in charge here.' He turned to Dorothy.

'I hope so.' She opened her medical bag and brought out the injection equipment. Because the glass vials held enough treatment for a dozen people, she broke the top off carefully and decanted the rest into a sterile specimen bottle. The little one, six-year-old Polly, whimpered, but once Dorothy sat down next to her and explained what would happen, and that it would make her better, she tolerated the injection. The older girl, eight-year-old Branwen, was more stoic.

'Will the medicine make the baby better, too?' Polly said drowsily, and Dorothy put her hand on her forehead.

'I hope so. One tablet, in water, every four hours,' she said, handing over soluble aspirin to her father. 'That will help with the fever.'

'And the balsam?' Mr Allen asked. 'It does help with the cough.'

Dorothy glanced up at Dr McBride and he rolled his eyes a little. 'I will make you up a linctus for the girls,' she compromised. 'But please stop using medicines that are not provided by a medical practitioner.'

'Nurse Oppy makes it,' he said earnestly. 'It's in a big bottle, at the front of the cupboard.'

Dorothy reassured him, but when she got outside and the door was shut, she couldn't hold it in. 'That *dreadful* woman, preying on these ignorant people.'

'They can't help being ignorant. How are you going to handle this Mrs Oppy?'

'I am going to evict her, and fire her, and threaten her with prosecution.'

'Hold on there, tiger. She may have acted wrongly, but are you sure she's not just as ignorant as the other folks around here? The twentieth century seems to have passed the place by.'

He followed her along the road as she tried to think of one

argument. 'If she hadn't strung those poor people along by selling them her mixture, they might have sought medical attention sooner.'

'How? You weren't here, the last locum left a month ago. I met him, wet behind the ears doesn't cover it, he looked straight out of school.'

She stopped. 'No. You're right. But they probably would have taken the baby to the hospital sooner.'

'How is the baby?'

'Extremely ill. I would say moribund already by the time I saw her. She's not expected to last the night.' He was beside her as they walked up the road to the Doctor's House. 'Can I at least offer you a cup of tea?'

His laugh was a little rumble. 'I was hoping you'd offer me coffee. I can't get a taste for... *tea*.'

She was inviting a man into her home, late at night. She had a momentary qualm, but successfully squashed it. 'I think I might have a little,' she said, having seen half a tin of instant when she was cleaning. 'But perhaps it's a bit late?'

'It's just the right time,' he said, a laugh in his voice. '*I* don't want to miss the showdown with Mrs Oppy.'

13

PRESENT DAY, 28 APRIL

Eleanor knocked on the farmhouse door, wondering if Ruby would open it, although it was a school day. It was opened by Bruno Roskelly, who at least looked cleaner and better dressed in jeans and a shirt. He also looked younger. She noticed his hair was shorter, and that it suited him.

'Ms Markham,' he said, his voice neutral. 'Please come in.'

He led the way to a kitchen, with old Formica units. The house itself looked old; the windows were made of small panes overlooking a garden filled with rows of vegetables.

'Call me Eleanor, please. I love your garden,' she said. 'The worst thing about living in an apartment in London is no outside space.' She turned to him. 'I do have a balcony and a few pots, but just herbs.'

'Ruby does most of it.' He waved at a coffee pot. 'I've just made fresh if you'd like some?'

'Thank you.'

'We could drink it outside. It's not too cold.'

Mindful that Ruby had said he had to clean up the house, she agreed, in case he hadn't made it around the rest of the rooms. 'As I wrote in my proposal—'

He cut her off with a wave. 'I read your letter, and the terms are generous. I suppose I could move the sheep temporarily, although they won't like it. They have always had their freedom. They might bellow all through your festival.'

She smiled. 'We once had a milking herd going back and forwards over the camping ground. People loved it, they wanted to help, but the clean-up was a lot of work. And we'll start the music gently so we don't scare the sheep.'

He brought two mugs out to a garden bench under the window that looked out over raised beds and fruit bushes. Beyond was a small field full of trees, with a few chickens pecking between them. He put her cup on one arm of the seat and sat at the other end. They looked over the scene, sipping the coffee. It was stronger than she would have chosen but good.

'The thing is, I need the money,' he said quietly. 'Farming doesn't bring in enough, and I've had some losses. The house needs some work, Ruby wants to go on a school skiing trip...' He had made an effort, Eleanor noticed as she watched him. His muscular arms and hands were clean, his hair neat.

She was moved that he would be so open with her. 'I understand. The hope – the committee's hope – is that it would be an annual event. So, you would have an ongoing income for the farm.'

'I see.' He drank some more coffee, looking away from her. As he squinted across the sunlit field, she saw that his lashes were long. She couldn't tell what he was thinking until he spoke. 'I suppose we could give it a try.'

'And, if that was the case, the festival might make some beneficial changes to the land. Like running water pipes or electricity lines, fixing fences, things like that.'

He frowned. 'All those strangers tramping about on my land,' he said, finally. 'I don't like it. They would be right *there*,' he said, pointing at the fence beyond the trees. 'Staring in at my windows. And Ruby, how do I keep her safe?'

'Mr Roskelly, we're not inviting football hooligans. They will be paying guests. Most festivals are incredibly good-natured and relaxed. If we can keep the drugs to a minimum and the alcohol under control – there will be stewards doing that the whole time – it will be lovely.'

'How can you control the drugs?' He looked haunted.

She smiled reassuringly. 'Since everyone has to come over by ferry, we will have sniffer dogs and handlers checking bags and passengers onto the ferry with local police support. There will still be some drugs, from the islanders themselves, but they are already here.'

'The islanders?'

'Mr Roskelly—'

'Bruno.'

'Bruno, there are drugs *everywhere*, even here. We are very aware and take lots of measures to make sure everyone is safe.'

'I know that. It's not something you like to think about when you have a child.' He looked into the distance again. He seemed very depressed, as if he hated the idea and was being forced into it. 'I've had people I've known all my life phoning me up to persuade me to do it,' he said.

She could feel a sympathy for his sadness, wherever it came from. 'Can I show you what we have done at other festivals? Would that reassure you?'

He took a deep breath, put his coffee down, stood and turned to look down at her. 'I'll do it because I don't have any choice. I'm being pushed into it from all corners, even by my own daughter. But I want you to personally explain every stage to me, and listen to my conditions.'

'Of course.'

'To start with, Ruby is to have *nothing* to do with any part of the festival.'

.   .   .

Eleanor walked back along the coast road and beyond the harbour, and found a path down to the sea. Taking off her strappy, gold sandals, she walked on the cold sand, wet from the tide.

She was sad, upset at something she couldn't identify. Just sitting with Bruno had worried her, as if his sadness was infectious. And how on earth was she supposed to exclude Ruby, who could talk about little else but the festival? She sat on the harbour wall to brush the sand off and put her sandals on. But by the time she reached the road to the Doctor's House, she had shaken off most of the melancholy.

Sally had an appointment at the health centre, so she let herself in and looked on the table for the customary note. 'Back later. Put quiche in oven at half past twelve'.

She checked her phone; she was just a few minutes late, so she obeyed the instructions and started making a salad. Sally had been teaching her what herbs could go in a salad, so she added fresh green shoots of garlic chives, sage leaves and rosemary flowers.

There was fresh bread cooling, presumably for lunch, too, so she cut a couple of doorstep slices and put the butter on the garden table.

When Sally came in, she smiled at the sight of her. 'You look very domesticated,' she said. 'The leeks in the quiche are the last from the garden, they are so sweet. How did you get on with Bruno?'

'He'll agree in principle but he obviously hates the idea. And he absolutely doesn't want Ruby involved.'

Sally took out a mysterious-looking bottle and a jug of water from the fridge. 'Homemade lemonade,' she explained. 'I had lemons that looked a bit long in the tooth so I made some. I can understand why Bruno's worried.'

'Why?'

While they waited for the quiche to cook, Sally sat in her

usual chair in the garden, kicked off her shoes and closed her eyes. 'Oh, that's heaven. Why? Well, his wife ran off with someone she *met* at a festival, a big one in Cornwall. Apparently she let her hair down, got too drunk and slept with him.'

'That's not the fault of the *festival*,' Eleanor said. 'They could have met in the supermarket.'

'But they didn't. I know there were drugs involved. I don't know the whole story, but he was devastated, and until he got Ruby home again I thought he might do something drastic to get her back. But he was a complete wreck for months.'

'That's sad.' They sat in silence for a few moments, sipping the sharp but lovely lemonade. When the timer went off, Eleanor put her hand on Sally's wrist. 'Stay there, I'll get it.'

When she got back, they dished up the food, but Sally just had a sliver of quiche, a morsel of buttered bread and a little salad.

Eleanor watched her for a while as she ate, but Sally looked distracted and didn't talk as much as she normally did. 'So, are you OK to book all the rest of my visits? And the festival week as well, once we secure the dates.'

'Oh, of course. You know that. Come whenever you like,' Sally said, seeming to shake off the strange mood. 'And tomorrow, we'll try that little seafood place on Morwen, the Crab Shack. Have you ever been there? The fishermen run it, but they sell a lot of the catch to the hotel there, Chancel Hall, out of season.'

'Then cook for themselves in the summer?'

'Exactly. Years ago, when the fisherman's father and grandfather ran the business down on the quay, I was one of their early customers. They used to pull their boats high up the beach, and haul them back down to go fishing. The old man was still moving those boats into his eighties.'

Eleanor smiled at her. 'Don't tell me, he lived to a hundred and nine.'

'Nope. He got drunk, fell off the quay and hit his head. He washed out on the tide. Just the way he would have wanted to go.'

Eleanor's smile faded. 'How do I tell Ruby she can't get involved in the festival?'

Sally considered her question for a while, picking over the best bits of the salad and nibbling. Finally, she looked up. 'Tell her the truth, whether she likes it or not,' she said. 'I've always thought she's got an old head on young shoulders.'

Eleanor started to clear the table, knowing Sally was right but also knowing Bruno might see it differently. And she didn't want to go against his wishes when he still hadn't signed the paperwork.

14

MARCH 1943

Dorothy slowed down as she stormed back to the Doctor's House, and Dr McBride had to jog to catch up with her. He was still determined to see her engage with Mrs Oppy.

'I'm guessing the relationship with your staff isn't going well?' There was so much humour in his deep voice she turned around to stare at him through the last of the twilight.

'Are you presuming to *laugh* at me?' she snapped back.

He held up both hands defensively. 'Oh, I wouldn't dare. I'm betting on you to win this fight.'

She stomped up to the house, only slowing as she pushed the gate open and looked at the dark house, surrounded by its drifts of dead weeds and with the cobalt sky behind just showing a few stars. She couldn't think where to start.

'You're right. She was peddling false hope,' he murmured right behind her. She could feel his warm presence blocking out a sharp breeze that suggested there would be frost tomorrow.

'Yes,' she said, without turning around. 'She was.' The thought of the baby fighting for its life in the hospital put energy into her push at the front door, which slammed back against the wall.

'Mrs Oppy?' she shouted, and the door to the kitchen creaked open. She stood there, all in black like Mrs Danvers from that film, *Rebecca*. Dorothy had seen it in London. Mrs Oppy's hands were folded in front of her just the same.

Dorothy took a deep breath and channelled her anger, laced with grief at the future of a dying baby. 'Mrs Oppy, you are dismissed. You will leave the cottage in the garden, and the employment of the surgery, by the morning. Please return any items that were in the inventory of sale. Including any *medicines* you have been' – she swallowed the first three words she thought of – '*illegally* providing.'

The woman walked forward, ignoring Dr McBride. 'If you sack me, how many patients will walk through that door? They don't trust you now. You need my good opinion. You'll be bankrupt within a year. *Doctor*.'

Dorothy stood her ground, even though she was so close she could smell the onions on the woman's breath and the sweat from her body. She moderated her voice. 'If you are still here, and the items are not returned, I will be forced to call upon the police.'

Mrs Oppy sneered. 'You think the sergeant will do what *you* tell him to? I looked after his mam when he was born, I know every member of his family. His father is ill with consumption, but he won't come here to some fancy London woman doctor. How many people have asked to see you this week?'

'You have broken the law,' Dorothy said, undeterred. 'Perhaps we should put it to the test?'

Mrs Oppy continued to stare at her, her nostrils flared. 'Oh, I'll go. You couldn't pay me to stay with one of your kind. Disgusting, I call it.'

She swept her long skirts and stalked out the back door, leaving it open. Dorothy's hands were shaking as she locked it. *She has keys for all the doors*. Looking up to the top of the door, she found a bolt that wasn't painted over. Wrenching it, she managed to get it half across.

When she turned around, Dr McBride wasn't smiling. The single lamp in the kitchen gave him a severe expression. 'You shouldn't let that woman get away with bad-mouthing you all over the island,' he said. He reached over her head and finished pushing the bolt over the door.

'She's right, though. No one has made an appointment since I've arrived,' she said. 'There's a semi-retired doctor on St Petroc's. His receptionist has written to me every day, asking for the records of previous patients of the practice.'

'Go and see him,' he recommended, leaning on the kitchen table. 'If you can impress him, he'll advocate for you. Sit down, you're shaking.'

'I'm so *angry*.' Her voice wobbled with tears.

'You were magnificent,' he said, smiling again. 'It will take time, but that passion will win them over. And what you're doing for those children with diphtheria.'

'In the meantime, I'm running out of money,' she said, half laughing through the prickle in her eyes.

'There I *can* help. My right-hand man has just shattered his femur falling off a roof, and his junior has been called home to Iowa. Frankly, he's not cut out for medicine. He'll end up a psychiatrist. How's your surgical training?'

'Eight years in the Royal London, four in Chelsea Women's Hospital.' She sat down, exhausted. 'I'm a bit rusty but I can cut and sew.' She wiggled her fingers. 'I have little hands, and I did well in embroidery at school.'

He laughed out loud. 'I can give you a couple of shifts a week, covering for me and Peaty. We're starting to get wounded men from the front sent to our wards, and some of them are pretty bad. I'll pay you as a trainee to start, see how good your needlework is.'

She remembered her last year at the Chelsea. 'In 1941, the

hospital was bombed. I went with the victims to the Middlesex to operate. You don't forget that sort of work.' She looked up at him. 'The work would be very helpful.'

He smiled down at her. 'Why the funny look?'

She pushed her hair out of her eyes. 'The lamplight makes you look jaundiced,' she replied.

'So my wife used to say,' he said, standing tall. 'What was that nonsense from the Oppy woman about not wanting to work in your house?'

She looked away from him as her heart lurched at the words. *My wife.*

She thought back to the pictures she had put up in her bedroom of her fellow students. They had become as close as sisters, as family. 'I have no idea,' she lied. 'I certainly don't have the time to be *disgusting*.'

'Well, see me out and make sure the door is locked. I wouldn't be surprised if that old woman was vengeful.'

'If I'm found dead in my bed, you can be a witness to her hostility,' she said, ushering him out into the chill air. She pulled her coat over her clothes and watched him walk to the gate, turning and waving, before he disappeared.

A shiver crept under her skin. *Married.*

15

PRESENT DAY, 29 APRIL

Eleanor walked into the brightly painted Carlin Outdoor Adventure Centre with her folders of projections and information. It was attached to an older stone building, and surrounded by slabs of rock sunk into the grass as seats. She was met by the centre manager, Kayleigh, an attractive woman in her thirties with a blonde ponytail, who immediately made Eleanor welcome.

'Come through to the office,' she said, leading the way through a bright refectory with folding doors open to an outside dining area. 'We have a group of young people arriving very shortly, but the group leaders will deal with them.' She led Eleanor past the commercial kitchen, gleaming in stainless steel, and through into a small room that smelled of coffee. Sally insisted on herbal and fruit teas in the morning, so the scent made her mouth water.

Kayleigh laughed at her expression. 'I'm assuming you'd like a coffee?'

'Yes, please,' Eleanor said, hand on heart. 'I'm caffeine deprived at the moment.'

Kayleigh cleared some space on the desk for the folders. 'We've had meetings about the idea of the festival and we're very keen in theory, but we are struggling with the date. We have established bookings all through August, for local kids whose parents need childcare. It's our busiest time. We take children from all over the islands for a summer club.'

'One of my colleagues has come up with a suggestion. Would it be possible, for that one week, for the childcare to move to the school? We'd make it worth the school's while, and you already have the staff.'

'We run a very active programme. They might have to miss the water, the canoeing and sports elements,' she explained. 'We don't want to short-change our own children. Including mine.' She looked down at her lists.

Eleanor opened up a brochure in the folder. 'We will be offering various events for children booked into the festival. The teams are all insured and have their own equipment – they could do extra sessions at the school for the local children. See, these are favourites of mine – Jump and Juggle. They offer circus skills and all sorts of outdoor acrobatics.'

Kayleigh looked through the brochure, then Eleanor passed her another showing kids running around surrounded by enormous rainbow bubbles.

'These are called Bubblemasters. They are artists that work with bubbles. I've seen them put a child inside one, it made a fantastic photo. It's in there somewhere. They also do balloon art with children.'

By the time they had put together an embryo of a package of events for the summer club, Eleanor was ready for another hot drink and the guided tour. A new group of year 5 and 6 students had just arrived by ship, some looking pale and green after the ferry. They sat in the refectory enjoying biscuits and fruit drinks while they listened to a talk on what they would be doing. The programme sounded excellent.

'I would have loved this when I was at school,' she murmured to Kayleigh.

'I did,' she answered, before stepping forward and introducing herself to the group. 'My office is back there if you need anything. Or you can ask any of the instructors or hostel staff, and they will be happy to help you,' she said to them.

One of the instructors then began a hilarious surfing demonstration – on a table – and Kayleigh turned back to Eleanor. 'I'll show you the hostel accommodation we have in case you need it. Obviously, our own kids come home every night so we don't use it in the summer.'

'We always need more space than I expect,' Eleanor said. 'Many of our entertainment teams normally bring camper vans, but obviously that's impossible.' The hostel was actually two low buildings set in a fenced-off grassy area, quite a way from the centre. 'They could be accommodated back here very well. Along with some of our technicians.'

'These were originally barracks for American soldiers during the war,' Kayleigh said, showing her around. 'They've been completely rebuilt now, of course.' She pushed a door open into bright, modern rooms with a few individual showers.

'Did you grow up here? On the islands?'

Kayleigh leaned against the doorway. 'St Brannock's born and bred. This place was being extended with the reception building when I left college. I started in the old farmhouse kitchen as a Saturday girl and worked my way up.'

'Do you know Bruno Roskelly?'

Kayleigh nodded but her expression changed. 'I knew him at school.'

'How? I mean,' Eleanor stammered a bit, 'he looks a *lot* older than you.'

'No, he was only two or three years ahead of me. Bruno was like the Labrador of the school. Goofy, funny, kind. And he used to be good-looking before he let himself go. He's a big softy. I remember he always took weeks off school to help his mum and dad with the lambing, even when he was eight or nine. Everyone liked him.'

'So what happened?'

'It sounds crazy, but he married the wrong girl. He fell in love with someone who came here each year on holiday, one of our summer swallows. Her family disapproved of the farming life, they thought they should all move to the mainland. I suppose they were right.'

'But he has Ruby.'

'I know, isn't she great? She's one of our new generation of Saturday elves.'

'He's agreed in principle to let us have the fields for the festival.'

'I'd get that nailed down and in writing if I were you. He's been volatile since Michelle left. Ruby is the centre of his life, she anchors him here and helps him focus on the farm, especially since his father died. I don't know if he can handle the festival, though.'

Eleanor didn't want to be nosy. On the other hand, she was interested; she could feel a tug towards him. 'He says Ruby can't have anything to do with the festival. I don't know how to persuade him to let her get involved in a small way.'

Kayleigh walked towards the main building, leaving Eleanor to follow. 'Ruby never does *anything* in a small way.'

Back at the Doctor's House, Eleanor sat in the sunny garden, topping up her tan. It made her bleached hair look even whiter, but she didn't care. She checked her watch. Normally, so close to lunch time, Sally would be bustling about in the kitchen. When Eleanor checked, the stove was off, none of the delicious produce from the garden prepared on the table. Some weird feeling, maybe instinct, crept into her. It made her skin prickle.

She headed upstairs, softly in case Sally had gone for a nap. She found her lying on her bed, but not asleep, and obviously in pain. 'Sally!'

'Oh, don't fuss, I'm fine. I must have eaten something that didn't agree with me.'

'What's wrong?' Eleanor sat on the side of the bed. 'You went to the doctor the other day, and you haven't eaten much since.'

'Well, we've been enjoying all that lovely food for the festival,' Sally said. 'I haven't got room for anything at home. I haven't got over those moules marinière yet. He said I might need a plainer diet for a while.'

'We can do that. So, the doctor said you were basically all right?'

Sally was quiet for a moment. 'I might have to have some tests.'

Eleanor felt like she had been thumped in the chest. She sat, waiting.

Sally continued. 'My mother died of stomach cancer, you know.'

'I didn't.'

'Hopefully it's not that, or anything serious. It's just very painful at the moment.' She smiled, and put her hand on Eleanor's. Her fingers were so small, they looked like a child's. 'It's probably all that rich food we've been having. And the scones! And the cakes at the hotel on Morwen, so delicious. Too much for my poor old stomach...'

Eleanor found herself back at the moment her mother was told she had breast cancer, the promise of treatments that slowly lost their lustre as the disease kept growing, shrinking Diana down to a husk.

'I hope so,' Eleanor said, tears clouding her vision.

'Oh, sweetheart, don't worry yet,' Sally said, sitting forward to allow Eleanor to gently hug her. 'It will all be fine.'

It was so surreal; Sally had been a stranger a couple of months ago, and now she was like a favourite aunt. 'I met the manager of the Carlin Centre,' Eleanor said, wiping her eyes with the back of her hand, smearing her mascara a little. 'Oh, what a mess I've made.'

Sally found her a tissue from a box and watched as Eleanor repaired the damage in her dressing table mirror. 'I don't know why you wear so much eye make-up,' Sally said. She hardly wore any at all.

'Well, I'm not pretty as such. So I go for different, maybe *interesting*.' She critically examined herself in the mirror.

'I think you're very pretty. But the hair. It's very short, I'm not sure it suits you.'

'You actually *do* sound like my mother now. Mum always said I was going for a David Bowie look.'

'What colour is it underneath all that bleach?'

'Just dirty blonde,' Eleanor said. 'Ordinary.'

'Yes, but *you* aren't,' Sally said. 'You're one of the most interesting and vivid and funny people I've met in a long time. You remind me of my mother, in some ways. You don't need to *dress* extraordinary to *be* extraordinary.'

'Thank you,' she said, moved. 'Now, can I get you anything?'

'Downstairs, in my handbag, is a new prescription. That should help. I've been banned from taking aspirin.' Sally laughed. 'Honestly, I feel better just for seeing you. I miss you when you go back to London. How did you get on with Kayleigh?'

'Oh, she's lovely. Maybe, while I'm back in London, you could answer a few of her questions, make notes on anything she suggests? You could message me or email.' She knew perfectly well Sally refused to rely on technology and waited for the reply.

'I shall write reports, weekly, on handmade paper with a fountain pen,' Sally said with dignity. 'And you can buy the stamps.'

16

MARCH 1943

Baby Bathsheba's life was delicately balanced between a cascade of organ failures and intensive treatment in hospital. Her mother stayed beside her night and day, and was reassured now that her own older sister had arrived from another island, Morwen, to care for the children and the house in Silver Street.

Dorothy visited the home at least twice a day. To begin with, both children got worse. Whenever Dorothy visited, supplies had been left outside by neighbours and friends: bags of coal and logs, a few cans of food, a bottle of milk.

Branwen, who was eight, was managing to eat broths and puddings to build her strength. Dorothy warmed to the child, who had enormous brown eyes and masses of dark curls and wanted to sit on her aunt's lap and be read to until she dozed off.

The younger child, Polly, was more seriously ill. Dorothy arranged her bed by the window and insisted it stayed open, to let the cold air reduce some of the alarming swelling at the back of her throat. With soothing cold drinks and aspirin, all she could do was minimise the symptoms. If her throat closed completely, she would need surgical intervention, and the cottage hospital didn't have the facilities to help her breathe.

As she opened the front door, on her way to make her evening visit to the Allens, a woman in a dark coat and hat appeared, hand raised ready to knock.

'Hello? May I help you?'

'Can I come in?' the woman whispered, looking around as if she didn't want to be seen outside the Doctor's House. Dorothy let her in, shutting the door as she took her hat off. She was young, but she had that peculiar prematurely old look that Dorothy knew came with poverty. Living hand to mouth was a constant stress, and it showed. She also looked too pale and thin, as though frequent childbearing had ground her down.

'How may I help you?'

'I'm expecting a baby.' She waited, as if Dorothy would know what she wanted immediately.

'I see. Do you need maternity care? I have a leaflet here...' She reached into her bag.

'No! I don't *want* to need maternity care,' the woman said, slapping at the proffered paper from Dorothy's hand. She looked distraught.

As a female doctor, Dorothy had been approached this way by desperate women many times. 'It is illegal, and immoral, to end a viable pregnancy,' she explained gently. 'But I can support you and help you deliver a healthy baby.'

'I nearly died last time,' the woman said, her eyes darting around the hall. 'My baby *did* die. I've got four children. I can't go through it again.' Her voice was high with distress. 'You *have* to help me.'

Dorothy led her towards the examination room. 'Please come in. How old are you, my dear?'

'What does that matter?' the woman said, biting her lip, looking back at the door.

'Sit down, please. Come in and talk to me,' Dorothy said. 'I have a little time. But then I must be off, we have a serious case in the town.'

'Maybe I should get diphtheria like Polly Allen, then I might lose the baby.' Her voice was high with distress.

'Or you might die, and leave your children behind, without a mother. Come on, we can deal with this together.'

'Where's Nurse Oppy?' she asked. 'I just need a word with the nurse. She would help me.'

Dorothy shut her eyes in distress. Was Mrs Oppy guilty of more than just passing off quack cures as medicine? She shook off the idea. 'What's your name? Perhaps I have your notes here.'

The woman was shaking. 'Beryl Livingstone,' she said, sinking into a chair and covering her face. 'I know I'll die,' she moaned through her fingers. 'I can't do it again.'

Her notes were clear. Five pregnancies in seven years, contraction of her pelvis due to rickets, traumatic forceps delivery with her last child. She was pale with anaemia, desperately thin from repeated childbearing and probably exhaustion. Her oldest child was only six. Despite her lined face, she was only twenty-four years old.

'Right, Beryl. You will come and see me at ten tomorrow, and we will discuss your care. And you must put any idea of harming the baby out of your mind.'

'It's not a baby yet!' Beryl said, looking up sharply. 'Nurse Oppy says it's just helping the body miscarry naturally.'

'And miscarriage that comes at the end of a knitting needle or some poison is not only unnatural, but criminal. You could be arrested.' The woman started sobbing again and rocking in the chair. Dorothy put her hand on her shoulder. 'I really can help. You must let me.'

'I might as well jump in the sea,' the woman cried.

Dorothy crouched down to her level. 'I promise you, you will feel better tomorrow, after we've looked at all the safe – and legal – options. Will you come tomorrow? Promise me you will give me a chance to help, at least for the sake of your children and husband.'

Beryl retrieved a handkerchief from her coat pocket and blew her nose. She couldn't speak, but nodded.

They walked to the door; Beryl's shoulders slumped as if she felt defeated. 'You will tell Mrs Allen that we are all thinking of her? She is in all our prayers, especially with the baby.'

'I will,' Dorothy said, her own eyes prickling with tears at the probable outcome for baby Bathsheba.

The following morning, a note came down from the doctor at the hospital that Bathsheba had died, peacefully, in her mother's arms. *At least Mrs Allen was there.* Dorothy could still see the little pinched face, feel the tiny bundle in her hands. She took a moment to let a few tears loose as she listed her tasks for the day.

A letter in the post promised that an engineer would be arriving the next day to connect the surgery phone line, which would make life considerably easier. Dorothy walked down to see the Allen family. It was hard to hold back her own grief to support both parents, who were in great distress. She was able to administer a sedative to the exhausted mother, knowing that only sleep would begin to restore her now. Branwen was improving, starting to take more food and drink. Dorothy forbade her from getting up to play, but allowed some stories and games in her bed.

Little Polly was not recovering. She struggled to breathe, the back of her throat obstructed by a thick membrane, the same type that had suffocated her baby sister. Not knowing what else to do, Dorothy administered a second, larger dose of the anti-toxin. She longed for a second opinion, but it was clear that the local hospital was thinly staffed and they had already failed to save Bathsheba.

'Mr Allen?' The children's father was sat outside the cottage on a bench, waiting for the tide that rules any fisherman's life. 'If I send you with a letter up to the aerodrome for the American base hospital, could you take it?'

'I will,' he said, jumping up. 'Anything for my girls.' Inaction was probably harder than doing something. Anything.

'It's for Dr McBride,' she said, pulling out a notebook and a pen. 'I have to go back to the surgery to see a patient, but I will come back as soon as I can.'

She jotted down her request.

Dear Dr McBride,

I find the middle Allen child is not responding and have administered a larger dose of antitoxin. The pseudo-membrane of diphtheria is well developed and the tissues are necrotic. She is feverish and fighting to breathe, barely drinking a few sips of water. I fear she may need a tracheal airway to be induced, and I have neither the experience nor the equipment. I hope you can advise.

Yours etc,

D. Harding-Rowe

She checked on Polly one last time. 'Cold air and water can help,' she said, but she was very worried. The child had hardly bothered about the needle into a tiny vein and the slow infusion of antitoxin, and her whole body was fighting to breathe.

She was losing the battle.

17

PRESENT DAY, 5 MAY

Eleanor had just packed her bag to go back to London by helicopter and train, but she was finding it difficult to leave. The island had a magnetic attraction for her. She could leave her windows open at night and hear the birds waking up, a distant cockerel from the farm, the wind rustling through the plants on the pergola over the patio. Her flat would feel empty now, without her mother regularly popping in or staying for a weekend. She had lived with Eleanor in the last months of her life and they were always laughing and joking, right to the end. The place felt hollow, cold now.

She was worried about Sally, too.

The doorbell rang, making her jump. Sally's friends and Ruby tended to just barge in. She was surprised to see Liz and Andrea from the committee waiting on the doorstep.

'I'm glad we caught you. Sally said you were leaving today.'

'Is something wrong?'

'Not at all. We found something new about the Allens.'

Andrea walked past her and headed for the kitchen. 'Shall I put the kettle on?'

Eleanor looked at her watch. She would have to jog down to

the airport if she left it too late. 'I only have a few minutes,' she warned. 'Is the kitchen all right?'

'Oh, I love Sally's kitchen,' Liz said, looking around. 'I used to do my homework at this table when we were both at school. Of course, we made her mother help us. She was really good at maths.'

'We've been looking at some of the weathered gravestones that are hard to read,' Andrea explained, putting a notebook on the table. 'Our local historian suggested holding a mirror underneath to see the shadows, where the faint indentations remain. I took photographs. Here's a printout of a grave we missed.'

At first Eleanor couldn't see much but a speckled, lichened piece of stone. Then a few lines and curves became visible. She couldn't read the first word, but the second one took shape. 'Allen!'

'It's a baby, Bathsheba. The gravestone was paid for by the local community. She was just three months old,' Liz said, looking over her shoulder.

'This is in relation to the diphtheria outbreak,' Eleanor said, looking up at Andrea. 'You got me some articles, there are more in the library, I meant to check them out.'

'I asked the librarian. It's got him quite interested. He also looked for other Allens on the islands,' she said. 'There was an Allen girl after the war. She went away to live with relatives when she was young. I think she was unwell; I think it might have been TB because all her classmates had to go to Cornwall to have chest X-rays.'

'This is the same Allen from the article?' Eleanor said.

'It could be...' Andrea said. 'Poor little scrap, diphtheria can be deadly. And it killed her baby sister. That can't have been easy for the family.'

Eleanor would have loved to talk more but she didn't want to miss the helicopter. 'Look, I have to go. Please make yourself something to drink, Sally will be back soon.'

The two women looked at each other. 'Sally hasn't had anything to say about this?'

Eleanor leaned back and folded her arms. 'She told me her adoptive mother delivered my mother at the Doctor's House.'

'It was a home for unmarried mothers back then,' Liz said. 'I would ask Sally about her mother's records. Dr Dorothy must have kept lots of journals and notes – maybe some are still in the house somewhere.'

Eleanor dragged her bag with the wonky wheel the last few hundred yards to the helicopter. They glanced at her ticket, took the bag and waved her aboard.

'Just made it!' she panted.

The front seat was taken by Ruby – she recognised the hair. The dark head next to hers must be Bruno's. She strapped herself in, as Ruby looked around and waved, then said something to Bruno. He didn't look around. Eleanor didn't have enough time to do anything except check a few emails in the fifteen-minute flight, but Ruby bounced up to her at the Penzance heliport.

'Hi, are you going back to London?'

Eleanor smiled at her enthusiasm. 'I have to get back to my proper job. Are you off somewhere nice?'

Ruby made a little face. 'I'm going to Bodmin to see my mum. It's OK, it's just different staying there. I like my new little sisters, though.'

Bruno walked up to them, looking reluctant. He nodded to her.

She couldn't help smiling. 'Mr Roskelly, I was hoping to get those papers signed so we can start bookings...'

'Dad!' Ruby erupted. 'You said you would.'

He looked away. 'I've been busy.'

Eleanor put her best work expression on. 'We can't book the

Carlin Centre until you do, or confirm the dates for the website. And we already have hundreds of people queued up to buy tickets.'

'Dad. Please?'

He turned to Ruby. 'I don't know why you're so bothered, *you* aren't going.'

Eleanor could see the change in her expression. 'No, thanks to you I'll probably be working at the school, looking after the summer club kids.'

He took a deep breath. 'OK. I'll do it as soon as I get back. Can I drop the papers at Sally's? I'm working on her trees tomorrow.'

'Thank you,' Eleanor said. She could breathe easier once the contracts were all confirmed. The Bubblemasters team were already close to being double-booked for the best dates. 'Let me know if you have any questions at all. We aim to make the whole process as pain-free for our landlords as possible.'

'Come on, Ruby, we don't want to miss the train.' He glanced at Eleanor, not meeting her eyes, and nodded before walking away. Eleanor waved to the girl as she followed her father out onto the road, looking back at Eleanor and making funny faces.

For a few moments, she couldn't take her eyes off his shoulders, bent forward as if in defeat. She wanted him to be pleased about the farm being leased, and benefit from the festival. She just had to find a way to make it happen...

The next day, Eleanor called Sally.

'Any luck with Bruno and those papers?' she asked.

'He popped them through the door this morning. They weren't in an envelope, so I saw them. They are all signed.'

'Great! My assistant will book everything and confirm the

ferries. I'll be back in a couple of weeks. Probably on the eighteenth. Is that OK?'

'It should be.'

'That works out well, then. Did you see Liz?' She tried to think back to what Liz and Andrea had said about the doctor's records.

'They were here when I got back, a nice surprise.'

'I was wondering...' She tried to phrase the question right. 'Liz said I should ask you about my mother's birth, but you've already told me what you know, haven't you?'

The phone was silent for so long that Eleanor thought the call must have dropped out before Sally finally spoke again. 'I don't really *know* anything.'

'Liz thought you might have records from back in your mother's day?'

Again, a long silence.

'I was born in 1953,' she said finally. 'I was adopted.'

'OK.'

'But I had a brother, Junior. He was born in 1945.' Eleanor could hear her sighing at the other end of the phone. 'There were rumours about a *Mary* Allen. I think she was sent away to a hospital.'

'Liz said one of the family had some sort of lung disease? Maybe tuberculosis?'

'Back then, it wasn't so easy to treat. They used to send you to a special sanatorium.' She sighed. 'Look, I'll dig out what's left of Mum's old records, although they are in the loft, so they might have been wrecked by mice. You can have a look through them.'

'Please don't go up into the loft, you might fall,' Eleanor said. 'Let me do it, when I get back.'

'All right. We'll do it together, then.'

.   .   .

Before Eleanor returned to the island, she went to the graveyard in London to be there when the stonemasons set her mother's headstone up. Diana hadn't discovered any relatives from her birth family by the time she died. She still had a few relatives from her adoptive family, and an old friend from university who had attended the small funeral six months earlier. With a few of Diana's students they made up a group for the simple, heartfelt ceremony to install the gravestone she had ordered. Eleanor had agonised over every word on the dedication.

The masons stood back as she welcomed people, and a cousin read a poem before they all walked down to the pub leaving the experts to seat and secure the simple stone. Eleanor and Diana had chosen the carving of a dove, symbolic of her mother's escape from never feeling like she belonged anywhere, except with Eleanor, her one blood relative. Both Diana's adoptive parents were elderly, and hadn't felt able to make the journey to the graveyard.

She linked arms with Lacey, Eleanor's flame-haired best friend through high school, and occasional holiday companion when they were both between boyfriends. They walked to the pub.

After thanking the other people for coming, Eleanor found a small table in a corner and sighed. Lacey put down two glasses of wine. 'So, how are you doing? You look well. You even have a tan.'

'I'm better. I've gone back to work properly, setting up a festival on the Atlantic Islands.'

'Are they the ones off Scotland? Or France?'

Eleanor rolled her eyes. 'It's amazing you passed geography at school, honestly. They are off *Cornwall*. A long way off, too. It's a proper boat ride to get there, two or three hours. I flew, I'm still scared of water.'

'So, what are they like?'

Eleanor was about to give a flippant answer, but couldn't.

She sipped her wine. 'Beautiful, really. I've been on the beach a lot. The festival is going to be amazing, even if it's tiny.'

Lacey clinked her glass. 'Drink up. We can squeeze another glass in.'

'I want to go back, you know, to see the stone.'

Lacey nodded. 'We can do that, too.'

Eleanor sat down to a second glass. 'I can't believe it's nine months already. I still expect her to be at the flat when I get there.'

Lacey took a few moments to answer. 'Neither can I, really. You were so close. I suppose it's being an only child. And not having a dad.'

The tears welled up, blurring Eleanor's view of the pub. 'I've found out a few things about her. In fact, I've been sleeping in the room where she was born. I think.'

'That's strange...' Lacey said, handing her a tissue.

'The house where I stay was the old mother and baby home,' she explained. 'And my hostess is the adopted daughter of the woman who delivered her. There's this whole group of people, who sort of know – or are related – to everyone else.'

'Are they friendly? I'm imagining duelling banjos right now.'

Eleanor smiled through the last of her tears. 'They're lovely – well, most of them are. There's this farmer who just took a dislike to me the moment we met. Which is unfortunate because we're renting his land.'

'Is he grizzled and mad?' Lacey waved for another glass of wine and Eleanor wondered if she was all right. 'Eighty years old?'

'Actually, he's quite – not exactly good-looking but attractive in a very macho way. He's an outdoorsman, hard-working farmer, protective dad. A bit older than me.'

That raised Lacey's eyebrows. 'Macho? Outdoorsman? Not exactly your type. Wait, do you *fancy* him?'

'Well, I'm not *dating* him, we're in a business relationship!' Eleanor sighed. 'Oh, all right, I *do* fancy him a bit. But he's pretty uncompromising about his daughter. Ruby, who is adorable by the way, wants to go to the festival and he won't let her near it.'

'How old is the kid?' The mother of two children herself, Lacey seemed to focus on the difficulty for Eleanor straight away.

'She's fourteen going on twenty-four.' She thought back to seeing the two of them, so relaxed together, father and daughter, like her own relationship with her single parent. But that close-ness could lead to misunderstandings and lack of privacy.

'Don't get involved,' Lacey said. 'He's her father and fourteen is a difficult age. Just get the land and stay out of his way.'

'You're right,' Eleanor said, draining her glass. 'Come on, they said they needed an hour to tidy up the grave. And I need to say a proper goodbye.'

18

Walking to the surgery for her appointment with Beryl Livingstone, Dorothy considered her request for help. Every doctor came up against the problem of unwanted pregnancy, and whatever one's personal view of the religious aspects, the law was clear.

It was apparent from the notes that the poor woman should have been delivered by caesarean for her last child, after two days of obstructed labour. She had suffered terribly, and also bled severely. It was a miracle to Dorothy that despite her poor condition, life had found a way to plant an unplanned and unwanted seed in her womb. But it was almost impossible to teach these uneducated, poor women about family planning, even if their husbands agreed. By the time they arrived at the doctor, many married women were depleted by constant child-bearing, and many had suffered physical injury by having babies too close together. Yet many also considered children a gift from God and the natural burden of women. Having done a few training sessions in a Marie Stopes clinic, Dorothy was still undecided on the topic.

'Mrs Livingstone,' she greeted her at the front door. 'Thank you for waiting.'

'Is it the diphtheria? The Allen girls?' She looked worried. 'Only, my children play with them all the time.'

'There is a very small, contained outbreak. Your children will all be given a vaccination at the school tomorrow,' she said, as soothingly as she could. 'But right now, we need to talk about *you*.'

She led her into the examination room. 'If you could just hop onto the couch and I'll feel your abdomen.' When Beryl looked even more worried, she explained. 'Just your tummy. Now, how many weeks is it since your last monthly?'

'It must be four months,' she whispered. 'My last baby was born in August.'

'It is very soon to have another child,' Dorothy said, feeling through the woman's dress to the small, firm roundness that confirmed her pregnancy. 'But with medical support, all may still be well.'

Beryl started whimpering. 'I told you, I'll die. I nearly died last time.'

Dorothy helped her sit up. 'Not at all,' she reassured, as cheerfully as she could manage. 'But you may have to come into hospital once your pains start to have an operation for the baby to be safely born. You will be asleep through the whole thing, and your baby will be out in no time and safely in the care of experienced doctors.' She waved at the chair. 'Do sit down.'

Dorothy explained that as her pregnancies had gone on, the babies had become bigger. 'You're a slim woman, with narrow hips,' she explained. 'We'll examine you nearer your due date to see if the baby can safely pass through the birth canal.'

Beryl wasn't really listening. 'Could my son have survived if I had been in hospital last time?' she asked, her eyes wide and filled with tears.

'Possibly. I'm so sorry about your baby boy,' she said gently.

'But we know what the problem is now, and will make absolutely sure you get the best possible care.'

The doctor must have known how dangerous the birth would have been last time, and Dorothy wondered why no one had helped Beryl. Perhaps the doctor, with his senility, didn't have a competent locum at the time, or an experienced midwife. She would study the notes later, to see if the family had fallen back upon the cheap but ignorant assistance of Mrs Oppy or someone of her ilk.

'My cousin had to go to Penzance to have that operation,' Beryl said, looking even more worried. 'She was away for a month and couldn't do anything for ages afterwards.'

'Leave that to me,' Dorothy said, making a note. 'I will speak to the doctors at the hospital, see if we can arrange your care here. And the operation, especially if it's planned before you go into labour, is very safe. Most people are well recovered in a few weeks and back to normal in a few months.'

She could see Beryl chewing her lower lip, looking away. 'I just can't face it, Doctor, not any of it...'

'I do understand this must be very badly timed news. Once this baby is born, perhaps we can talk about preventing future pregnancies when you feel well enough.' She could see thoughts crossing the pinched, pale face. 'Mrs Livingstone, if you lose your baby at this stage, I would be honour bound and legally obliged to let the police know, and there would be an investigation,' she said gently.

Beryl stood up, clutching her handbag to her chest. 'I should have just gone to Nurse Oppy.' Her voice was bitter. 'They told me in the town you wouldn't help.'

'I *will* help you,' Dorothy said, with more confidence. 'I just won't break the law and put us both in prison.'

. . .

At lunchtime, a young man in American uniform on a bicycle dropped a note off.

> *Dear Dr Rowe (I feel we are well enough acquainted to use this abbreviation),*
>
> *A number of our patients are air crew who have suffered respiratory tract burns, therefore we have a range of suitable tubes. We do not, unfortunately, have children's sizes, but can surely adapt something. I have experience of the procedure and would be happy to teach you. I would remind you that your first shift at the base hospital will be tomorrow night at 7 p.m., if we have not met before over the Allen child.*
>
> *Yours,*
>
> *Hector McBride*

The note was a relief. Polly Allen was getting worse, much worse, her lips blue and her whole chest and throat muscles heaving for air through the narrowed airway. Having asked for advice and help at the local hospital, Dorothy was told they couldn't do the necessary tracheostomy. There were also no beds available for infectious patients.

Dorothy was relieved that Polly could be referred to the American hospital. Not only were they ready to take her in, but they sent an ambulance, albeit with canvas sides, for the short journey along the coast road and into the base. Riding in the back with the child, holding an oxygen mask on her face, Dorothy was thrown around on the wooden bench seat. Polly was jolted out of her feverish daze and looked around in panic, her clawed hand gripping Dorothy's wrist. She wailed a few times, a sad croak, and Dorothy found herself murmuring nonsense to keep her quiet.

'When you are all better, you will go home, won't they be pleased to see you! And Branwen will have recovered, and the medicine has already stopped Cecy from catching the disease. Soon you will all be able to go to school and play with your friends again.'

The truck jerked to a halt and someone pulled back the canvas. They slid the child out on her stretcher and Dorothy climbed down. The first person she saw was Hector, his face as serious and concerned as she had seen it, focused on the child. She was shaken by her reaction to him. She was so pleased to see him, overwhelmed at how handsome and kind he looked.

'Well done for getting her here in one piece,' he said, a stethoscope already pressed to Polly's chest. 'The heart doesn't seem to be involved yet, so that antitoxin is doing its work.'

'It's her throat,' Dorothy said, crouching down to the child's level. 'Just let the doctor see your throat, dear.'

As the child half opened her mouth, the putrid smell of the dead tissue was diagnostic in itself.

'Let's get her much more comfortable,' McBride said, and Dorothy held her hand as they carried her straight into a treatment room. 'I'm going to give her a whiff of chloroform, we haven't got time for much else,' he said. 'I'll get a better look and if we need to, pass a tube into her trachea directly. It would be too dangerous to intubate through the infected tissue, she'll likely bleed. Do you want to gown up and assist, Doctor?'

A male orderly showed her where to scrub up and gown up, as McBride did the same. Dr Peaty stayed with the child, holding the oxygen mask to her face, the sweet scent of the anaesthetic permeating the air. By the time Dorothy returned, the little girl was gasping into the mask, her eyes terrified.

'It's going to be so much better in a minute,' Dorothy said. 'Then you will feel more comfortable.' A little of the terror faded from Polly's face, and her fingers dug into Dorothy's arm again. 'Dr Peaty is just going to help you fall asleep, and when you wake up, it will be over.'

McBride came in, gloved hands in the air to keep them clean. 'We've mocked up several sizes of tubes,' he said through his mask, watching as Polly's eyelids fluttered closed. 'We need Wells forceps, scalpels and the usual hooks and scissors...' He was confident and informative as he explained what he was going to do, but never patronising. 'Put her head back a bit. Watch this, Peaty,' he said, as he made a tiny incision. He showed Dorothy what he was doing, let her feel for the features in the neck, and gauging the tube, cleared just enough space to insert it into the matching incision in the exposed windpipe. Dorothy secured the tube with tape, and immediately, a whoosh of air came through the tube, then another. Polly's lips started to pink up.

'The trick is to avoid too much bleeding,' Hector said, showing her a few stained swabs. 'A few spoonfuls is all she can spare.' He smiled. 'You'll do the next one. Let's get her to a side room and instruct the nurses. She'll need watching for a few hours.'

'I'll stay with her to explain why she can't talk,' Dorothy said. 'She's dehydrated, too. A bottle of saline would help.'

He patted her on the shoulder as he walked by, and pulled his gown off. 'I'll keep you company.'

Her shoulder stayed warm, until she reminded herself. *Married.*

19

PRESENT DAY, 17 MAY

Eleanor returned to the Doctor's House a day earlier than she had expected, after a voicemail from Sally. She had said something about going away, but she didn't answer her phone when Eleanor called. For a moment, Eleanor wondered whether to call Ruby, but she didn't have a number for her. She took Sally's constant invitations to treat the place like her own to heart, and turned up on Sunday afternoon.

The sun was out, and the water around the islands was almost luminous, glowing shades of aquamarine. The helicopter pilot was chatty, pointing out the bottle-green reefs, the submerged sandbanks and almost one thousand stacks and islets. Eleanor didn't want to look at the dark water below. She dragged her bag from the heliport along the high street, cursing the broken wheel, which she had meant to replace. Turning onto Springfield Lane she noticed the windows were all shut, as if Sally had already left.

The door was locked, but the spare key was where Sally had pointed it out, hanging on a rusty hook among the stems of the climbing rose around the door.

'Hello? Sally!'

A draught was running through the house. Stepping into the kitchen, she saw the back door open. The idea that she might find Sally collapsed outside made her heart race, but as she stepped outside, she saw Sally poring over a book at the garden table. She looked up, surprise, fear, then relief flying across her face.

'Oh, it's you, maid.' Sally stood, and when Eleanor leaned down to hug her, she could feel how thin she had become. 'Oh, I *am* pleased to see you. I was just going to leave a note out for you for tomorrow,' she said. 'I'm going into hospital.'

Eleanor led her back to the table and sat next to her. 'What's going on? You're not right, I can tell. You've lost more weight.'

Sally patted her hand. 'It's silly, really, I can't eat anything without the pain coming back. They want to do a lot of tests, all at the same time.'

'Well, that's good,' Eleanor said, putting her hand over Sally's. Suddenly she seemed so much older, seventy at least.

'It turns out I'm anaemic. I'm bleeding somewhere and they think it's my stomach.' Her eyes were shining with tears. 'It's how my mother's cancer started.'

'Do they think it is cancer? Could it be something else?' Sally's fingers were cold, even in the warmth of the garden.

'They don't know.' Sally's voice faded for a moment. 'I don't feel right. I don't feel like me.'

Eleanor had recently been trying to construct family trees from the knowledge she could tie down to the Allens. 'Was this your biological mother?' she asked. 'The one with stomach cancer?'

'Oh, I see what you mean,' she answered, though she looked uncertain. 'No. I never found out who my mother was. No, it was Dr Dorothy.'

'Well, you can't have inherited it from her,' Eleanor said, and felt the teapot on the table. It was cold and almost empty.

'Tell me what herbs you'd like in your tea,' she prompted, standing up.

'I never even thought of that. How silly was I being?'

'What are the odds that two unrelated people would get the same disease at more or less the same age, in the same house?' Eleanor said, gathering up the pot and the cups.

Sally followed her into the kitchen. 'Don't bother with the tea.' She opened her arms for a hug. Eleanor's chin could just sit gently on the top of Sally's head. 'Let's go out to Mrs Keiller's café for a scone and cream.'

'If you want,' Eleanor said, shoving the bag out of the way. 'Are the tests tomorrow?'

'No food or drink from midnight. Then I have to report to the day unit for eight o'clock. No breakfast, not even water. I shall be so thirsty.'

'I'll take you,' Eleanor said. 'We'll get a taxi.'

'It's OK, Bruno is driving me.'

'Well, I'll come too, and keep you company. You know you would rather have me there than Bruno.'

'It might be a long wait,' Sally warned. 'And you have lots of work to do.'

'Actually, I do need to walk the grounds with our site manager. Mr Roskelly – Bruno – will want to be part of all those decisions. It might make him unbend a bit towards me.'

'Do you think he's leaning away from you?' Sally started to smile. 'He just thinks you're very important and efficient. And unapproachable and clever. But he must see how pretty and kind you are – under all that make-up.'

Eleanor held out her crooked arm for Sally and pulled the door to behind them. 'Hardly *any* make-up, I'll have you know. And I'm *very* approachable.'

'Maybe he thinks you're out of his league,' Sally commented.

Eleanor shook her head. 'I'm sure he finds me massively

annoying, and he believes I'm encouraging Ruby to defy him over the festival.'

Sally led her onto the high street. 'He keeps bringing you up in conversation. Mostly along the lines of "who does she think she is" and "what does a towny know about farming". But still, he's interested. And he thinks you have influence over Ruby.'

'Well, he should talk to his daughter,' Eleanor said as they entered the café. 'She's a smart girl, she'll find a way to defy him. They all do at that age.'

The woman running the café was in her eighties, maybe more. Sally introduced Mrs Keiller to Eleanor, who relayed their order to the staff member behind the counter then walked back to join them. She was white-haired and looked a hundred years old, but walked with a bounce in her step.

'Sally tells me you want to know about Mary Allen. I think we knew her as Polly, if you mean the girl who nearly died of diphtheria. I was just a baby then. Back when my mother and grandmother ran the shop. Mrs Keillers have run the café for nearly two hundred years.' Her dark eyes twinkled.

Eleanor smiled. 'This is so kind. Thank you,' she said, smiling at Sally. 'Both of you. I'm not sure how Polly Allen of the forties fits in with my mother, born Hecta Allen, but it feels like they are connected.'

'Oh, they *must* be.' Mrs Keiller said. 'I don't know that much, mind.' She held a hand up defensively. 'And I don't like to gossip—'

'This isn't gossip,' Sally intervened. 'This is *family*.'

'Well, then. When I was a very young woman, I met a young man. We were both really young and, well, really ignorant.' She leaned back as a tea tray was delivered to the table. She checked each component and nodded. The young waitress looked relieved when she was finally dismissed. 'One day, I realised I might be in the family way, but I didn't want anyone to know. So, instead of going to the health centre, I popped into the Doctor's House to see Dr Dorothy.' Her face, even at her advanced age, went quite pink.

'I see,' Eleanor said, looking at Sally, who shrugged. 'Did she help?'

'In a way, because she spoke kindly to my father and the young man and I were married shortly after.' Mrs Keiller said. 'But I saw Polly Allen there, who had moved to the mainland years before and just came back for holidays. I knew her well because her older sister babysat for my family. Polly was so shocked to see me, she even begged me not to tell anyone she was on the island.'

'Why did she leave St Brannock's?' Eleanor asked.

'She'd been living away with her aunt,' Mrs Keiller said. 'Because she had had breathing problems since getting ill as a child. She went away when she was about ten or eleven, and I heard she was staying with relatives in Truro who lived near the hospital. Then she turned up at the Doctor's House probably ten years later, and I could see she was expecting. This was a few months before the place opened up as Springfield Maternity Home. I can't tell you how much people wanted to cover up that sort of thing.'

'I can't find any birth records with Polly on them,' Eleanor said.

'Well, her mother's name was Cecily,' Mrs Keiller said. 'Mrs Cecily Allen – I know because her eldest was also called Cecy, and used to mind me as a child when the café was open. Polly was probably a nickname, too.'

'Well, that sounds very likely the same family,' Sally said. 'Shall I pour this tea before it gets cold?'

Eleanor was too excited to respond. 'Have you ever heard the name before? H-E-C-T-A, Hecta?'

Mrs Keiller shook her head. 'Maybe it's in gratitude to the old doctor here, Dr Hector. Maybe he delivered the baby.' She glanced at Sally.

'I don't know much about the doctors,' Eleanor said.

'They did a lot of good for the islands,' Mrs Keiller said. '*She* got us all vaccinated. The whole family of girls were stricken with it, not just Polly. We all had to get jabs. I don't remember it, but my older brothers complained of the injections.'

'Could they be from the same family?' Eleanor asked, her heart racing. She was keen to divert the conversation back to the Allens.

'Well, there was Branwen, if I remember right, the middle girl. She was a lovely girl, settled down in Cornwall, had two sets of twins, imagine that! Cecy, the oldest, married a local boy, he joined the police, was a good lad and in the church choir. Polly just squeaked through the illness and had a bad chest, and the parents had two younger boys after. Nice family but there was a story there, with poor Polly always going backwards and forwards to the hospital when she was young. She was never well enough to go to school here, in case she picked up a bug.'

All Eleanor could think was: *Any one of these girls could have been my grandmother or even great-grandmother.*

20

MARCH 1943

By two o'clock in the morning, Hector McBride recommended that Dorothy go home and get some sleep. Polly was stable and breathing easily through the tube. With sufficient sedation, she would not pull at it, but to be sure a nurse would be on hand throughout the night.

Dorothy knew he was right, but she had enjoyed his company. She had chatted quietly with him, talking about his work at the hospital. She had even confided her difficulty with Beryl Livingstone and her very unwanted pregnancy.

Hector had strong beliefs. 'I don't say it's never wrong,' he said. 'When a child will be born with no hope of life, or where the mother's life is in danger. But it's a moral question, too big for me.'

'You've never been asked?'

'Not by a woman. But by one or two young men who had got their girls into trouble, when I was still in training. How about you?'

She rolled her eyes. 'I worked in a discreet and expensive private women's hospital. I knew it went on, although I couldn't tell you which doctors performed them. But rumours ran around that many titled young ladies, even European royalty, occasionally sent their wayward daughters to us with "irregular menstrual periods". But no, not me, not my close friends and colleagues.'

He stretched, and she found herself enjoying the sight. He was like a skinny white cat in his doctor's coat. She smiled at him, which he noticed when he turned to her.

'Don't judge me. I've done four out of the last six nights.'

'Not at all.' She smiled, gathering up her coat and bag. 'I've been enjoying rather too many evenings without a single night call.'

'Still no patients?'

She smiled grimly. 'I'm going to tackle this other doctor tomorrow, to see what's going on. I can't imagine he can see *every* patient on the islands.'

'I have every faith in you,' he said, smiling sleepily. 'After that showdown with Mrs Oppy.'

The next day, Dorothy took the small boat over to St Petroc's on the incoming tide. The sea was dark and brooding; clouds overhead threatened rain, making the journey seem longer and colder than she was prepared for. The island was different to St Brannock's, with its busy foreshore and harbour. The houses here had shutters at most of the windows and looked like a row of closed faces, stretching along the narrow quay and small timber jetty. Most of the small houses were painted white or pink, the whitewash revealing the stone and cob underneath in places.

Dorothy asked the way to the doctor's surgery, and was shown up a steep lane just off the quay. At the top, a larger house, two storeys and painted a cheerful pink, looked down over the whole community, over the fishing boats bobbing on their buoys, and piles of fishing nets and tackle stacked along the sea. An older woman, about seventy, met her at the door.

'Yes?'

'My name is Dr Harding-Rowe,' she said. 'I was hoping to see Dr Penrose.'

The woman peered over her glasses at her. She was bent forward like a prawn, with thin white hair falling in her eyes. 'Oh, you're the new doctor on St Brannock's. Well, my dear, Simon will be very pleased to meet you.' But there was doubt in her voice. 'He's just with a patient right now, but that's the last one this morning. You know, he was almost retired before the war. He could do with less work at his time of life.'

He was in his mid-seventies, Dorothy estimated, as she took his hand twenty minutes later. She recognised the patient from St Brannock's, who scuttled away with a red face after tipping his cap to her.

'Michael Ellis,' the doctor said wearily, waving a hand after him. 'He should cut back on the drink. He's one of yours.'

'No one will come to me,' she said blankly.

'Well, if I drop dead of overwork, they will have to,' he said with a dry voice. 'Is it too early for sherry or would you prefer tea?'

She opted for tea. He led her upstairs to a living room and study that looked over the sea. 'My wife will bring it,' he explained, before sinking into a chair in front of the window.

She sat down on a comfortable couch, admiring the view of grey clouds scudding over shadows on the sea. 'It looks like a storm is coming.'

'First rule of being an island doctor,' he said, waving a pipe at her. 'Listen to the shipping forecast. The fishing community all depend on it. If good weather comes after several bad days, your surgery will be empty. They all have to chase the fish.'

She filed away the idea. 'I'm not even sure I have a radio

set,' she said, thinking out loud. Presumably another thing Mrs
Oppy had taken.

'Old George Lavenham had one. First piece of advice he
gave me fifteen years ago, and now I'm passing it on to you.'

'I've heard the previous doctor had a nurse.'

'A proper, board-certified trained nurse, Nurse Penhaligon,
and an assistant, Nurse Harper. She's working for me two days
a week but she would be better working for you full-time. Have
you met your local midwife? She's very experienced, although
back in her day, training was less important. She's good, reliable.
She even borrows books from me from time to time.'

'I'll speak to her. I do have one obstetric patient. She previously had a very obstructed labour, lost the baby. She's pregnant
again.'

'Poor lass. You need to talk to the hospital before that Oppy
woman gets her hands on her.'

'Ah. Mrs Oppy,' Dorothy said wryly.

She smiled at Mrs Penrose when she set a tea tray down on
a small table.

'I'm just doing your lunch, Doctor,' she reminded him.
'Don't forget.'

'There will be enough for you, if you care to stay,' he said to
Dorothy, leaning his head back against the chair. She could see
then that his tan was more jaundice, that his thin body had a
firm, swollen belly just covered by his high-waisted trousers.

'Should you be working, Doctor?' she said, as politely as she
could. 'I believe you retired?'

'I kept a small local clinic going two mornings a week, but
the main surgery is on St Brannock's.' He gave her a knowing,
amused look. 'We're overloaded here. You need to convince
your flock to come to you.'

'The board said they wouldn't come to me because I am a
woman,' she admitted.

'Maybe some of the older men won't want to open their

shirts or drop their trousers for a woman, but if they are ill enough, they will have to.' He shook his head wearily. 'No, what you need is a fiancé.'

'I beg your pardon?'

He smiled at her. 'This is an old-fashioned, traditional community. A woman, living alone and not married, they're suspicious. It's like a chicken with two heads – they might pay to see one as a curiosity, but they don't want to buy one. It's not what they expect, it's not natural to them.'

'There's old-fashioned, then there's *Victorian*,' she muttered.

'And the Oppy woman is spreading rumours that you're an invert, that your interest lies in other women.'

She'd been afraid that's what Mrs Oppy had meant when she referred to her as 'disgusting'. She would have seen the pictures of her fellow students, their graduation pictures, all women hugging and laughing on a trip to Baden-Baden.

'It's none of their business if I'm married, engaged or single,' she said firmly. 'Or where my passions lie, for that matter. I'm trained in *medicine*. I have certificates in *surgery*. I have worked in hospitals for fifteen years.'

'Yes. That's the other problem. Being in general practice means much more than hanging up your shingle and expecting grateful patients to form an orderly queue. They know you've bought a business, that you intend to make money from them.'

'I'd like a living, but I'm not expecting to make a *profit*.' She was startled by the idea.

'You need to start raising your profile, get to know the important people in the community. The Lord Lieutenant, the base commander, the vicar, the teachers, the employers and various committees and clubs that run the place. Don't be shy. They will accept you, and then that approval will trickle down to your patients. It's very hard for a family to find five shillings for an appointment, so try opening a free clinic.'

She could see the sense of what he was saying, but as an introverted person, she'd never had the time or inclination to socialise outside of work. The idea made her muscles tense up. 'I'm not sure where to start...'

'You've already made a beginning with the diphtheria vaccinations. The local board are planning to get enough antitoxin to inoculate all the island children. That was your doing. That could be your first free clinic, and you can visit the other off-islands, work with the schools and meet the mothers.'

She looked at the dark shadows under his eyes. 'Thank you for that. Can I do anything for you?'

'No, my race is run. I'll probably need a bit of morphine at the end, but I'm managing for now. The work has been a good distraction, to be honest.'

'Can I ask...?'

'Carcinoma of the liver. I was a big drinker when I was a student, never lost the habit. It's a bit late to care, so I still have the odd sherry.'

'You know where to find me. I've had the phone put back on at the surgery.' She thought about the idea of a clinic, a flicker of warmth and excitement starting to spread.

His eyes drifted closed. She stood up and shook his arm gently. 'Don't forget your lunch, Doctor,' she said. 'And thank you.'

21

PRESENT DAY, 18 MAY

'When is her appointment?' Bruno growled in the early morning, as Sally went back for yet one more thing she needed. It turned out to be a pink stone, to add to the velvet bag of crystals she had already put in her case.

Eleanor shook her head at him. 'We'll just be a couple of minutes late,' she said, 'no more.'

'I'm so thirsty,' Sally said on one of her scurries through the hall. 'And I can't find the book I was reading.'

'We packed it first,' Eleanor said. 'Anyway, you'll have me to talk to some of the time, then you'll have this test, then you can have a nap. They'll give you a sedative, if you want it.'

'I want to know what they are *doing* to me,' Sally said, stopping in the hallway, hands clasping and unclasping. 'I don't think I can do it.'

'I *know* you can,' Eleanor said, taking one of her hands, shaking it to make her point.

For a long time Sally stared into her eyes, then shook off her fear for a moment. 'Of course. I suppose hundreds of girls said that when they came here to have their babies.'

'Exactly. And your test takes forty-five minutes. I don't know much about childbirth, but I think it takes a lot longer.'

Sally laughed as Bruno picked up her bag, his expression both exasperated and affectionate. 'You probably know more about childbirth than either of us,' she said, looking up into his face.

'I know it went on for ages,' he said, guiding her out of the door. 'And I got shouted at *a lot*.'

Eleanor laughed at his comical grimace, and somehow they managed to get Sally seated, reassured her that she didn't need to go back for anything, and that she would be home by evening. Eleanor got in the back seat with her, and Sally gripped her hand tight.

'But what if they find something… nasty?' Sally asked, her face screwed up with anxiety.

'We'll deal with it, if they do. But they might find something very treatable. Remember what the doctor said? Maybe it's an ulcer.'

'I didn't hear most of what he said,' Sally admitted. 'I just heard the word "cancer" and my ears slammed shut.'

Bruno eased the car onto the main road in the town, towards the small hospital. Eleanor could feel Sally shaking.

'So, remember, they are going to spray your throat with some special local anaesthetic so you don't feel anything,' she said. 'And you'll be mostly asleep.'

'You haven't had it done,' Sally grumbled. 'I'm scared.'

Eleanor took a deep breath. 'I had a test a bit like it, once.'

Sally looked suspicious. 'As frightening as putting a camera into your stomach?'

Eleanor winced. 'Worse. They had to check I didn't have bowel cancer.'

She could see the skin around Bruno's ears stretch as he grinned and started to chuckle.

'What... Oh.' Even Sally smiled. 'Poor thing. You must have been terrified.'

'I'd rather have the test than the disease.' Eleanor thought back to the experience. 'It was more embarrassing than painful, but I definitely opted for the sedative so I missed most of it. My boyfriend at the time said I should have asked for a DVD of the procedure.'

'But you were all right?' Sally was staring at her, her eyes wide. 'There wasn't anything wrong?'

'I was fine. It was a precaution, that's all. Just like yours. We'll all feel so much better tonight.'

Bruno parked the car, and opened Sally's door. 'Come on. Don't keep your doctor waiting, he's probably got half a dozen to do before lunch.'

Sally clutched Eleanor's arm as they walked up to the sliding doors, and Bruno took her other arm.

'You're always telling me to do the hard things,' he said to Sally. 'Like letting the festival onto my farm. Now it's your turn. Let's get it over with.'

Eleanor and Bruno delivered the shaking Sally into the hands of a reassuring nurse, then found themselves left in the waiting area.

'Are you going to stay?' he asked.

'She's first, they're taking her straight in,' she answered. 'It's funny, I feel at a complete loose end now.' She was almost in tears; Sally's emotions had been infectious. It felt good to have Bruno there. 'Suddenly I realise she might have cancer.'

'She might,' he said. 'Or she might not. But it's her illness. We just have to be here for her. It's not like *we've* got cancer.'

'It's not as easy as that,' Eleanor said, even though she knew he was right. 'My mother died of cancer last year. It's a tough journey.'

'I'm sorry. But it's *her* journey,' he repeated, awkwardly patting her arm. 'Let's not plan her funeral just yet – she might just have an infection or something.'

'Not very sympathetic, are you?' she huffed.

'Not at all,' he said. 'I'm a farmer, not much room for sentiment there. Let's get some breakfast, I couldn't eat or drink anything if Sally couldn't.'

'Nor me,' she said, reluctantly following him back to the car. 'Breakfast where?'

'Mrs Keiller's café,' he said, as they both got in the front.

'What about all your farming?' She put her seat belt on as he started the car.

'All done hours ago,' he said. 'I'll go around again this afternoon, and check on them this evening. But they all looked fairly lively at six this morning.'

'I was up at six, too,' she said, leaning her head back against the headrest. 'Trying to stop Sally eating something "accidentally" so she couldn't go into hospital.'

He pulled up in one of the few spaces on the quay. 'Come on. I'm owed a big coffee at the very least.'

As Bruno drank his coffee and consumed a bacon sandwich, Eleanor picked her way through a croissant. He was full of contradictions, on the one hand being rude to her, pushing her away, then being both firm and encouraging with Sally.

'You've obviously known Sally for a long time,' she observed, as he took another gulp of coffee.

'On and off. She's only moved back to the Doctor's House full-time since the old lady died. Must be twenty years ago, or even more.'

'The old lady?'

'Dr Dorothy. Our local GP. She adopted Sally, which you probably already know, so she grew up there. Then Sally left the islands for a few years, came back and rented a few houses over the years. She practised as a herbalist, I think, but she was qualified as a nurse as well.'

'She moved in after her mother died?'

He nodded. 'She visited regularly before. She'd always been around, staying for days or weekends, taking her mother on holiday. I think she rented these other places just to get a bit of alone time.'

There was something secretive about Sally, something she hadn't said. 'But she didn't meet anyone?'

'Just Nessa.'

Eleanor put her head on one side. Bruno was a very efficient eater, no mess, no crumbs but enormous bites. 'Who's Nessa?'

'Didn't Sally mention her? Lovely lady, great sense of humour. We never found out much about her previous life,' he mumbled through his food. 'Except she came from up north on the mainland, Yorkshire, I think. She started working with Dr Dorothy as the receptionist and secretary, that's how she met Sally. Nessa and Sally moved in together afterwards, so there was a bit of gossip. When the doctor got ill, they were both helping her, helping to nurse her.'

'I'm glad she had someone, anyway. She's such a sociable person, even if she pretends to be a recluse.'

He looked at her over his coffee. 'What happened to the unsympathetic boyfriend?'

'He's long gone. How about Ruby? Any special boys yet?'

His face dropped. 'Certainly not. She's too young for all that.'

She put her cup down. 'Don't you remember being a teenager?'

'I remember what fourteen-year-old boys are like,' he said. 'You didn't grow up on an island where everyone knows everyone.'

'No, I grew up in London with CCTV and neighbourhood watch. In a street with no proper gardens where everyone knew what you were up to. We couldn't even kiss behind the bike sheds – they were alarmed to deter burglars.'

He glanced up at her. 'Sounds horrible.'

'I loved it, most of the time. Then we moved to a sleepy village in Sussex and yes, everyone was eyeing up the new girl, all the time.'

'So, what were you like at fourteen?' He was staring at her, as if he was really interested.

'Honestly? A bit young for my age. I had pets, I played in an all-girl band, I did Irish dancing for four years. A boy held my hand all the way home when I was twelve, I didn't get a proper kiss until I was fifteen.'

'I can't keep up with Ruby. She's desperate to grow up, she wants to leave school and get a job. She wants to travel, even though I know she loves the islands.'

She could see how anxious he was, and softened her tone. 'She's such a sensible girl, you don't need to hold onto her too much. Then she'll always want to come back to you.'

'I tried that with her mother,' he said bitterly, the temperature between them falling.

'Ruby is her own person,' Eleanor said. 'I think she's a remarkable young woman. You can trust her judgement.'

He finished his drink and stood up so abruptly the chair scraped back a foot. 'When she's grown up, maybe. But until then she's my child, and I intend to keep her safe.'

Having checked by phone that Sally was fine, sleeping after her procedure, Eleanor walked back to the house. Bruno hadn't offered her a lift, just walked off, and she wanted to clear her head. Sally's anxiety had infected her a little, along with Bruno's fears for Ruby.

By the time she got to the Doctor's House, she had run out of anger and was just sad for Bruno, and worried about Sally.

Despite having only known her for a short time, she felt very attached to her. Maybe it was some connection with her mother, the closeness of them being born in the same house. Sally was as warm and affectionate as Diana, and had the same mischievous sense of humour.

The kitchen seemed very quiet when she got in, but a box she hadn't noticed when she got Sally ready to go to the hospital was sat on the table. A Post-it note on the top read 'Eleanor'.

The cardboard box had an advertising logo on it that looked like it had fallen out of the sixties. Sally must have put it there this morning. On the top, in faded pen, was the word 'Adoptions'.

The sticky tape holding the top closed had almost crumbled away. She opened it with great care. She was scared to look inside.

The box was filled with envelopes. There were simple names on each, with a date. She opened the first one, peeking in the top, feeling like she was breaking some sacred confidence. 'Elizabeth Court. 14 May 1954. Boy, Arthur. 7 lb 11 oz'.

Inside was a folded piece of blue paper and a couple of old photographs. They depicted a stiff-looking girl, who looked about sixteen, holding a tiny baby up to the camera. The second picture was a close-up of her holding the infant to her face. Her eyes were swollen and her agony was palpable. Maybe this was taken when she was about to give up her baby. The paper was a folded letter, far too personal to read.

Eleanor flipped through the envelopes as they moved through the years, slotted sideways into the box. They covered 1953 to 1970. *One of these might be Sally's. One of these could be Mum's.*

The envelopes were yellowing with age. 'Meredith Shoot. 24 September 1967. Boy, Alan. 7 lb 3 oz. Morwen'.

Her fingers shook as she sorted through the papers. Towards

the back, there were a few dated 1970. She leafed through them, her own breath coming short and noisy in the silent room.

'Alys Allen. 22 April 1970. Girl, Hecta. 5 lb 13 oz'.

Eleanor realised she was holding her breath and was feeling sick. She put the slim envelope on the table and stared at it. It wasn't sealed. Maybe she could just slide out the contents and see the frightened girl – her grandmother – and the baby that would grow up to be her mother. Her hands were sweaty; she wiped them down her thighs, then carefully tipped up the envelope.

It was empty.

22

APRIL 1943

Dorothy returned to St Brannock's Island with a new enthusiasm for the task ahead. Even the bumpy water and odd splash of spray enlivened her, although she was happy to reach land. She realised she had allowed herself to get affected by, of all people, Mrs Oppy. On the way home, she called in at the post office to ask where she was residing.

'She's up at Green Lane, staying with her sister. Pair of old witches, if you ask me.'

Dorothy smiled and turned back to the postmistress. 'What makes you say that?'

'Well, they've never done nothing that didn't favour themselves,' she said, sniffing. 'I used to look in on the old doctor. I was never sure the old biddy wasn't robbing him blind.'

'I'm also looking for the nurse who used to work with Dr Lavenham? I would like to employ a couple of staff.'

'Sister Penhaligon? She's a lovely woman, a bit strict but she knows what she's doing. She's working up at the hospital now, but maybe she'd like to come back, if the terms were right.' She jotted down the address.

The terms wouldn't be better, because so far there was no

income. But perhaps getting the patients back was worth an investment of the last of her savings.

The walk up the steep lane didn't even take the spring out of her step. Tonight she would start at the hospital and – she could admit it, just to herself – would enjoy the company of Hector McBride, even if he *was* married.

The hospital had been designed for men. The only ladies' bathroom was for the ward clerks and nurses, but Dorothy didn't mind changing in there. Her first hour of the shift had been uneventful, and Dr McBride had joined her for the handover. The most unwell patient had been unstable all day, and on her examination had been diagnosed with a serious bleed into his wound, a haematoma, causing him enormous pain. She decided he needed to go back into theatre, to drain the blood and find where it was coming from. Ten minutes later, a troublesome blood vessel had been neatly tied off – her hands never shook when she was at work – and McBride was praising her technique. Leaving the patient in the hands of the nurses, McBride suggested they go outside for a smoke.

It had been years since she had smoked. But the idea of standing in the fresh air talking with him was too tempting, and she accepted the cigarette and stood next to him, looking over the aerodrome and the sea beyond. Every star seemed to be reflected in it, the mirrored moon wobbling as the waves rolled in.

'You're a good surgeon. Why do you want to look after sore throats and creaky joints?' he asked.

'Well, sore throats can kill children,' she said. 'Although not Polly Allen, I see.'

'No, I think we'll be sending her home tomorrow, once we take the tube out. She's doing well. So, why buy a general practice?'

For a long time Dorothy tried to find the words. 'I didn't want to be pigeonholed,' she finally said. 'I liked the medical work, but my job was mostly about being charming and polite to a lot of unhappy wealthy women.'

'You don't find being charming and polite satisfying?'

She laughed. 'I'm just not very good at it.' She lit the cigarette then handed the lighter back. 'I don't really like it. I gave up socialising before the war.'

'I don't see you as trivial or social, if that's what you mean. You come across as truthful. And direct. I haven't forgotten you seeing that woman off your property.'

That made her smile. 'I'm fairly certain Mrs Oppy robbed the house first. I've been told there was a radio set but I haven't seen it. At least I have the phone working now.'

'Was she living in the house with you?'

'No, she had a cottage in the grounds. Well, not much more than a stone shed. Her son was staying with her and I didn't want to tackle them both.'

'Do you want to search the place properly tomorrow? I have some hours off in the afternoon, if you will have caught up with your sleep by then.'

She agreed, relieved that she wouldn't have to tackle the place by herself. She hadn't a key, and Mrs Oppy had left the place locked up tight.

'We might even find your radio,' he said, blowing smoke away from her.

They stood in companionable silence while he finished the cigarette.

'Can I ask you something?' she said. 'I don't want to sound forward. Just as colleagues...'

'You want to know if I'm still married.'

She let the silence grow darker and thicker. She felt foolish; it was an inappropriate question, too forward. She must be bright red; her cheeks were burning. She was glad of the night.

He spoke first. 'I *was* married. When I was young, just a student. She was the daughter of friends of my parents. I knew her all my life. She died four years ago.'

'I'm sorry,' was all Dorothy could squeak out.

'Don't be. Our affection, if that was what we felt, burned out many years before that. We had nothing in common, and I'm afraid she was rather stupid. There, it sounds respectable enough in the dark.'

A widower. Despite herself, her heart did a little skip. 'I'm still sorry for you. That must have been hard.'

'I wasn't even there. She had a silly accident, fell over while gardening. She got a small infection, then she felt unwell, feverish, was in pain. Her father was a doctor, too. He looked after her but then he diagnosed septicaemia. Nothing he gave her worked. She died two days later. I just got home in time to say goodbye, but the poor girl didn't know I was there.'

He must have loved her, somewhat anyway, she thought, the tender way he spoke about her.

'Did you... have any children?'

'A boy, Robert. He lives with his maternal grandparents.' He turned away, his voice softer. 'They had always wanted a son, but had three girls. He's fifteen now, getting ready to go to college. I felt at least I could let them have that, since their beloved daughter was gone.'

'Will he become a doctor?' she asked, her voice coming out soft. She felt him turn towards her.

'I suppose he'll always be trying to work out how we could have saved her,' he said softly. 'We all seem to have a reason for becoming a medic.'

'Me too,' she confessed. 'My father had a stroke when he was young, forty-nine. I was convinced there must be a treatment that would restore him.'

She could hear him take a deep breath before he changed

the subject. 'So, we're going to look for this radio tomorrow. Two o'clock?'

'Two o'clock would be fine,' she said, trying not to sound too eager. She stared across the aerodrome buildings and down to the farmers' fields, the ghostly sheep criss-crossing the grass.

He's widowed.

23

PRESENT DAY, 19 MAY

Sally had come home subdued and worried about the outcome of her tests. It turned out she was anaemic, and they had taken various biopsies and done scans.

Eleanor decided to stay and work on the islands, rather than head straight back to London. She didn't want to leave Sally until she had the results, whatever they would mean. She had to talk to food vendors and the construction company that would put up the stages and marquees. They already had a plan to run water pipes with sinks along the western edge of Bruno's fields, with armoured electric cables to provide basic lighting around the site.

She worked at her laptop on the kitchen table, while Sally wandered about making some lunch. Eleanor was worried about her; she drifted around starting things, then would forget what she was doing.

When the phone rang, they both jumped. Sally answered it, one hand pressed to her heart, and put it on speaker.

'Sally? It's Dr Mark Benz here. How are you?'

To Eleanor, this always seemed like the stupidest question, but Sally tried to answer it.

'You know, all right, just waiting...'

'You'll be glad to hear there is no evidence of cancer at all.' He said other things, but Eleanor and Sally just locked eyes, then moved in for a hug, the doctor's words somewhat muffled, pressed between them. Finally Sally was able to speak.

'Thank you so much,' she said, quite breathlessly.

'You're not listening,' he said, but there was humour in his voice. 'You *do* have an ulcer, and you will need treatment. It's been bleeding, that's probably why you're so anaemic. It won't be a quick fix but we can treat it.'

'Thank you,' Sally repeated. 'I'll take the treatment, thank you.'

'I've made an appointment for you. I'll catch up with you tomorrow, ten thirty.'

As he rang off, Eleanor hugged Sally again, tears welling up. 'Thank goodness. But you have to *promise* to take the medicine.'

'Oh, I will,' Sally said, a little impish smile on her face for the first time in days. 'Alongside some liquorice, aloe vera and other herbs.' The smile faded. 'I never thought I would get an ulcer, I'm not really a stressed person, but the last couple of years, with Nessa... It all got too much for me. I was so worried it was cancer.' She looked down, wiped her eyes with the back of her hand. 'Goodness, what a drama.'

Eleanor felt sick with relief, especially coming so near to her own mother's anniversary. 'I don't need to go home for a few days, so I'll make sure you get your medicine and set up a pill box so you remember to take it.'

Sally sank down into her favourite chair. 'I feel quite wobbly. But you don't have to stay to look after me.'

'Well, I still want to look through the rest of the papers, to see if I can find Mum's records.'

'I really thought they would be there,' Sally said, closing her eyes. 'I didn't look in the box. I was afraid...' Her voice trailed away. 'I've never wanted to know who my real mother was.'

'Do you think your record is in there?'

Sally opened her eyes and looked up at her. 'No. Ma made me an album of baby pictures but never mentioned whose baby I was. I knew I was adopted but I really didn't want to know who gave me up. Threw me away.' She looked away, her face screwed up with some emotion Eleanor couldn't identify.

'I'm sure it wasn't like that at all. I'd love to see your baby pictures, and I'm sure your birth mother didn't just *give* you away.' She took a deep breath. 'My mother used to say she was given the gift of a wonderful family by a young girl who had less to offer her. She just wishes she could have met her, to say thank you. Just to know her.'

Sally's eyes filled with tears. 'I hope it was like that, it's a lovely way to think of it. And really, that was what it was like for me too. I – I just wondered if my epilepsy put her off, that was all. Go and get the album. It's next to my bed. I keep it there since Nessa died.'

Eleanor had stood up, but sat back down with a thump. 'Nessa? Bruno mentioned her.'

'She was my love. I'm sure someone's told you in the town that I ran away with another woman and lived gloriously, happily with her for years.'

'Actually, Bruno did say something.' Something about the expression on Sally's face made her tear up. 'When did she die?'

'Nearly two years ago. She was eleven years older than me, which never mattered, not for decades. Then, suddenly, it did. She started getting forgetful, then would get lost. Eventually, her son – she had two children and a husband before she met me – wanted her put in a home, nearer the family. I was very welcome to visit, they always said that, but after a while I couldn't face going.' She looked at Eleanor, her eyes pouring with tears. 'I wanted her here, nearby. But it's so hard when the person you love more than anyone doesn't recognise you. It was sort of a relief when she died two years later, but then the grief started and it was torture.'

'Torture?' Eleanor asked.

'When I was visiting her, I could dream that one day she would suddenly regain her memory and call out for me. But once she was dead, that fantasy was over. Ma had died, and I was just here, in this big house, on my own. I decided to set up a bed and breakfast, to help with the bills.'

'So we're both grieving.' The house seemed larger now, echoey; the high ceilings made the place seem aloof. 'How did you manage this house on your own?'

'Friends helped. I tidied up a room – your room first – and let it out to lonely travellers or romantic couples. I started cooking again once I had someone to make breakfasts for. I worked hard in the garden to make it lovely for my visitors and started replanting my herb garden. The house brought me back to life, and many of the guests became friends.' She stood up, her shoulders rounded as if she was worn down by the stress of the last few days, of the story she was telling. 'And now it has brought me you.' She hugged Eleanor. 'The daughter of my old age. Such a corny phrase, yet it seems to be true.'

Eleanor hugged her back. 'It's a privilege to be thought of as your family,' she said.

She felt like the house – and its owner – were an inextricable part of her life already.

Since she was still on the islands, Eleanor had agreed to go along to one of the planning meetings run by the festival committee. She was astonished by how many little side events were planned – there were posters and messages online about cake competitions, art shows, music events, even a sandcastle contest.

This meeting was especially for the music events on the

other islands – called the off-islands by the locals. She was across a table from a tall, broad, grey-haired man with beads in his beard like a Viking.

'Mitch Tate,' he said simply, and shook her hand. 'Everyone calls me Elk.'

'I know you've been doing a lot of the back-room planning with Joey,' she said, 'with getting bookings.'

He shrugged. 'Just a few old friends that owe me a favour or two. And a couple of people I used to play with.'

'Well, the line-up is amazing.'

He frowned a little and leaned forward, looking a bit intimidating. 'But we still want to see more local musicians, the young ones coming up.'

She found herself nodding. 'Absolutely. Our bookings team have it all in hand, and they will pay them all. We don't ask anyone to perform for free.'

'It's ridiculous that money-making festivals expect people to work for free,' he growled. 'For the' – he made air quotes with his huge hands – '*exposure*.'

'They will all get a biography on the website, too, and links to their agents, where they have them.'

A young woman spoke up, pretty in Indian cotton with dreadlocks down her back. 'I'm Tara Tresillick. There are events on each of the islands. I was hoping we'd get some publicity for those, too. I'm involved in a few gigs and a dance session.'

'We are just working on the booklet the ticket holders will get. All of the events registered with Sunlight Festivals will be in there. We will have booklets distributed around the islands, too. People will need to buy a day ticket to attend the actual festival, but these side events are all either free or priced locally.'

As they went through the list of bookings and she explained

where they would go in the timetable, she could see the event in her mind. It was still raggedy, lots of spaces on stages and gaps in the programme where several acts wanted the same slot. But everyone would be listened to and as many as possible accommodated.

Every pub seemed to have bands or individuals performing for free beer and a hat passed around. Several venues were offering open-mike events or jamming sessions with local musicians, including a couple run by Elk. The school was putting on a musical talent show and the winning band would play on the first afternoon on the small stage. Shanty singers would feature each day. A Breton folk band was coming over and staying with musician friends, and would perform on the first evening. She was beginning to feel the connection between Brittany and the Atlantic Islands, the same traditions of fishing and music and, always, the sea.

She could see how it was all going to weave together.

Before she left to go back to London, Eleanor walked down the hill to the snicket that led to the farm gate. She'd got to know the sheepdog, Haze, so when she reached the farm she was met by a hysterically barking, wagging whirlwind of black and white fluff.

Bruno looked out of the open door to see who was there, then stopped. 'Side gate's open,' he said, then shouted, 'Haze, shut up!'

The barking stopped but the fawning and rolling onto her back for a belly rub continued. Eleanor finally reached the door covered in long dog hairs. 'I'm just off to London,' she called through the doorway.

'You can come in!' he called back. She found him washing up in the long kitchen, a smaller version of Sally's but with ugly units that looked like they had fallen out of the eighties.

Eleanor couldn't help it; she was redesigning as she stood there. 'I just wondered if you could look in on Sally.'

'I always do,' he said, turning to stare at her. Her heart did a little jump. 'We did manage to get along all right before you came, you know.'

'Of course. But she's in a strange mood at the moment, a bit flattened by the illness, and the treatment is a bit rough. She's not a big fan of antibiotics.'

'She's actually taking them?' He dried his hands and walked towards her. He was average height with a muscular build; he shouldn't have projected such a powerful presence. But somehow, he filled the space.

'So far,' she said, feeling her heart race. She was a bit embarrassed at the effect he had on her. He was just so *male*. 'I do sit over her and count them, though. And she's just been a bit... melancholy. Talking about the past.'

'Nessa?' He waved her into a living room which was less untidy than she'd expected. It looked straight on to one of the fields she was going to rent, and sheep were nosing their way along the wire fence a few metres from the windowsill. 'I'm surprised she talked about her. It's a bit raw, I think.'

'We've sort of... bonded. We're both products of the mother and baby home. She was born there, and my mother was, too. Anyway, I thought I would give you my card, my numbers are on there. Call me if I can help.'

'I have a number for you already.'

'That's the office, about the land. That one's got my private number on it.' He took the card and stared at it.

'I'll stick it on the fridge,' he said. 'Ruby will be in every day, too – she's been popping in to check on Sally after school.'

'I know,' she replied. Awkwardly, because Ruby had made a beeline for her every day, had even started teaching her a bit of gardening and chatting about the line-up of bands coming to the festival. While she had been looking forward to hearing the music over the hedge, Bruno had suggested sending her off the island to her mother's. Eleanor hadn't dared put forward an opinion, but she had a feeling Ruby would get her own way somehow.

'How long will you be away?' he said, not looking at her, as if he didn't care either way.

'Two weeks.'

He glanced at her with a sudden smile. 'We'll see you then.'

24

APRIL 1943

Dr McBride – Hector, as he had asked her to call him outside of the hospital – was waiting for her at the front door of the Doctor's House to help her tackle the cottage. She had just been to see the Allen girls now Polly had been brought home.

'How are your patients?'

Polly, so close to death just three days ago, now had a bandage on her neck but could breathe easily. She was already livelier for being at home, and Dorothy had impressed upon the parents that she needed plenty of rest. Branwen was pale but recovering well. The family had once again turned its attention to the loss of baby Bathsheba, and Mrs Allen looked worn and defeated. Only time could heal that loss.

'All as well as one would expect,' Dorothy said. 'The baby's funeral is tomorrow. I think I'll go, as I was invited.' She unlocked the door, pushed it open. The old house was strangely welcoming for the first time; up until now, she'd always half expected Mrs Oppy to be there.

'I'd like to come also, if that would be allowed?'

'You saved Polly's life,' she said. 'I'm sure you would be very welcome.'

'I don't want to give the wrong impression,' he said, walking through to the kitchen after her. 'If we turn up together.'

'Why—' Then she caught his meaning. 'We're colleagues. We both serve this community. And we don't have to *arrive* together.'

He watched as she put her bag down on the table then turned to fill the kettle. 'One day, I'd quite like to turn up *together*. Maybe at a restaurant, or a bar.'

She turned to him and couldn't help smiling. 'Are you suggesting we go on a *date*?' She felt quite light and giddy, rather as she had as a young student, admiring all the male students who wouldn't even talk to her.

'Why not? Although the gossip would get around these islands like wildfire. Can you imagine, having a cream tea at the café? The proprietor would probably ask what my intentions were.'

She wondered what a date with Hector would be like. She put the heavy kettle on the hotplate, glad she had relit it when she came home after her shift. 'They might gossip about *you*, but no one is talking about me. It's almost as if I didn't come here to help.'

'That's because you're letting Mrs Oppy tell your story,' he said, and his voice was serious. 'Of the uppity London doctor who thinks she knows it all and put an honest, hard-working nurse out of a job. You need to talk to Dr Bristow at the hospital. He's been having a running battle with her the last few weeks.'

'*Mr* Bristow and I didn't really hit it off,' she said, looking in the row of rusted tins near the kettle. 'He doesn't believe in women doctors. He'd be horrified if he knew I was operating.'

'Oh, he knows,' Hector said, looking around the room. 'I told him.'

That made her smile. 'I only really have tea.' She peered at the coagulated remains of instant coffee in a rusted tin and rejected it. 'I brought it from London, it's rather good.' She lifted down the new tin at the end of the row. 'I think mice have got in most of the stores.'

'Are you listening to me?'

She turned to him, flushing warmly. 'I am. I'm going to do something about Mrs Oppy *and* Mr Bristow. But first, I am going to have a cup of tea. Then I'm going to break into the cottage and see if there's any incriminating evidence.'

'And I'm here to help? Will I be expected to strongarm the door?'

'You, sir, are to testify to any evidence I do collect,' she said sharply, which made him laugh. 'How hard can it be? Burglars do it all the time.'

It turned out to be quite difficult, and even with both of them shoulder to shoulder they needed a crowbar. Dorothy almost fell into the doorway, but Hector caught her arm.

'Thank you,' she said, panting, aware of his hand on hers.

'Let's see what's inside.' His eyes wrinkled up in that way she found attractive.

There was one room downstairs, just a living and cooking space with a fold-out camp bed, presumably for her son when he was at home. Up steep steps was a single bedroom, with a tiny window overlooking the back of the main house. As she had expected, in a corner of the bedroom, under a heap of news-papers, was a large brown radio set.

'Why would she even *want* this?' she asked Hector, standing at the top of the steps, the floor groaning as she moved across the speckled boards. 'There is no electricity here. And everything's got woodworm.'

'I suppose she thought she could sell it. But everyone would know it belonged to you, so maybe she decided against it. I think you need to come down,' he said, easing his foot off the top step. 'This place is close to falling to pieces. It's creaking.'

'Take this,' she said, heaving the radio into his hands. 'I'm just going to look around.'

Under the bed she found what seemed to be half the pharmacy cupboard – canisters of powders and chemicals, bottles of tinctures. There were also a few surgical instruments, none clean. None seemed suitable for interfering with a pregnancy, but several large syringes certainly could be involved.

She brought down as much as she could carry. 'Anything downstairs?'

He was looking at the top book of a small pile. '*A Student's Handbook of Obstetric Medicine and Surgery*,' he said. He looked inside the flyleaf. 'Eighteen ninety-nine. It might have been your predecessor's textbook at medical school. He went to Edinburgh.' He pronounced it *Edin-burg*.

'*Edin-borough*,' she corrected. 'So did I. Considerably later, though.'

'I imagine so. How old *are* you?' It was either an outrageously rude question, from a gentleman to a lady, or a purely scientific enquiry.

'How old are *you*?' she fired back.

'Forty-seven.'

She laughed. 'It's very rude to ask a lady her age. But as a doctor, I can tell you I'm thirty-eight.'

'You don't look it,' he said, staring at her face, at her hair and neck.

'Plump women often look younger,' she said simply, regurgitating her mother's wisdom on the subject.

'Thin men look past their age, halfway to their dotage,' he said, although his easy movements always made him appear younger.

'Men seem to get more distinguished as they age.' She collected another small pile of books. 'Women just get old. Oh, here's *Bateby's Bones*! I had a later edition of this.'

He took the book off the pile, laid it on the small table. 'I did too,' he said. 'I don't think of you as plump, Dorothy. I think of you as hiding a lovely figure under a lot of tweed and woollen stockings.'

She blushed; she was sure her face was fiery red. She'd had a few flattering remarks in the past but mostly from predatory colleagues or patients. 'Well, it's a uniform. I want to be taken seriously as a doctor, not as a woman. And there isn't much heating here.'

'They might like you just as much – even more – if you dressed in a more relaxed manner.' He smiled wryly. '*I* would like to see you in something more informal.'

Dorothy was flustered. She didn't know how to respond to such an overture after years of denying her own femininity to be taken seriously as a doctor.

'Well, let me think about it.' She resolved that maybe it was time to ask her mother to send down a trunk of clothes from home, all those dresses and shoes that Mama thought necessary for socialising in London. 'I didn't bring much to the island with me,' she explained, suddenly shy. 'Just stuff that was easy to launder and put on. But I intend to make the local patients see me, even in tweed.'

'Well, I would like to see you socially, whatever you wear.'

25

PRESENT DAY, 20 JUNE

After three weeks away, Eleanor thought how lovely it was to be going back to the islands. She was starting to wonder if having a holiday home here would be a perfect retreat, especially as she would be close to Sally and Ruby. And Bruno.

She filed the idea away. The brochure was as finalised as it could be at this stage, the website was up, tickets were flying away, and it was obvious they would make their target. The company's agents had secured the artist bookings, found musicians places to stay, and the power and water services were organised.

June was even more beautiful on the islands, she thought, as she stepped off the helicopter. It was the light, reflected from all sides off the sea, an extra glow in the sunshine. It lit up patches of flowers in the fields, and every hedge was a riot of blossom. Ruby ran in for a hug.

'You're back!' she shouted unnecessarily. 'Me and Sally came to meet you.'

Sally walked over, looking less pale and a little less drained than when Eleanor had last seen her. She enfolded Sally in a hug, too.

'You look a little better already,' she said, holding Sally at arm's length.

'Yes, well, I hate the medicine,' she replied. 'But my herbs are working alongside it so I'm making good progress. Bruno and Ruby have been looking after me.' *Bullying me*, she mouthed over Ruby's head.

'I'm here to do some interviews for the press,' Eleanor said to Ruby. 'Want to help?'

'Maybe Dad wouldn't... no, Dad *would* be OK with it. I'll make it into a project for school.' She reached for Eleanor's bag. 'Honestly, you should fix that squeaky wheel on your bag. I like your dress. You look great, too.'

For no reason whatsoever, Eleanor had chosen a wild print dress and strappy sandals for returning to the island. She looked down at it. 'Oh, this? Well, it's usually warmer on the islands than I expect.'

'You should come swimming with us!' Ruby said excitedly.

Sally took her arm. 'You should. I might come down for a paddle myself.'

'I didn't bring a costume.' Deep down, the shivers started. Eleanor had never learned to swim, not after a boy ducked her in Tooting Bec lido. 'I might stick to paddling.'

'Well, the tide is just coming up,' Sally said reassuringly, as if she'd picked up on Eleanor's anxiety. 'And lunch is in the oven. Ruby made it.'

'It's mac and cheese,' Ruby shouted back, now a dozen metres ahead.

'How are you really?' Eleanor said.

'I've been sad. The house seemed very empty when you went back. After all the stress, I suppose it was an anticlimax.' She added, 'A good anticlimax, though – no cancer!'

'And you had Ruby. And Bruno,' she added lightly.

Sally nodded, holding onto Eleanor's arm as she turned the corner. 'And *Bruno*,' she said, sneaking a glance at Eleanor.

'He's been doing my shopping, and he ran around with a broom when I dropped a bag of sugar. He's not much of a housewife. We have ants coming in all the time now.'

'I found out something about Polly Allen on the internet,' Eleanor said, unable to keep it in any longer. 'She was a patient in a hospital in Cornwall. St Adwenna's Sanatorium.'

'The TB hospital?' Sally asked, stopping so abruptly she dragged Eleanor to a halt.

'Well, it was a hospital for respiratory illnesses. She was there for three years.'

'People used to joke at school of being sent to the hospital,' Sally said, shuddering. 'You know I had seizures when I was a baby?'

'You said.' Eleanor could see tears starting in Sally's eyes. 'Did they tease you about it?'

'All the time,' she answered. 'They said the only reason I didn't get sent away to a hospital was because my mother was the doctor.'

'Poor you,' Eleanor said, and they started up the lane. 'I had a conversation online with a hospital historian. He can't break confidentiality because Polly could conceivably still be alive, but he answered my questions about the sort of problems that the hospital helped. Diphtheria could do a lot of permanent damage to children. I didn't know that.'

'That's interesting,' Sally said, and her sadness seemed to have been lifted by the change of subject. 'Come on in and sit. I'll pick some salad from the garden. We've just got our first baby cucumbers.'

Ruby had dragged the suitcase into the consulting room, and had walked through the French doors to the garden. She came back with a basket full of vegetables, from fern-topped carrots to glossy cucumbers and lime-green mangetout.

'You grew all these?' Eleanor asked, and copied Sally in biting into a fresh peapod. 'Wow.'

'Me and Sally did,' Ruby said. 'She's the clever one at growing baby plants from seed. I plant them out and look after them.'

Sally washed the vegetables and put clean carrots on the table. 'Chop them into sticks, please,' she said to Eleanor, handing her a small knife and chopping board. 'They don't need peeling.'

The baby carrots sent up a wave of sweetness, each one with a different scent and colour. She worked her way through the vegetables as washed lettuce, sliced cucumber and a few spring onions were placed on a large platter. The toasted cheese smells from the oven complemented them and her mouth started to water.

'Dad will be in soon,' Ruby said, and Eleanor's heart gave a little skip.

'Good, there's loads of food.' She couldn't think why she had this reaction. Back in London she had lain awake trying to work it out. Bruno was rude, rough and ready, and he was too strict with Ruby, but there was something darkly attractive there. Back home, she'd decided it was because he was a bit wounded by his lost marriage. Or he had a lot of *Wuthering Heights'* Heathcliff going on. Either way, she'd lost a bit of sleep, and was determined to think of him firmly as a business partner.

She had just put the plates out when she heard him stomp in and take off his boots. Sally kept an area by the front door for him, with an extra doormat.

'Oh,' he said, when he walked into the kitchen. 'You're back.' His voice was neutral, and she couldn't tell if he was pleased to see her or not. She tried to ignore the reaction her body was having, her muscles relaxing and her heart skipping about. She felt like a schoolgirl. 'I like your dress,' he said.

'You can always borrow it,' she offered breezily.

The corner of his mouth twitched upwards. 'That's

not... very funny,' he said, and with complete seriousness he added, 'It's not my size.'

She laughed as Ruby came in from the garden and headed for the sink to wash her hands. A small bowl of edible flowers just needed a quick rinse before brightening up the huge salad.

'Hi, Dad,' she said, with a cool air. 'How's Daisy and Maisie?'

'No stitches, just a haircut.' He looked over at Eleanor. 'One of our ewes cut herself on an old bit of wire. Left by someone replacing the fence – he just dropped it on the grass.'

'I'm sorry.' She was immediately anxious. 'I'll have a word with them. Is there any permanent damage?'

'No,' he said, looking at Ruby. 'And all the blood on the lamb was from the ewe. I'll keep an eye on them.' He didn't seem angry.

'Would you like us to check all the fences in case there's any more rubbish left?' Eleanor added.

'No. I checked, that was all there was. Unfortunate, but anyone could have dropped a piece in the long grass. They've done a good job, saved me replacing a whole run of fencing from my father's time.'

'But you must have been upset, I'm sorry about that,' Eleanor said, lifting the heavy dish out of the oven and putting it on a trivet on the table. 'Wow, Ruby, this smells gorgeous!'

Ruby turned and beamed at her. 'It's my own three-cheese blend.'

'I was upset because Daisy was injured,' he said, sitting down to the table. 'Then I saw the blood on the lamb, Maisie, and I was even more upset. But a quick wash and antiseptic spray and we were done.'

'You did stomp up and down and shout, "That beep-beep Eleanor..."' Ruby said.

'Ruby!' Eleanor couldn't help stepping in. 'I'm sure I would have done the same. Come and have some of your lovely food.'

'Smells good,' Bruno said, eyeing her quickly.

Sally put a hand up. 'I want to say something first.'

They all stalled what they were doing, Bruno and Eleanor holding serving implements in mid-air.

'OK.' Eleanor exchanged confused glances with the other two.

'I... have decided to live,' Sally announced.

'That's... good,' Ruby said. 'Weren't you going to before?'

Sally held out her plate for the colourful salad. 'Well, I wasn't really doing anything *about* living. I started to think I was getting old, out of breath even going for a walk, then the pain started. I thought I was going to die like my mother did.'

'But you had an ulcer.' Eleanor said.

'Yes, but *why* did I have an ulcer? And why did I have anaemia? I had stopped *living*.'

Bruno helped himself to some of the cheesy pasta. 'After Nessa left?'

'Even before. After my mother died and Ruby's mother left, all in the same year. *You* were like a bear in a trap, Nessa was starting to get confused, and then her family, her *next of kin* made the decision to take her away from me.'

Eleanor could feel the emotion running around the table. That was how it had felt when her mother's sand trickled out of her timer, and the pain became impossible to treat at home. 'Nessa was ill, but you weren't,' she said. 'Mourning is necessary, but at some point, you have to reclaim your life. Maybe even find new friends, new *loves*.'

'That's either very wise, dear, or a bit trite. There isn't anyone else like Nessa.'

'Of course not,' Eleanor said. 'But you can still find companionship, friends, laughter, fun. You said you've decided to live. What are you going to do with the time you have left?'

'I think I'll travel.' Sally laughed at the expression on Bruno's face. 'Don't get too excited, I don't think I'm ready for a round-the-world trip yet. But I have an old friend in North Devon, she's been asking me to visit for – oh, forty years. We write lovely letters.'

They all laughed. 'It's a start,' Eleanor said. 'Then you could come a bit further and stay with me. I have a spare...' There it was, the lightning flash of grief at the memory of her mother's room.

Sally looked at her, knowingly. 'Well, that would be inter-esting. I haven't been to London for years.'

'I bet they don't wear crinolines and top hats any more, even,' Ruby joked, and took a huge bite of the salad. 'What's this pink dressing on the rocket? I love it.'

'Raspberry vinegar,' Sally said. 'How old did you think I was, again?'

Ruby shrugged. 'Anyone over thirty is pretty old.'

Eleanor caught Bruno's eye and they both smiled. There was warmth and a sense of family spreading around the room.

'Well, despite *my* advancing age, I'm racing at the Pilot Gig World Championship at the end of the month,' he said. 'Does anyone want to come and cheer for me?'

'Oh, Dad! Don't be so embarrassing,' moaned Ruby. Eleanor laughed.

Sally nodded. 'We'll all be there. If poor Daisy the sheep is up to it, she'll be very welcome, too.'

That made Ruby splutter over her fruit juice.

'Maybe I'll hang around for that,' Eleanor said.

'There's a good chance I'll come last, fall in and crash the boat,' he said, his eyes sparkling with humour.

'Well, I definitely don't want to miss *that*.' She knew she was flirting, and it felt fine.

Bruno sneaked a look at her and they both smiled. She had no idea what it meant, but it meant *something*.

26

APRIL 1943

The one restaurant on the island that still did something like silver service was in the main town, run by an elderly couple who had once, they assured Dorothy and Hector, served at Claridge's. Sadly, the chef didn't come with them, and the fare was sparse and fish-based.

Dorothy and Hector started with mussels, which had no wine or cream to liven them, and were rather overcooked. Then a thick pie filled with mixed fish with a sauce that tasted a lot like powdered milk, and finally a stodgy suet pudding and packet custard with very little sugar.

'You Brits are really suffering with rationing, aren't you?' Hector said, prodding the pudding around the bowl.

The conversation had started with medicine, and Dorothy had lost herself in comparing notes about their training, exchanging stories about exams, bullying consultants and deteriorating dissection subjects. She'd forgotten she was wearing a watered silk gown that looked ostentatious, over-dressed and smelled of mothballs. It was also not warm enough. She couldn't face wearing her fur – it would have looked ludicrously out of place – but she had put on her grandmother's pink pearls, looped three times around her neck.

'Less so in London,' she said, 'but it's still miserable. I can't help thinking the island children wouldn't be so susceptible to infection if they were better nourished.'

He sat back, abandoning the dessert. 'This hasn't been a very romantic date,' he said, with a small smile. 'I'm afraid this is not how we would have done it back in the States.'

'How would it be different?' Dorothy asked, unable to comment on the first statement.

'I don't know. Dancing, maybe?'

'I don't dance,' she told him. 'I never learned, not really. We did a bit of country dancing at school, but I've never needed the minuet socially.'

'It doesn't sound like you've spent a lot of time at *all*, socially.'

She pushed her plate away. 'You probably realise, my parents are quite comfortably off. In London, the expectation was that I would grow up and get married, produce nicely bred and behaved grandchildren – and die of boredom.'

'So, you became a doctor. At considerable expense and effort.'

She smiled at the memory. 'I don't want you to think that it was *that* difficult. The law had changed, we were tolerated reluctantly, and my parents paid the fees. I don't think they expected me to actually *practise* medicine, just listen to well-to-do women moan about their minor ailments and their husbands, then go home to a pleasant life. And meet a handsome doctor and get married.'

'You never threw caution to the wind, did something that they wouldn't understand?'

'After studying, we all needed to let our hair down. I was in a great group of female students, all wrestling with misogyny and even violence on occasion. It bonded us. We went walking in the Alps, swimming in the Mediterranean, rented cottages and *pensioni*. Two of our class went to America, where the situation is easier. One died – TB, dreadfully fast – and two of our number got married and left the profession. That just left me and my friend Frances.' She thought back to the most awkward times around the end of their friendship, when Frances declared her affection for Dorothy. 'She wanted more than I could give, to do missionary work abroad.'

He seemed to look straight into her, see her heart. 'But that's not you?'

'I'm not religious,' she said, the most she could put into words.

He waved at the waiter for the bill. 'And no gentleman friends?'

She smiled as she shook her head. 'When you are very young, you dream about the other students until you realise they are as stupid and rude as the boys at school. There was...' She couldn't believe she had started to voice the thought. 'You're very easy to talk to. But that isn't my story.'

'Who's going to tell it?' he said, standing up and holding her coat for her. 'When I was young I didn't have time for girls, so my mother would introduce me to a new one each time I came home. Second weekend of the month, dinner with my parents and brother, pep talk from my dad and meet a new girl for Sunday lunch.'

'Didn't you like any of them?'

He held the door open, and she walked into the cold air.

'I liked most of them, but that's as far as it went. I couldn't tell interesting anecdotes about dissecting someone or contaminating the lab by dropping a plate of typhoid bacteria—'

She put her hand over her mouth to stifle the laugh. 'You didn't!'

'I was a klutz,' he laughed as they walked into the darkness. 'Right up until I operated on a living patient – they trusted me with removing a harmless lipoma – when the shakes and nerves just disappeared.'

She slipped her hand into his elbow when he crooked it, hoping the darkness would cover the blush that was warming her right up to her ears. She couldn't believe she was in a silk dress, smart shoes and on a *date*.

'That time flew by for me,' she confided to him. 'When my childhood friends paired up like swans, I was glad, it made life easier.'

'Easier, how?'

'Well, all that longing and speculating and awkwardness with young men,' she said, to the darkness. 'I'm sure you weren't shy, but I was crippled with stammering and knew I was plain. I didn't fit in.'

'I was shy, too. What do young men say to girls, anyway? I should have met you back then, we could have compared suturing techniques.'

'Mattress or subcutaneous?' she answered.

He feigned pulling back in pretend horror. 'To think I was going to let you loose on a couple of skin grafts tomorrow!'

She chuckled, the first easy laugh of a long time. It sounded like a girl's laugh again. 'My stitching is excellent. Years of sewing samplers.'

They walked along the high street in silence, and for once, she didn't feel a pressure to say something clever or socially acceptable. His arm was warm in her hand, and he blocked the cold breeze. They were halfway up the lane before the darkness emboldened her.

'There was someone once,' she murmured. 'A senior doctor, in my last year of training. I knew he was married, of course, but he paid me a lot of attention. Young people are always attractive, aren't they? And I was a rabbit to be bagged by the hunter. He went through most of the younger nurses, too.'

'What did you do?' They stopped outside the garden gate.

She winced when she remembered. 'He invited me out for a bite at the local café. Nothing posh, nothing expensive, just friends. Food was plentiful before the war – it seems strange now. He carried my heavy bag; I'd taken revision texts into work and done a forty-eight-hour shift. My landlady was out, but I still told him no men were allowed in the house.'

The memory opened like a book she couldn't bear to read.

'He went to your room anyway.'

'He said it was just a joke, he was laughing and teasing me as he carried my books up. He attacked me before I had even got to the top of the stairs. He half dragged me into the room, and I managed to twist away from him, falling onto the bed.'

Hector seemed to be holding his breath. 'What happened?'

'I kicked him in the left patella and then got another boot into his iliac crest.' She smiled grimly. 'He stumbled back and fell down the stairs.'

'Thank God. So, you won?'

'Not really. He failed my practical surgery practicum, and I had to repeat it at another hospital.' She let go of his arm, and suddenly she felt colder. She fumbled in her pocket for the door key. 'I often wonder, if I had just given in, perhaps my career wouldn't have been dragged down by that bad report.'

'You wouldn't have, though?'

She shrugged. 'It's not as if I hadn't thought about it, daydreamed about the handsome doctor falling for me. I knew the biology of it. But I knew instantly that was all he wanted, and I didn't. Maybe I'm a bit cold like that. It was the last time I trusted a man.'

'I promise I won't push my way in,' he said, leaning on the door frame.

She laughed. 'I didn't mean that about *you*!'

'Well, I am not that sort of man,' he said, but his voice was serious. 'I've never forced anyone into anything in my life.' He lifted his hand, just visible in the low light from the hall lamp, and brushed it down her face. 'But that doesn't mean I'm not attracted to you.'

Her breath caught in her throat.

'If this was a proper date, I'd ask to kiss you,' he said, in a conversational voice. 'But I think I'll leave it to you to decide if or when that's appropriate.'

She struggled to find her voice. 'This – this *is* a proper date,' she managed to whisper.

'Oh. Well, then.' He smiled as he leaned forward. After a few seconds, she moved a little nearer and he closed the gap, brushing her lips with his. Her eyes closed involuntarily and flew open when he pulled back.

'See you tomorrow,' he said, walking a few steps towards the gate, and waving over his head until he disappeared into the darkness.

She pressed her fingers to her tingling lips, catching a breath she seemed to have missed.

27

PRESENT DAY, 22 JUNE

The next morning, Eleanor walked down the hill to talk to Kayleigh. Four modest buildings surrounded a central house that looked at least three hundred years old. Grey stone, slate roof, a row of windows each side of the portico with an open door and a welcome sign. Kayleigh met her and showed her into a wide hallway with doors to two large rooms either side.

'This was originally Carlin Manor Farm,' Kayleigh said. 'We don't use the dorms much, but they're good storage. Kids nowadays need charging points and daily showers.' She rolled her eyes.

'So, what do they get up to here?'

Kayleigh launched into the facilities at the centre. 'We have a climbing wall and zip lines, we do coasteering, surfing, canoeing and paddleboarding. We provide quite a lot of nature education to school groups, rockpooling, bird counts, treasure hunts, that sort of thing. Basically, we keep them all so busy they don't have time to get into mischief.'

'That sounds great. I might have loved all that when I was a kid, it might even have got me swimming.'

Kayleigh put her head on one side. 'You can't swim? Kids

here all learn to swim at primary level. You live on an island, you could take a hundred boat trips a year. You need to be able to swim really well – and do water safety, too. We have an outside pool here, and we host swimming lessons for all the primary-aged children throughout the year.'

'I just hated the smell and all the echoey shouting at the pool,' Eleanor confessed.

'Well, we run private lessons. I can give you some times and dates.'

Eleanor waved it off with a laugh. They looked at a room which could be used as a help centre.

'Through here,' Kayleigh said, opening a further door, 'is what we'll use as a medical room. We have a fridge for medication.'

'We'll have a trained nurse and a first aider on duty at all times, and there will be a protected route if needed, for the ambulance. We'll put down bark chippings in case it rains.'

'We have disabled access into both these rooms and the sports centre,' Kayleigh said, pointing out a couple of large pieces of equipment. 'We have a large, accessible bathroom at the back as well as loos.'

'Oh, that's great,' Eleanor said.

'We're as inclusive as we can be,' Kayleigh said. 'How are you finding the island? You seem to be here a lot.'

'Whenever I can,' Eleanor said. 'I've had a tough year, and this has been my "easing myself back into work" project. And I love staying with Sally.'

'Everyone loves Sally,' Kayleigh said. 'She's had her losses, too.'

'Did you ever meet Nessa?'

Kayleigh grinned. 'On this island? You meet *everyone*. I loved her. She used to run a poetry competition on the islands, and talk people like me into judging it. I don't know anything about poetry, but every now and then I'd find a poem I loved.

So, I was learning alongside everyone else. She was this intense ball of light. When she started to dim, we knew something was wrong.'

'Dementia?'

'Yes, but a rare one. Sally called it galloping dementia because it advanced so quickly. She was moved to a home on the mainland.'

Eleanor knew how much Nessa's loss had hurt Sally. It had made her look hard at what she was doing with her own grief. 'I know this is a long shot, but do you know of anyone called Polly or possibly Mary Allen?'

Kayleigh frowned and fell silent. 'I think I've heard of Polly somewhere. Have you been to the library? They have a great archive of local history there.'

'I'll look it up,' Eleanor said, unsure why the idea of more research was putting her off. Maybe she didn't want to find out that her grandmother was a madwoman or had committed some crime.

On her way back to the Doctor's House, Eleanor walked past the library in the civic building, and almost didn't go in. But if Sally could decide to live and enjoy life, despite her over-whelming loss, she could definitely just have a quick look.

The librarian was a quiet woman with a long silver plait. 'You'll need the local history archive downstairs.' She smiled. 'You're in luck, Tony's in there now, although he normally closes the room in ten minutes.'

'I don't want to bother him...' Eleanor started to say, now feeling cold at the thought.

'Nonsense! You will make his day.' She beckoned Eleanor to the stairs. They led down into a basement with books and papers all around, and two high windows illuminating the ceiling – and drifting dust.

'Hi Tony!' she called from the middle of the stairs. 'I have someone looking for family history, Eleanor Markham.'

'The lady who is organising this blasted festival?' A small, spare man in his sixties looked over tortoiseshell glasses, but smiled.

'I am. Sorry,' Eleanor said, smiling back.

'I suppose we need the publicity,' he conceded. 'A couple of people have mentioned you were looking into the Allen family?'

That made her laugh out loud. 'How on earth do you keep a secret on the islands?'

He rolled his eyes. 'It's not easy. So, you think you are the granddaughter of an unknown Allen, here on the islands? Do you feel the pull to the islands?'

'I sort of do!' she said, laughing. She sat in the chair next to him at a crowded table with a laptop, two piles of books and banks of papers. 'My mother was researching her birth family when she died. Her birth name was Hecta Allen, from the birth certificate. Her mother was Alys Allen.' She spelled it out.

'I'm sorry to hear that you lost her.' His voice was gentle. He fired up the laptop and peered over his glasses. 'It definitely sounds like the same family. The first thing you should consider is that your grandmother Alys – is that right? – may have lived and got pregnant on the mainland. Girls travelled here to stay for the last months of their pregnancy. That way, they could keep it a secret from their communities back home.'

She was taken aback; it was such a plausible idea. 'How many girls?'

'Up to about a third of babies born at Springfield came from Cornwall or even Devon. It's hard to believe being pregnant and unmarried was such a big deal, but it was.'

'Do you think that's what happened this time?'

'I actually don't. It's the spelling of Alys that sort of gives it away.' He signed into a genealogy website. 'Have you got the certificate?'

She brought her tablet out of her bag and opened her family tree file. 'I think Polly was a very common name back then, and it might have been a nickname for Mary.'

'Polly and Molly were both nicknames for Mary. Imagine you were having a baby who was going to be adopted, and you knew they would probably get a new name. But on the original birth certificate, you could add names that would give away the wider family, in case they ever got to see it.'

Eleanor ran her fingers over the handwritten information. 'So Alys *and* Hecta could be family names?'

'I've already done a search for Alys out of curiosity when Sally mentioned you. The traditional spelling of Alice was quite common in the islands and there are many in Cornwall and Somerset. But Alys with a Y was a rare spelling.' He brought up a list of names and two Alyses stood out. 'One was born in 1913, one in 1888. Mother and daughter. Cecily Alys Hayle married George Allen, 1931. It was a family name, her mother was Katerina Alys Hayle, born 1888.'

'I've seen a gravestone for a Katerina. What do we know about Cecily Alys Hayle?'

'Her first child was...' His fingers sped over the keys. 'Also Cecily. Pretty name, born eighteen months after the wedding. Branwen born in 1935, Mary was born 1937. That's very close to your relative, isn't it?'

She read the entry carefully. 'They were all born in Silver Street. Where's that?'

'There was a row of hovels down the road by the old pub. The houses have gone now, the supermarket is on the site. But there are some pre-war photographs in the library. I'll get the book for you.'

A sepia picture showed a tiny cottage, the walls looking like the outside plaster was falling off. A small child in a pinafore was leaning against the door jamb. *That could be my grand-*

mother. Eleanor's heart sped up as she tried to make out the features.

'Number 4, Silver Street,' she said. 'I've seen that address before, about a baby that died, in a newspaper. One of the local ladies found her memorial in the graveyard. There was an outbreak of diphtheria.'

'Exactly. I found that article, too – it's from a national paper. But here's what the local paper, the *Island Press* had to say. They followed the aftermath.'

Today, the last child in the islands has been vaccinated with diphtheria antitoxin. Vulnerable adults have also been immunised free of charge through the board of health, and inoculations were administered by Dr Harding-Rowe, the islands' general practitioner. This devastating illness took the life of one St Brannock's baby, Bathsheba Allen, and left another, Polly Allen, with permanent lung injuries. She is currently being cared for in a special hospital in Redruth which caters for these impediments. We hope that no other child will be so affected.

'This was from 1945, just before VE Day,' he explained. 'Many children were left with brain damage, throat issues and even heart and lung problems. The hospital, I think, was a respiratory hospital.'

Eleanor was moved. This poor child had almost died, and must have been left with terrible problems if she couldn't live at home. 'I tracked this young Allen girl – Polly – to a hospital in Redruth. Who would have paid for that?'

'I think there was a lady almoner at the cottage hospital who would have arranged it. They were in charge of the charitable trusts that ran the hospitals. There might be records up there.'

'I chatted to the archivist at the hospital,' Eleanor said, making some notes. 'You've given me some great leads.'

'There's another thing you could think about,' he said, closing the laptop. 'The name "Hecta". As I said, it's pretty unusual.'

'Maybe the *father* was called Hector?' she hazarded.

'Well, there was a Hector on the island during the war, a doctor at the US base hospital.'

She noted him down. 'Sally mentioned him. Could he be the dad?'

'I doubt it, he'd be quite old by 1969, 1970. But the name is deliberate. Maybe the mother was very grateful to him, or he helped her in some way?'

Eleanor leaned back. 'How does she relate to Polly or Mary?'

'That's a good question. If we say the birth certificate is for Mary Allen, born here in 1937 and definitely in the same family, that's the only real candidate as your ancestor. That *must* be the Polly who got diphtheria and nearly died, because we know what happened to all of her sisters.'

The idea made Eleanor catch her breath. 'So, my grand-mother might have called her baby Hecta so she could find her? If she ever went looking.'

'Maybe...' He opened the laptop again. He clicked on a file with a flourish. 'And here... is *Cecily* Alys Allen, who might be your great-grandmother. Born Cecily Hayle in 1913.'

The grainy black-and-white photograph was of a small group of children, unsmiling, staring into the camera in a school picture. 'Wow!' Eleanor scanned the picture. 'What year was this?'

'1922, just after the census, so she was about nine years old. It helps that there were only three girls about that age at the school, and those two in the left-hand corner are identical twins.'

That left a serious-looking, dark-haired girl in a dark dress, white apron and heavy-looking boots. All the children had shoes that looked uncomfortably heavy and maybe handed down. She had what Eleanor thought of as an 'island' look, like Sally.

That could be my great-grandmother.

'Hello, Cecily,' Eleanor murmured.

28

APRIL 1943

Mrs Oppy knocked on the surgery door in response to a note left at her lodgings.

Dorothy opened the door and the ex-housekeeper walked straight into the kitchen, sat down and put her handbag on her knees.

'This is about the wages owing, is it?' Mrs Oppy asked, looking around the room with disdain.

Dorothy had put some of the crockery away in cupboards, rather than have it all shelved on the dresser gathering dust, and had instead used the top two shelves for books, leaving just one for china. She had found a set with a pretty pattern of yellow roses in a downstairs cupboard, and was using them.

'Mrs Oppy, we both know that there were no wages agreed since I bought the practice.'

'What about all the weeks I nursed the old doctor, then? Never a penny, not even from his relatives.'

'Perhaps they gave you room and board instead of wages, since you – and your son – were living in the cottage for free? I told you before, you must take it up with Dr Lavenham's solicitor.'

Dorothy felt better standing. Mrs Oppy was several inches taller and gave off a faint threat.

'*Cottage?*' The woman sneered. 'More like an old shed.'

'Indeed,' Dorothy said firmly. 'And I am glad you have found accommodation elsewhere. I want to talk to you about the medicines you dispensed in the absence of the doctor.'

'All agreed with one or the other of the locums,' she snapped. 'Just a bit of cough linctus and the like.'

'Well, are their prescriptions written up on the patient records?'

Mrs Oppy stared up at her defiantly. 'I have no idea if the doctors made proper notes. My responsibility was just to dispense them.'

'But you're not...' Dorothy took a deep breath. 'Only a trained dispenser or chemist may give out medicines. And only a qualified doctor or nurse may prescribe for patients. The same for the midwife.'

'In my mother's day, experience counted for more than book learning and certificates.' Mrs Oppy sniffed. 'She was a capital midwife, and laid out the dead, too.'

'Well, things have changed. I have been looking after a patient who is with child, four or so months gone.'

'Beryl Livingstone?' Mrs Oppy threw her shoulders back, sitting bolt upright with a disdainful look on her face. 'I wouldn't count any chickens. That family is very prone to miscarriages. Her mother was, too.' She stared directly at Dorothy. 'I knows you promised you would cut out her baby, come time, but hopefully she won't need that.'

Dorothy shook her head at the words. 'Mrs Oppy, if you go near Mrs Livingstone, if you tend to her in any way, I will get you arrested. If she miscarries, I will have her examined and report her – and *you* – to the police.'

'I knows all the police on these islands,' Mrs Oppy hissed,

standing up. 'I helped birth one of them, and my mother 'elped another.'

'My evidence would be given to the police in *Penzance*,' Dorothy answered, drawing herself up to her full height. 'I need to remind you that inducing the termination of a pregnancy incurs a prison sentence.'

Mrs Oppy leaned over the table, hissing her words so close that spittle hit Dorothy's face. 'And who will be responsible when Beryl goes out on the tide, unable to bear losing another child – or her own agony trying to birth that baby for days?'

'You can safely leave Mrs Livingstone to me,' Dorothy said, and Mrs Oppy drew back. 'It would be easier if you left the island.'

'Easier for *you*, you mean,' she said, snatching up her bag and walking to the kitchen door. 'But unlike you, I belongs here. When you go bankrupt because no one will come to you, not after what *I* tells them, I'll still be here. We got on perfectly well without *your* type, and we'll do so again.'

Your *type*? Dorothy could feel a bubble of humour rising up. 'I am an excellent and well-qualified doctor.' She smiled at her. 'Look, we don't have to be enemies, Mrs Oppy. I am happy to get my solicitor to contact the family of the practice's previous owner, if wages are really owing. But you cannot practise *any* type of medicine here on the islands.'

Mrs Oppy stalked to the front door and wrenched it open. 'You'll get your comeuppance. I know of your type, and no one will allow their wives, or their children, near *you*.'

'Except the Allens,' Dorothy said, walking to the doorway.

'They are from *Morwen*,' Mrs Oppy spat, clearly furious. 'And no one will forget you let their baby die.'

Having coloured in the dozen posters she had created, Dorothy walked into the town to persuade people to put them up. The waiting room in the hospital put one in a prominent place, then the post office and shop put one each in their windows. The café wasn't so keen at first – apparently, public health and tea and scones didn't go together – but she managed to persuade Mrs Keiller, whose grandson had been the injured fisherman she had helped.

Free vaccinations, baby weighing and child health checks were prominent on the poster. She had drawn wonky teddies on each to catch the children's attention. Walking through the town, she also persuaded the pubs and the tiny shop right on the end of the island, as well as a couple of prominent citizens, to display the posters. The vicar's wife promised that her husband would mention the clinics on Sunday.

She then tackled the board of health's representative of the National Insurance scheme for the working men. Shamefully, fewer than half the island men qualified – the stamp price of a few pence a week was too high. Their wives were not automatically covered unless they worked and paid their own insurance. Children were generally not covered anywhere. The board representative was not unsympathetic; they already supported the voluntary hospital through an almoner, but saw the general practice as a business. They did offer some samples of free vitamins for the children's clinic and advised her to speak to her natural allies, the midwife and nurse who had done a lot of the work with the old doctor. Cod liver oil and orange juice concentrate were to be offered more widely to all children, as well as more milk, but the government scheme didn't always reach the islands. She would have to fight for it.

It was a nice surprise when she got back to the surgery to find a woman with a small child waiting by the door. A simple case of impetigo – a scabby rash on the child's face – was painted with gentian violet, two shillings and sixpence paid for the appointment and sixpence more for the bottle of violet dye.

'Apply widely over the whole area,' Dorothy advised. 'But

don't get it in his eyes, and don't let him rub his eyes until the purple is dry. Just reapply each day for a week, and it should go by itself.'

'But he can go to school?' his harassed mother asked. 'Only I got shifts down on the quay, gutting and salting fish.'

'Could he stay with a relative, or friend?'

'My mother's dead, my mother-in-law is ill. All my friends are either working with the fishing boats or down the cannery.'

Dorothy looked at the boy, nine years old, gaps in his teeth and mostly purple-headed. 'He really can't go to school because he'll pass it on to the other children. Perhaps the teacher could give him something else to do, away from the others?'

The mother huffed about it, but Dorothy couldn't see what else would work. 'But you did the right thing bringing him,' she said at the doorway. 'Impetigo can spread through a whole family. It can even be serious,' she called to the woman's back as she walked briskly away, muttering.

The boy turned and put his tongue out, shocking pink against the violet. Dorothy stuck out hers in response.

29

PRESENT DAY, 27 JUNE

Eleanor had just finished filling out a fifty-three-page insurance document, one of the slowest and least liked tasks for the festival. Now she had to tackle the valuation of the farmland they were renting and identify any risks from the sheep themselves. She had never heard of half the diseases sheep could get, let alone pass on.

She arranged to meet Bruno at the quay, where he was apparently working. She slipped flat shoes on, perked her lipstick up and brushed her longer hair. She was letting the natural dark blonde grow in a bit – she fancied herself as more of a country girl for the duration.

She said goodbye to Sally, who was busy drying bunches of herbs, and walked into town. She found Bruno sitting outside the pub, relaxing with a beer in his hand, squinting into the midday sun.

'I thought farming was an around-the-clock job,' she joked, sitting beside him. 'I expected to have to walk down to the farm.'

'Oh, I'm still working. We've just taken a cut of hay, so I'm checking the weather isn't going to stop it drying.' He glanced up at the perfectly blue sky. 'You need to keep an eye on it.' He smiled in a way that made her stomach fill with butterflies.

'Well, I have more questions to ask you, if you don't mind. Can you help me with my form?' She handed it over, with a pen. 'It's all about animal husbandry, so I thought you'd know more than I would.'

He skipped through the pages, cutting through the boxes with decisive strokes. 'No – no and no,' he said, hesitating over page two. 'Do they really think one of my sheep is likely to kill someone? Or that your music lovers might kill a sheep?'

'We have to assess the risk.'

'Pretty well *zero*,' he said. 'I suppose one of your visitors might steal a sheep, but they'd have to be nuts and we'd notice. Honestly, I struggle to pick up an adult ewe, and the lambs are faster than I am.'

They raced through the form; most of the questions didn't apply to sheep, and he didn't spray with chemicals or own any dangerous animals like bulls. 'My two rams are on their summer holidays over on the eastern side of the island,' he concluded, signing the form. 'There you are.'

'Thank you,' she said, putting the bulky folder back in her bag. 'About five more to do.'

'Would you like to walk along the harbour wall?' he asked. 'I want to show you what's happening in the field we moved the sheep to.'

'OK.' She was happy to get away from her computer. 'I'll drop my bag home on the way.'

'Bring a swimsuit,' he said. 'You might fancy a dip. The beach is lovely at this time of year and the water's starting to warm up. It's so hot today.'

'I... I can't swim,' she said, her face growing warm. 'I know, it's stupid... and everyone on the islands swims like a fish...'

'No, they don't,' he answered. 'Over the last twenty years or so, we have had four drownings, *all* locals. It's not even about whether they can swim, it's about currents and rip tides and the cold water. You should at least learn to float.'

She shuddered at the thought. 'If I can't swim, what makes you think I could float?'

'Everyone can float. It saves lives. If I can risk my land and my livelihood because you persuaded me – with one arm up behind my back – you can at least trust me enough to give floating a go. For your own safety.' He was standing close enough for her to feel his body heat, and her resolve was weakening.

'But I don't even have a swimsuit!' she argued feebly.

'You can swim in that natty outfit you go running in,' he said, smiling at her. His eyes were kind, his face was kind – but a little quirk of his lips said he was amused as well. 'I'll look after you, even if you're scared.'

'I'm not scared,' she lied. 'I'm *busy*. But if it bothers you that much…'

'That's the girl,' he said. 'Facing our fears is always helpful. I had to face mine about renting you the fields.'

She followed him to Sally's house, her heart racing at the threat of drowning. *But you weren't going to die if renting out the fields went wrong.*

Sally thought it was an excellent idea. So much so that she decided to go with them.

'Where are we going?' she asked. 'The water's still very cold.'

'I thought it might be more comfortable to start in the Carlin Centre pool,' he confessed. 'Obviously, if she's a natural, we can head straight down to the beach.'

Eleanor threw a towel at him. 'You set me up!'

'Ruby's meeting us there after school,' he said, grinning.

Eleanor stomped into her room, grabbed some exercise clothes out of the hamper and went back into the kitchen. 'So, I'm going to make a fool of myself in public?'

'What do you think I'll be doing, racing gigs?' he said. 'I haven't practised for months and I must be a stone heftier than last time I got into the boat. I could sink it!'

Sally laughed but Eleanor followed them, her steps getting heavier and more reluctant. Her heart was beating faster, and cold sweat was creeping down her back. *I cannot swim. I'll die.* Along with that fear was the complication that Bruno would see her being a hysterical idiot. He might have to touch her, not the way she had imagined, but to stop her falling. She had imagined meeting him on the festival ground, head high and wearing tie-dyed silks, in her element. *Why do I even care?*

She was just about to take a stand and assertively refuse when she realised they had stopped for her to catch up.

'You're really scared?' he said, his voice gentle. She nodded, and he pressed her hand for a second. 'I get that. Most adults who haven't learned to swim have a fear rather than an inability to do so. But almost everyone can swim.'

'How do you know so much?'

'I teach swimming in the centre,' he said, smiling at her. 'And life-saving. We aim to get everyone at least floating by the end of their first lesson. We can't send kids out on paddleboards and canoes if they panic when they fall in. Panic gets you killed.' He moved a little closer, his voice soft. 'At least let me try. Give me a chance, in the shallow end.'

She managed another nod. The three of them set off down to the activity centre again.

'I feel stupid,' she said to Sally and Bruno. 'I just never try things I can't do. I'm always prepared for anything I tackle.'

'You *are* prepared.' Sally smiled at her. 'You've brought a swimming instructor and an old dear to hold you up.'

'I've trained all the lifeguards at the centre and on the beach up there,' Bruno added.

'Not just a farmer, then,' Eleanor said through clenched teeth.

'Everyone does several jobs here,' he said, grinning. He looked so much younger, she distractedly noticed, when he was smiling. 'We diversify, you know.'

Having changed into her crop top and shorts in the changing room, hoping they would remain opaque when wet, Eleanor eased herself into the warm water at the shallowest end of the pool, hanging onto the side.

'I'm sorry I'm being such a wuss,' she said to Sally, who was resplendent in a flowery bathing suit with a skirt, hair covered in a floral bathing cap.

'Don't be silly,' Sally said, launching herself into a brisk breaststroke towards the deeper water.

Bruno walked out of the changing room in a pair of long shorts. She was momentarily distracted by his stocky, powerful physique – from lifting all those bales of hay and lambs, she thought – before her foot slipped a few inches and she froze in panic.

'You're OK,' he said, wading towards her.

She noticed the sign in a panic: one metre deep. *What is it people say? You can drown in a few inches of water*.

'If you fall over, you'll naturally hold your breath and stand back up.'

'Will I?' she said, her breath coming so fast she felt dizzy, and she was shivering. The water wasn't freezing, but it wasn't bathwater either.

'That's what you're going to be able to do after today,' he said, moving closer. She grabbed his forearm and hung on.

'I'm not!' she snapped, with certainty.

'You've washed your face before, had a shower, a bath. You've held your breath many times.' He reached out his other hand. 'You can do this.'

His arms were mahogany brown and muscular; she felt

reassured by his complete confidence. She still squeaked when he walked backwards into slightly deeper water, the cold creeping up to her chest.

'Bruno,' she gasped, her hands clamped onto him. She had been holding her breath in panic.

He stopped and she could feel the cold ebbing away as she calmed down. 'What's the worst thing that could happen?' he asked.

'If I fall over, I'll breathe in water.' She spoke through clenched teeth. She wanted to cling to him.

'You won't. Not here, in the pool. Just splash a bit of water on your face. Get used to the temperature.'

Her fingers on his arm had cramped and she had to loosen them slowly. She ran a wet hand over her face. Then, holding her breath, she splashed on a little more, as if she was rinsing off cleanser. 'I don't even like baths that much,' she confided. 'I prefer showers. It's so much quicker...' She grabbed his hand tightly.

Sally swam past her, then turned around and swam back. 'Well done,' she called cheerfully, then dipped her head under-water for another stroke. Eleanor shivered.

'I love baths,' he said conversationally. 'I'd really like a hot tub in the garden. And Ruby is an absolute water baby.' He was walking back again, the water getting deeper and looking darker, and she grabbed his other hand.

'Bruno...' she begged.

'I won't take you out of your depth,' he said. 'And I promise I won't let go.'

'I fell in the sea once,' she stammered, the memory loading into her brain with the feeling of water around her. 'I was paddling, I was only four or five. A wave knocked me over.'

'What happened?' he said, in the same voice she had heard him use to calm his daft sheep if they got a leg stuck in the fence, or had got separated from the others.

'My mum picked me up, and I coughed and spluttered and threw up. I must have breathed in a whole mouthful of water.'

'You didn't,' he said calmly. 'Children have a reflex that closes their airways down, but their sinuses, mouth and nose get filled up. They cough and vomit to clear them.'

'I felt like I couldn't breathe.' She clung to his hand.

Ruby slid into the pool next to Sally and waved at her. She tried a smile but it was feeble.

'Because your airway was temporarily in spasm,' he explained. 'Then you started breathing again, because you're here now, aren't you? You can just hold your breath. If you hold your nose, it will keep the water out.'

'Sally wasn't, when she was swimming,' she said, more curious than scared now.

'No, she was breathing out through her nose,' he said, in the same gentle voice. It started to annoy her.

'What do I have to do to get out of the pool?'

'You're going to grip your nose, hold your breath and then bend your knees. I'll be holding your other hand the whole time.'

'I'm going to die,' she said, as Ruby swam over.

'No, you won't! I'll do it, too,' Ruby said. 'Here, borrow my goggles, then you can see what's happening. You'll be fine.'

It was hard to let go of Bruno's hand to put the goggles on. They instantly steamed up. She gripped his hand again the second she could.

'I'm coming, too!' Sally cried as she swam towards them.

'We'll go when you do. Take your time,' Bruno said. 'Try just dipping your face in first.'

She took a deep breath, let it out. It was almost impossible to pant with fear and hold her breath at the same time. She locked eyes with Bruno, dark eyes, long lashes clumped together with water. A long gasp of air, she shut her eyes and dipped her face forward into the water. When she opened her eyes, she could see her feet and his, reassuringly flat on the bottom of the pool. She flung her head back and breathed out with a whoosh.

'Well done,' he said, a big smile. 'Now, you're going to bend your legs and dip under the surface. You'll feel your hair floating. OK? Just for a count of three.'

Locking eyes with him, she bent her knees as he, too, sank into the water, his dark hair floating around his head, filled with air bubbles that looked like mercury. Ruby smiled underwater with both thumbs up.

Eleanor counted to three slowly, breathed out a trail of silver and pushed up. Bruno's hands steadied her as he rose with her. 'There you go!' he said, grinning, as she pressed a hand to her galloping heart. 'I'll take you to the shallows and you can practise. Ruby, do you want to help?'

'Love to,' she said, holding her hand out. Led by both of them, Eleanor got to the edge of the pool and let go of a whoosh of tension, transferring her grip to the side.

'He used to make me do that,' Ruby said, smiling broadly. 'Well done!'

'How long did it take you to learn to swim?'

'Well, we used to swim to the bottom of the pool, I'd kiss his nose, and then we'd bounce up to the surface again and laugh. That made it funny rather than scary. It's easier when you're six.'

That made Eleanor smile. And she wondered if kissing Bruno would distract her from the panic, too.

30

MAY 1943

When Dorothy opened the surgery door at eight o'clock to shake a duster out, she was surprised to see two women standing outside.

One was an elderly woman with a stick, leaning on the other's arm. 'It's my knee. The old doctor always lances it for me,' she explained, hobbling into the waiting room. 'I tried to treat it myself since the doctor died, but it's got worse.'

'Well, it would need sterile treatment and a proper dressing if it was infected,' Dorothy explained, helping the woman over the slight step leading to the examination room. 'If you could take a seat in the waiting room, Mrs...?' she said to the other woman.

'My name's Harper,' the woman said. 'And I is, strictly speaking, not here as a patient.'

'Oh.' The name was familiar to Dorothy. 'Nurse Harper?'

'That's me. Easy does it, mother,' she said to the old lady.

'Are you related?' Dorothy enquired as they helped her into a low chair.

The old woman cackled and wheezed a sort of laugh. 'Oh,

bless you, Doctor. That's what we call the old people here. Young women is maids, old women is mothers.'

'I'll just get your notes, Mrs...?'

'Flora Ellis,' the old lady said. 'Only it's Florrie, it always has been.'

'I'll get them,' Nurse Harper said, slipping to the records cupboard.

'I'll listen to your chest, before I look at that knee,' Dorothy said, getting her stethoscope out and slipping on her medical apron.

She was astonished at the crackles and whistles that came though the instrument, but the woman looked as well as could be expected for her advanced age. Her white hair was thinly distributed over a pink scalp; her fingers looked like knotted twine.

'How old are you, Mrs Ellis?'

The nurse, who had slipped her coat off, handed Dorothy a thick packet of notes. 'Mrs Ellis was born in 1842. Has a history of TB but has been well for many years.'

'Last time I got consumption was the year the queen had her jubilee.' Dorothy realised she was over one hundred years old. She looked like her features were lost in deeply tanned wrinkles, but faded blue eyes peeped out at her. 'Queen *Victoria*, that was,' she added helpfully.

'Well, that's a very good age,' Dorothy said, as the woman lifted her long skirts to reveal a stained bandage around her knee. Dorothy gently unwound it. The smell was vile, and the redness around the edge suggested the infection was spreading.

'I'm afraid I do need to see to that now,' Dorothy said, leaning back and catching sight of the nurse's half-smile. 'Nurse, if you are here to help, could you set up a tray for draining this infected lesion and applying an antiseptic dressing?'

The leg was soon drained and cleaned, although Dorothy had to hold her breath for a long time during the treatment. The orange acriflavine liquid was painted around the wound after it was flushed with saline. Finally, the nurse bandaged the leg with practised efficiency.

Mrs Ellis hadn't complained once, even though it must have hurt. 'I'd have preferred to put some sulfa powder in the wound,' Dorothy said, thinking aloud. 'I have ordered some, but it's in short supply with the war.'

'Never mind fancy drugs, my dear,' Mrs Ellis said. 'I just want to go to my grandson's christening before I die. Well, my *great*-great-grandson's christening, can you believe that?'

Dorothy struggled with the idea. 'How many children do you have?'

'Well, I has five married children but my eldest never could have any so just twelve grandchildren, then twenty-two great-grandchildren. And young Erik, born in January.' Her expression changed. 'Nine of them are serving, and two of my grand-daughters are in munitions.'

'Good grief,' Dorothy said faintly. 'How many will come to the church?'

'We can seat most, and the rest will be at the hall,' she said, then thanked Nurse Harper for tying up the final bandage. 'Of course, some of them live on the mainland now.' She made a little purse of her lips. 'But most of them will come over on tomorrow's boat. They'll get a special pass, even though it's the war.'

'They will,' the nurse confirmed. 'There are a few Ellises working on the ships.'

'And you should come, too, Doctor,' Mrs Ellis said, helped to her feet by the tall nurse. 'I'll save a pew near the front for you. And your husband?' she questioned without self-consciousness.

'No, I don't have a husband,' Dorothy said.

'Well, maybe you'll find one at the christening.' The old woman winked, then chuckled. 'My Erma was like you, late to the altar and look what happened? Two boys then twin girls!'

'Mrs Ellis...' Dorothy started to argue.

'Don't bother,' the nurse said, over the old lady's head. 'She quite deaf. She says whatever she likes.' She smiled. 'She always did.'

'Bring a friend, anyway,' Mrs Ellis said, shuffling to the door and holding onto the frame. 'I'll just get to the door and then my Samson will take me home on his milk cart. He's my grandson, he's a bit young for you but he's recently widowed,' she said hopefully, as she was helped along the hall.

'I'll see,' Dorothy said more loudly.

Nurse Harper smiled back at her. 'You should come. Nothing else will persuade the locals to come to a female doctor more than the endorsement of the Ellises. I'll just settle her on the cart and come back.'

Dorothy put the kettle on and set the instruments aside for washing in antiseptic and then steaming. By the time the nurse was back she had a pot of tea ready.

The nurse stood behind the table. She was tall and thin, somewhere in her late forties or early fifties, with a broad, weather-beaten face.

'I brought my registration papers,' Nurse Harper said. 'I trained in Truro and came to Penzance to work for a few years. When I married, I had to leave hospital nursing, but did extra training on the district. I came back here so my mother and mother-in-law could help with the children.'

'That's marvellous,' Dorothy said, feeling relief relax her, making her knees quite wobbly. 'It felt like I was just here on my own.'

'You have to pay me out of the surgery income,' Nurse Harper said, and took a breath. 'Dr Lavenham never put my wages up. But the new rate is five pounds and five shillings, forty-hour week, and the use of a bicycle to be provided.'

Dorothy would have agreed to more, but the bicycle confused her. 'I don't think there is a bike, is there?'

'Mrs Oppy was left in charge of the practice bicycle,' the nurse said, sitting at the table. 'It's probably been sold.'

'How was she ever allowed to work here?'

Nurse Harper shrugged and poured a splash of milk into each cup. 'Fresh milk?'

'I find a bottle on my doorstep every other day,' Dorothy said. 'I don't like to report it, or someone else could get into trouble. But it's very welcome.' She poured out the tea. 'I've been giving the extra to the Allen girls,' she explained. 'For medicinal purposes.'

'I saw young Polly sitting in the lane,' Nurse Harper said. 'She's still very frail. She gets out of breath easily.'

'She may have permanent lung damage. She was desperately close to dying.'

The nurse sipped some tea and closed her eyes in appreciation. 'Did you really put a breathing tube into her windpipe?'

'It's a new technique called a tracheostomy. Actually, I only watched. Dr McBride at the airbase did it. But I'm confident I could do it.'

'Dr Lavenham always sent surgical patients up to the cottage hospital, leaving me to argue with the lady almoner. He was never confident of surgery. His predecessor used to do tonsils on kitchen tables.'

Dorothy laughed. 'Well, I'm glad we don't have to do that any more! No, we needed the American hospital because the local one couldn't take someone who was so infectious. Especially after the baby died.'

'You'll win them over. But one thing... Your clothes.'

Dorothy looked down at her tartan skirt in cream and green, her green blouse and her apron, now grubby. 'My *clothes*?'

Nurse Harper finished her tea and rose to her feet. 'Mrs Ellis is right. You give the impression of someone who is – to be blunt – an older lady. Not a family person,' she said delicately. 'Could you invite a male friend to sit with you? It would reassure the locals.'

'You are joking?'

Nurse Harper snapped on a brooch that held a cape over her shoulders. 'This may be the modern era and the nineteen-forties, but these people are stuck in the *eighteen*-forties. It would make you seem more like them, and less like a rich Londoner who might give up and go home at any minute.'

'I'm not going anywhere,' Dorothy snapped back, even surprising herself. 'Could you start work tomorrow? We need to organise a mother and baby clinic.'

The nurse raised her eyebrows. 'An excellent idea. I'll see if our local midwife is free to come and talk to you. Can you think of someone to invite to the christening?'

Dorothy laughed. 'If I don't, I shall have Samson Ellis to fall back on!'

31

PRESENT DAY, 29 JUNE

Eleanor spread the site maps over the large kitchen table to plot where vendors, stages and facilities would go. Liz Retallack had come over to sign off on the plan, but she was in the garden chatting to Sally, the two of them giggling away among the newly ripening vine flowers on the pergola.

'Right,' she called out the open back door. 'This is my best draft,' she explained, moving another square of card – South Indian Street Food – into line with the meandering path that would be created with biodegradable bark chippings.

Liz and Sally came in, holding fragrant herbal teas. Sally had made Eleanor something called a cold tisane, brewed overnight. It was bright yellow, and Sally had insisted she drank it to help her deal with stress. She wasn't sure she needed it, but it was delicious nonetheless.

Liz asked intelligent questions and nodded her approval for all of the island stalls and stands. After getting Eleanor involved, she had stepped back a bit from the planning. She looked tired. 'We had hoped to get more local bands playing,' she said. 'Have you managed to do that?'

'There's a huge festival of music going on all over the

islands. It's amazing what the islanders have come up with. In pubs and venues, cafés, the youth club on St Piran's, restaurants, village halls all over.'

'I don't really go into pubs much,' Liz admitted. 'And I prefer classical.'

'Second day, stage two, three thirty.' Eleanor pointed to the enlarged brochure on her screen. 'If It Ain't Baroque – period strings and recorders doing medieval dance music. If you like jazz, we have a whole day around the town in different cafés, pubs and gardens. The vicar is hosting an outside event with big-band music, and...'

Liz held up her hand and pulled the list over towards her. 'I see! What else? What about art and dancing?'

'The Mermaid's Purse on Morwen has organised a dance-off on the quay for local morris dancers in the evening of day one. The ballet school are doing a gala performance on the main stage, in the morning of day three, and all parents get a free pass. Every spare wall in the town and in social venues across all the islands is showing artists' work, from woodcarving to ceramics and painting. We have visiting artists, too – some who have exhibited in the Royal Academy, and some of those are running workshops.'

'My goodness! You certainly know your stuff,' Liz said. 'I didn't realise it would be so far-reaching. Everyone seems to be doing something.' She looked down at her long fingers and twisted a wedding ring. 'Except me. Andrea's doing history walks around the church and graveyard, she tells me, the day before the festival starts. And another friend is organising spiritual music at different churches each day. And the churches are doing bell-ringing.'

'Is everything all right?' Eleanor looked at Sally, who looked away. 'Would you *like* to be involved with anything?'

Liz cleared her throat. 'I would love to, but my husband has been ill. I can't leave him alone for long.'

'We could organise people to keep him company?' Sally offered. 'Everyone will understand.'

'I think he'd get agitated...' Liz said uncertainly, then glanced at Eleanor. 'It's dementia, you see,' she said quietly. 'People don't know, not yet. He can still play the organ at the church, he loves that, even if he struggles to talk sometimes. He still recalls all the hymns.'

'Could he be involved at one of the church music events?' Eleanor said.

'Oh, I don't think so. He wouldn't want people to know he is having difficulties.'

'You're getting quite stuck indoors,' Sally said. 'Believe me, I know how protective you feel about someone with dementia. The old Michael might hate people knowing, but I doubt if the new Michael will mind as much.' She looked at Eleanor. 'He isn't the only one in our church with problems. We could make a dementia choir, almost, if we included loved ones and carers.'

Liz looked away, dabbed her eyes with a tissue. 'Goodness. I hadn't thought about that. My granddaughter sometimes sings with him, "Amazing Grace" and that sort of uplifting music. Just at home. He never forgets a word.'

'I can squeeze it in the programme,' Eleanor said. 'If you can keep the group name to fifteen characters.'

'I don't know,' Liz said. 'But I'll think about it.' She stood, and Eleanor did too, to be surprised by Liz leaning forward and kissing her cheek. 'You've been a ray of sunshine,' she murmured. 'Thank you.'

'Thank *you*, I've loved doing it,' was all Eleanor could stammer.

At the door, Liz turned to them. 'Are you two going to cheer the gig races tomorrow? We always used to. It should be fun, and there will be food on the beach.'

'Hot dogs,' Sally said. 'And a hog roast. You could bring Michael. He always loved the gig racing.'

'Well, he rowed in them for forty years,' Liz said. 'I think it might be too confusing for him to be in the crowd... Will you be there, Eleanor?'

'Ruby feels we need to cheer Bruno on. Apparently he hasn't been practising much this year.'

Liz smiled at that. 'He'll pay for it the next day,' she said. 'I hear you went swimming?'

Eleanor's face warmed in a blush. 'Not exactly *swimming*. I managed to stay underwater for a count of six. But I couldn't float, no matter how hard I tried, even with Ruby and Sally helping.'

'Well, keep at it. You're on an island now, you know. It might come in handy.'

'I sincerely hope not,' Eleanor said, alarmed.

Having been given online access to the library's archives, even the unsorted records, Eleanor sat on the bench in Sally's orchard. She swiped through documents and newspapers; many hadn't been fully digitised and weren't searchable. She was also finishing her second glass of wine after a delicious meal she and Sally had conjured out of what was looking a bit old in the bottom of the freezer.

'Hi there,' came a familiar voice across the grass. Eleanor looked around to see Bruno standing by the fence, hands in his jeans pockets.

'Hello yourself.' She pushed the laptop away and walked over. 'Finished farming for the day?'

'I was helping a friend move house all morning,' he said. 'The sheep are doing just fine. What are you up to?'

She looked back to the open laptop. 'Just doing some research into my mother's story here. I'm trying to find her birth parents.'

'Any luck?'

'Hecta Allen was the name on my mum's original birth certificate. Before she became Diana. I'm just looking for mentions of her mother, Alys, and her mother as well.'

He leaned on a fence post, folding his arms. 'There are still Allens living on Morwen, I think. I have a farming friend there, I could ask him – he might even be a cousin, the Ellises are related to everyone. Tink knows everyone on Morwen, he'll be over for the gigs.'

'Would you mind?'

He pulled his phone out of his pocket. 'I'll try him now. He has a toddler, though, so he might not be able to talk.'

'You don't have to right now...' she said, but found her hands balled into fists with hope that he would give her a contact.

'Hey, Tink. Bruno. I'm just asking for a friend. Is there anyone with the family name Allen still on the island?' He listened, nodded. 'Oh, right! I know her, a bit anyway. She's a teaching assistant at the high school.' The conversation went in the direction of farming enquiries, then he said goodbye and cut the call off.

'He knows a Jowannet Allen as was, she married a Lawson about ten years ago. She works at the high school over here. You could ask her how much of her family tree she knows.'

Eleanor jumped a little with glee then wobbled on the grass, caught the fence post. She put her hand to her lips. 'I may have had a bit too much wine. But it was the last bit of the bottle, not enough for a glass...'

He laughed, a low sound in the dusk. Dew was just starting to prickle on her face, the wind had dropped and the only sounds were the sheep and her own movement through the long grass.

His face changed and he looked at her intently, like he was trying to work something out. Suddenly, it seemed really easy to slide right up to him, inches away, either side of a strand of wire, and stare at him. He did have lovely dark eyes. 'Thank you!' She felt a bit dizzy. 'And thank you for the swimming—' Her gaze dropped to his mouth.

He moved forward and kissed her, and she froze, then leaned into the moment, savouring the feeling of his lips on hers. When he pulled back she almost leaned over to follow him. 'Mm.' She couldn't think of anything else to say.

'Red wine?' he said, a little breathless.

'Malbec,' she finally found.

'What I meant was, my pleasure,' he said. 'About the swimming. I'd better get back to Ruby.'

'Of course. And I need to take my laptop indoors before it gets all... dewy.'

She turned from him, walked back to the computer. *How much did I drink?* But the kiss was everything she had been dreaming about. When she sneaked a look over her shoulder, at the edge of the patio, he was looking back at her.

32

MAY 1943

One of the dresses that had come in a steamer trunk from Dorothy's parents actually belonged to her sister. Since they were now much the same size, she tried it on.

A dusty pink cotton shirtwaister, she thought it was called, it suited and flattered her. Unlike the silk evening dress she had worn, it didn't make her look like her mother. With it, in a small box, was a matching pillbox hat with hand embroidery. Hopefully it would be acceptable for a christening.

Recklessly, she had committed more money she didn't have to take on a cleaner three mornings a week. A seventeen-year-old called Jeannie Ellis, who was a source of knowledge about fashions.

'Oh, no, not those *shoes*, miss!' She was unable to call Dorothy 'Doctor', and instead treated her like a teacher. 'Those straw-coloured ones are much better.'

'I wore them to a wedding once,' Dorothy said, looking at them with doubt. 'They were very uncomfortable.'

'Then you need to practise wearing them at home,' Jeannie said. 'Soften them up. What about a jacket if it rains?'

'I don't have anything except my work coat.'

'Which is covered with mud. I'll brush that out when it dries properly,' Jeannie said. 'You should have hung it by the kitchen stove.'

It was like having a very bouncy nanny, explaining things that Dorothy hadn't worried about for years.

'I was wondering what to do with my hair,' Dorothy said, looking in the small mirror by the door. Her habit was to plait her thick, bushy hair – sandy blonde – and coil and pin it around her head. A single white strand had sprouted either side of her ears.

'I can set it in a side parting and rolls,' Jeannie said, standing in the kitchen doorway with an unlit cigarette in her hand. 'Look, we can shape your hair to come around that little hat.'

Dorothy sighed. 'I hate not knowing what you're talking about.'

'Don't you read *any* magazines?'

'The *British Medical Journal* and *The Lancet*, when I have time.' If they ever arrive, she added mentally. Everything took weeks from London, and her mother was sending them on with any post.

'What's the gentleman wearing?' Jeannie said with a smile.

Dorothy blushed at the memory of the carefully worded note – after many spoiled attempts – casually asking Hector McBride to accompany her as an exercise in public relations. 'I don't know. It doesn't matter, that's the only dress that works.'

'Well, I can come over for an extra hour in the morning and sort your hair out, and polish those shoes. We really need to wash that dress, it smells like mothballs.'

'I'll pay extra, because it's the weekend,' Dorothy said, knowing full well her reserves had dwindled to a couple of hundred pounds in the bank. But she had started getting paid a few shillings here and there from patients, and she was about to be recompensed by the board for the insured patients. At the end of the month, six night shifts up at the hospital would yield a little more.

'I don't mind the usual,' Jeannie said. 'I'm going to the christening anyway. Do you know the story?'

'No,' Dorothy replied, undoing the stiff plaits coiled around her head, ready to brush out.

'Well...' Jeannie started the story of a young sailor and his sweetheart – from another island, hardly the Montagues and Capulets. Then she let out a yelp. 'No!'

Dorothy froze. 'What?'

'Don't use a brush!' Jeannie said, taking it out of her hands. 'It will just go frizzy. Don't you have a comb?'

Dorothy was lost. 'I just need it tidy, I'm wearing a hat.'

'Let me help you wash and set it today, then it will be easier to do tomorrow.'

It had taken two hours to wash and moisturise her hair with a blend of almond oil from the medicine cabinet and one egg white. Then Jeannie detangled it with a comb she had previously thought better for grooming horses' tails. The girl had found her stories of being a medical student and having short hair hilarious, and was too polite to say *no wonder you're an old maid*.

The next morning, Jeannie created two smooth waves either side of the hat, at a jaunty angle, allowing some natural curls to cluster at the back of her head.

'I *do* look younger,' Dorothy said, staring at her reflection in the small, spotty mirror. This might be what she would have looked like without twenty years of working in a man's job, with doctors who didn't appreciate what she could do. Except Hector, who had recently complimented her on her technique reconstructing some poor fellow's ear, shot to bits with shrapnel.

'Let's get you dressed,' Jeannie said, gathering up the various tools of transformation.

Dorothy allowed herself to be guided by Jeannie, who looked fresh and young in a floral dress with a wide skirt. The fabric was worn and almost see-through in places – clearly it had been cleverly adapted from a previous outfit. There was no fabric available anywhere on the islands, no matter how many coupons you had.

'What about the jacket?' Jeannie asked, tying a scarf as an impromptu sash around the slightly baggy waist of Dorothy's sister's dress.

'I found my linen one in here,' Dorothy said, looking in the open wardrobe.

'No, this!' Jeannie said, wrapping a fur stole around her shoulders and posing, laughing. 'This is lovely.'

'My father gave it to me for my twenty-first birthday,' Dorothy said, remembering how awkward and stilted she felt at Rules, the beautiful restaurant where the rich went to see and be seen. 'But I can't wear it to a country christening. I mustn't take any attention away from the family.'

'They will *love* it,' Jeannie said, her face a picture of surprise. 'You'll be the guest of honour. It will make the whole church grander. Did you buy a present for the baby?'

'I found a little silver cup in Mr Bricknell's shop in the high street. I think it's Victorian,' she confessed.

'Let me polish it and wrap it up.' She pulled out the drawers on the dressing table and held something up. 'How about this?'

It was an old jewellery box, which now held her surgery medals from university. Jeannie unceremoniously tipped them out. 'Look, it's perfect!'

'Oh, very well,' Dorothy said, putting the medals in the drawer. 'And I'll wear my pearls.'

They had been a gift from an ancestor, a rope long enough to hang to her waist or be looped into two or three.

Jeannie's eyes grew round as she took them, like they might give her a shock. 'Oh, they're *lovely*, miss, and so heavy,' she said, awed as she lifted them.

The door rang. 'That will be Dr McBride,' Dorothy said, slipping into the now slightly softer shoes. 'I'll let him in. You'd better bring the pearls down, just give them a dust.'

He'd pushed open the door – it was never locked in the day if she was in – and watched her descend the stairs. 'Wow,' he said, with a tone of approval.

'Jeannie thinks I should dress like the guest of honour.' Warmth rose to her cheeks at the look on his face. 'I'm trying to advertise myself as the new doctor.'

'It really suits you,' he said. 'You look – younger, less worried, somehow.'

'Shifts at the hospital are helping my cash flow,' she admitted. 'And the patients are starting to trust me.'

Jeannie came down and gave her the heavy handful of pearls. Hector immediately stepped forward. 'Let me, please.'

She met his eyes. He unlooped the necklace and lifted it carefully over her hat. 'Twice?'

'Please.' His fingers brushed the skin on her neck, making her shiver.

'These are beautiful.'

'They were given to my great-great-grandmother on her wedding day,' she said, unable to look away.

'Well, they should be well used to church by now,' he said. 'There.'

He looked down, then glanced at her lips, and she wondered if, had Jeannie not been there, he might have kissed her.

Jeannie draped the fur around her shoulders. 'You could be going up the West End, like they say in the magazines,' she said, grinning. 'Wherever that is. You look nice, too, Dr McBride.'

He had a grey suit on, almost the same colour as his hair.

His blue eyes glowed under dark brows, to match a stripe in his tie.

'We'll make a splash in the local society papers.'

The short walk to the church wasn't comfortable in the tight shoes, but Dorothy knew instantly that Jeannie was right; the clothes lent an air of grandeur to the christening.

They were shown to a pew towards the front, and were generally greeted by everyone and introduced around by Jeannie and her great-grandmother, Mrs Ellis. The old lady was helped up to her pew by two strapping young grandsons, one of whom was introduced as Samson – a pleasant young man with two missing front teeth and a moth-eaten jersey. She couldn't help thinking they had both dodged a bullet.

Strangely, the community seemed extra polite to Dr McBride.

'They already accept you as their doctor,' he murmured to her, as the vicar waved at everyone to stand. 'I'm the interloper.'

The baby, a tiny scrap in a gown that looked much too big and a hundred years old, was passed around the new godparents, and the christening began. She couldn't help but notice that his little face looked thin.

'He looks a bit underweight, from here,' she said, craning her head.

'And tomorrow you can go back to being a doctor,' he murmured back. 'Maybe he was born a bit early? Follow up on Monday.'

The simple ceremony was surprisingly moving, and it brought many of her patients together in one room. She could see various problems that in a more prosperous community might have been treated. A man on crutches, another with a hacking cough at the back of the church, a woman sporting a suspiciously irregular mole on her face. Two small children had slightly bent legs, and there was another patch of impetigo.

These are my flock. These people need my knowledge and expertise.

McBride reached for her hand for a moment, held it, then tucked it into his arm. She couldn't work out if he was moved by the ceremony or just being friendly. He bent down to her ear and whispered, 'It's good if they think you have a gentleman friend.'

She knew he was right, but it made her flush with anger.

'And, I like being close to you,' he added, which made her warm in a different way.

It had been a very long time since she had been so close to a man. It was comfortable and exciting in the same moment. She leaned a little closer. 'As long as it's not just for show.'

He smiled back at her and she became aware that a lot of the congregation were looking at her. And old Mrs Ellis was sporting a very maternal smile.

33

PRESENT DAY, 30 JUNE

The gig racing – like everything else – was dependent on the tides, so Eleanor was rudely awakened early by Ruby bringing in a mug of tea.

'Come on, Sally's making toast to take down to the beach or we'll miss the first race. It's at eight fifteen.'

'What?' She sat, the idea of seeing Bruno already making her heart speed up. 'I'll get up, but only if it's the good marmalade,' she grumbled. By the time she'd got back from the bathroom, showered and dressed, she was ready to carry her breakfast with her down to the harbour.

The entire seafront was covered with the boats, each long enough for six rowers and a person at the back – the cox, she supposed. The boats were painted in all sorts of bright colours and designs, but they were all the same shape. A couple of motorboats were powering up and down, ushering the first few boats on the water into a sort of line. A gun was fired with a bang that echoed all around the bay, and they were off.

'Bruno isn't out there, is he?' Eleanor said, squinting at them.

'I hope not! They are the under-twenties ladies' teams.' Ruby laughed at her ignorance.

Eleanor took a big bite of toast with the good marmalade, just as Bruno walked up wearing shorts and a vest, looking athletic and tanned. His vest declared he was part of the Rare Vintage team. She struggled to swallow the bread while he grinned at her discomfort.

Ruby jumped up to hug him around the middle. 'When do you go, Dad?'

'Nine fifteen,' he said. 'The race will be running by then.'

'Race?' mumbled Eleanor past the crumbs.

'It's a current between the islands, in the Sound,' he said, pointing along the coast. 'The main current causes eddies and strange countercurrents – we have to contend with them.'

She felt cold across her shoulders; the darkest green meant the deepest water. 'Is it safe?'

He laughed. 'Nothing's *safe*. But as good as we can make it. Those two motor boats' – he pointed out to sea – 'will be looking out for us, and we have life jackets.'

'Well, be careful,' was all she could say with a dry mouth.

'I've been out on the water all my life,' he said. 'I am *very* careful.'

Ruby stood next to her, leaning against her shoulder. 'He's one of the safety officers for the day,' she said, smiling. 'Perhaps you can explain that you'll do the same for the festival. Making it totally safe for teenagers.'

Bruno rolled his eyes and stepped away. 'Good try.'

Sally shook her head. 'Don't antagonise him now,' she said. 'He'll come around.'

'He's talking about sending me to the mainland for the whole week,' Ruby grumbled. 'To stay with my mother and her new family. Like they even want me.'

'I'm sure they do,' Eleanor said.

'*She* said Dad should let me go to the festival, but he won't

listen to Mum,' Ruby said. 'He thinks I'm ten,' she aimed at
Bruno as he walked away.

'Are you rowing today?' Sally asked Ruby.

'No, I'm working at the activity centre later, serving lunch
and washing up,' Ruby said. 'You know, like a *grown-up*.'

As she went off with a couple of friends, Sally leaned in to
Eleanor. 'If you have to say you are a grown-up, you're not quite
there. But I wish he would let her come to the festival. Oh, here
come the boats again!'

The slim boats had almost disappeared on the shimmering
sea and were now edging around a red buoy. Five of them were
close together, only one had dropped back. The shouting
began.

Sally watched, shading her eyes. 'I think the Falmouth boat
is ahead. Look at the guide,' and she shoved a leaflet into
Eleanor's hands. The distinctive painted boats were all listed.

'There are hundreds here.' She tried to identify the lead
boat. 'Falmouth under-twenties ladies,' she confirmed. 'And
Dartmouth, followed by – is that yellow and green?' She leafed
through, looking for the boats. 'I can't work the others out.
Appledore and possibly Ilfracombe?' She looked again. 'Do they
really come all the way from Devon?'

'From all over the south. Some travel from France and the
Netherlands. They all come over on the ferry.' She started
waving to the two boats, neck and neck, jerkily racing along the
quay until one – the Dartmouth boat – just edged the lead
before a hooter went off.

'I love the gigs,' Sally said, before moving off to greet a
friend.

Eleanor walked along the harbour wall a little more. The
scene was so festive, bunting everywhere, boats moving on and
off trailers and into the water, people in matching T-shirts with
team names on. She felt strangely disconnected from it all. The
narrow boats looked very vulnerable.

A woman in a halter-neck dress that draped onto her sandals walked towards her. 'You must be Eleanor!'

'Yes,' she replied, not expecting the huge hug that pulled her in.

'I'm your cousin, Jo Lawson! Jowannet Allen as was. Oh, you're so tall, just like my auntie Rose. She's probably your cousin, too.'

'Are you sure we're related?'

'Sort of,' Jo said, letting go and grinning at her. 'I'm pretty sure we *are* connected, but I'm not sure *how*. All the Allens are. This deserves a fruit smoothie at the very least. What's your poison?'

'A smoothie with berries would be great,' Eleanor said weakly. As the woman charged off to one of the stands on the quay, she had to resist a weird impulse to run away, in case she was about to learn something disturbing or sad about her mother.

'I wasn't sure what you liked so I asked for the most popular berry one,' Jo said, when she returned. 'Strawberry, raspberry and blueberry. They'll bring it over.'

'Why are you so sure we're cousins?'

Jo nodded, her bright, dark eyes reminding her of Diana's, the deep widow's peak on her forehead echoing Eleanor's and Diana's hairlines. 'I'm pretty sure your grandmother and my grandfather were siblings.' She sat on the low wall. 'Their parents had three daughters – well, four if you count their baby that died – and two boys. My grandfather was called Robert.'

'The baby that died was Bathsheba,' Eleanor said. 'I saw the gravestone.'

'Well, after they all got ill, one of them was left disabled. Her name was Polly, she ended up living in Redruth. Her mother took Polly over to the mainland and her father stayed here and carried on fishing and looking after the kids.'

'What happened to Polly?'

'I've been asking around the family and all I know is Polly came back to the islands in secret – sort of, there aren't *really* any secrets – to have a baby. Then she went back to the mainland and for all we know, is still alive.'

Eleanor's eyes filled up with tears, and she stared out at the next boat race. *Alive?* 'She'd be very old...'

'Yes, but my grandfather, Robbie Allen, still exchanged Christmas cards with his sisters until he died a couple of years ago. Except for her sister Cecily, who died about ten, twelve years ago. I think Polly even went to the funeral. I think she was called Polly Trewin, then. You should talk to my gran, she still keeps in contact with everyone.'

'I would love to,' she said. 'If she'd be happy to talk about it.'

'I'll bring her to Sally's next time you're here, if you like. She's happy to do one of those DNA tests. She's very modern for seventy-eight. She's made up a family tree.'

'I knew there was another part of the Allen family on the islands. On Morwen,' Eleanor said.

'It's a Morwen name but most of the work was on the big island, so people moved. The Allens also mostly make baby girls, apparently, who change their names when they get married,' she said, grinning. 'Except me. Two boys.'

Eleanor caught one of her hands. 'I am so glad to meet you.' She searched the round face for traces of her mother, but she looked more like Sally than Diana.

Jo hugged her again.

Bruno's rowing race was between a whole group of other gigs, starting at different points. It was too confusing for Eleanor to work out, but Sally, who pushed an ice cream into her hand, pointed at his crew as they lined up to start.

The gun was fired and they started rowing, teams in perfect – or not quite perfect – time with each other. Several boats pulled away, including Bruno's, and Eleanor found herself joining in the shouting and cheering, even though she was worried. The water looked so rough, splashing into the boats at times. By the time his gig came in third, she was hoarse and relieved. When he returned to the quay, feted as if he was a hero by the locals, he made his way to them. Sally kissed him on the cheek, and Eleanor smiled.

'Very fast,' she said, laughing at his red face as he peeled his vest away from his body. 'Can we get you something?'

'Pint of Pirate's would be nice,' he said, still panting. 'Then I'm stewarding this afternoon for the main races.'

'What can I get you, Sally?' Eleanor asked.

'Orange juice would be lovely,' she said. 'Where's Ruby? Has she gone to work already?'

By the time Eleanor got back, they were in the middle of an argument that involved him folding his arms and Sally tapping her toe. 'She's almost a grown-up,' seemed to be Sally's argument.

'Look,' Eleanor said to them both. 'I know this is a well-worn discussion, but I have exciting news of my own which has left me rather… unsettled.'

'Thank you,' he said, reaching for the dark beer. 'What's this news?'

'I may have identified my mother's family,' she said, halfway between laughter and tears. 'I'm going to meet relatives of my possible grandmother, Polly Trewin. The family have started doing DNA tests. Perhaps I should submit one as well.'

'Is this the same Polly,' asked Sally, 'with the girls, so you only knew their married names? Was she an Allen, too? It was all before my time.'

'It sounds plausible,' she said. 'And their family names include Alys, which is on my mother's birth certificate.'

Sally looked away, and Eleanor wondered if she'd said the wrong thing.

34

AUGUST 1943

Three months after the christening, Dorothy walked into the little waiting room, which had eight people in it. Most would pay the minimum charge of a few shillings for the consultation, but the drugs cupboard had been cleared of a multitude of old medicines and stocked with fresh, useful ones. Leaning against the door frame was the tall figure of Hector. Dorothy's face became immodestly warm.

He'd been as gentlemanly and respectful as even her father would have expected. He had taken her out to eat several times, once with a few of his colleagues from the hospital. They had walked along the coast down to Carlin Manor Farm, where temporary accommodation for the garrison overlooked a magnificent beach, and he had held her hand. He had worked alongside her on reconstructions of the most terribly damaged young faces and bodies. He had held her when she sobbed after losing one of them on the table, even shed a few tears into her surgical cap himself.

Every time he left, he kissed her goodbye, the kisses getting longer and warmer and making her heart thump in her chest. She dreamed about him every night, thought about him all day. She hated what he must see, not a sophisticated woman but a flushed, hard-working doctor who had done nothing with her hair but shove it into a bun and ram it with a dozen hairpins.

'Hello, Dr McBride. Can I help you?' she said, struggling not to pat uselessly at her hair.

'I can wait,' he said. 'See your patients first. Actually—' For the first time since she'd known him, he seemed unsure. 'Would you mind if I sat in? With your patients' permission, of course.'

She instantly thought that of course they would rather have a male doctor consulting on their ailments. But a quick glance around the room immediately made her see her mistake. *She* was familiar, she was their doctor. *He* was a stranger, an outsider.

'If anyone is uncomfortable, I will ask Dr McBride to step out. But he is an eminent surgeon, and I do work with him regularly.'

No one objected, so she read the name on the next card. 'Mrs Ellis?'

Another Ellis. She needed a chart of the family tree.

More than an hour later, she had diagnosed a knee injury, an unexpected but very welcome pregnancy, nasty bronchitis that would be improved by the cessation of smoking foul-smelling tobacco through a pipe, a small child with a recovering ear infection, and a distressed woman bereaved by the war.

After the last patient left, she gathered up the fees: three IOUs, eighteen shillings and ninepence. Three of the patients at least would be paid for by the insurance scheme, and she might get funding for the child through the board, but it all took a huge amount of paperwork.

'That's general practice, huh?' Dr McBride said, shuffling his chair next to hers at the desk.

'It might seem trivial to you, but this is necessary care to create a healthier population.'

'It makes perfect sense to me,' he replied, pulling one of the forms towards himself. 'How much does the local insurance even pay?'

'Ten and six,' she said, filling in another one. 'But I'll keep that account open until he's completely better. I'm worried about him going back to work still coughing.'

'Why would he?'

She stared over at him. 'He earns maybe a pound or two a day, when they *can* fish. That depends on weather, tides and time of year. Not to mention enemy submarines and air attacks in the English Channel. He has no other form of income other than his wife's few shillings a week collecting seaweed.'

'Seaweed?'

She paused to look at his face. 'I can see you're horrified, but the locals supplement their income by drying and burning seaweed to make ash for glassmaking.'

'I'm not horrified,' he said. 'I'm thinking how resourceful these people are to make the best of their limited resources. There are poorer people in America, as well as richer. I'm just sad that people have to choose between food and medicine.'

Dorothy shuffled the patient record cards together, ready to file back in the drawers. More and more people had returned to her practice from Dr Penrose's on St Petroc's Island; she'd even picked up a few of his patients.

'I hope that one day, there will be some sort of universal health care here in Britain,' she said thoughtfully. 'Successive governments have been talking about it since Victoria was on the throne.'

'That would be something to work towards,' he said, his eyes shining.

'I'm sure you have something better in America,' she said,

raising an eyebrow. She was acutely aware of his knee next to hers, just touching.

'No, nothing like that, nor the will to do it,' he said, and his eyes seemed to capture her gaze. 'I think being here over the next few years might be amazing.'

'I hope it will be.'

He leaned a little closer.

'Hector...' Dorothy began.

He waited, as she gathered her thoughts.

'Why are you really here today?' she asked.

'I wanted to ask you something,' he said, and took one of her hands. His warm touch made her jump. 'Dorothy, you know I have been married.'

'I know,' she whispered, her breath caught in her throat.

'She was a lovely girl, but she had no idea what I did, really. She resented every late-night call-out, every long shift, me falling asleep in my soup after twelve hours' operating. If she hadn't died, I'm sure she would have divorced me.' He made a funny, sad twist of his lips. 'I know she had been seeing someone else before she died. We stood shoulder to shoulder at her graveside.'

'I'm sorry,' was all she could say, but she felt little anger towards the woman who couldn't be loyal to this man.

'I think I should have married a doctor. Someone who understands the crazy hours we work, the busy life, the high stakes for the patients. Someone like *you*.'

She pulled her hand away, doubt creeping in. 'I see.' She looked down, her fingers clamped together until the knuckles went white. 'Of course, you'll be able to stay after the war, then,' she carried on, her voice very flat, hurt at the idea of some sort of practical merger.

'No!' he said. 'I'm sorry, I just thought...' He leaned back in his chair, ran his fingers through his hair. 'Dorothy, you are a remarkable doctor and a fascinating woman.'

'I'm thirty-eight and ordinary,' she answered coolly. 'I know how people see me.'

'They don't *know* you like I do!' he said, eyes blazing again, jumping in his chair. 'I've seen you fight for someone's life, even though you were shaking with exhaustion and didn't know if you would win. I've seen you spend hours perfecting cosmetic stitching on a boy who looked like his face had been grilled. Then, in your sweaty overalls and leaning against the wall because you are too tired to walk, you are *beautiful*.' He moderated his voice a little. 'To me, anyway. I've been trying some English wooing, and I'm not doing very well.'

'You're doing better than you think,' she said, a little laughter wobbling her voice, even as her eyes filled up. 'I can't make the first move, you know. I'm a well-bred English lady of a certain age.'

'Well, I'm right here. Make a move. No one's here to see.'

She shuffled on her chair until her leg touched his, leaned into his open arms and kissed him. After a lot more kissing, she sat against his side, her head on his bony shoulder.

'I don't know if I can have children,' she warned. 'I'm not even sure if I *want* children.'

'I have a child already,' he said. 'He may not approve. But he's happy and settled at his grandparents and ready for college. Our lives will be full enough without children.'

'And I'm not giving up medicine if I do have one. I couldn't give up everything I've worked for.'

'I believe there are nannies,' he said, smiling down at her and kissing her again. 'And I could help. If we can, and if we want to.'

She settled into his arms. Birdsong through the open window became the only sound. His breathing grew slower and his arms more relaxed.

She pulled away. 'Are you falling asleep?'

'Sorry,' he mumbled. 'Twelve-hour surgery last night.

Fighter pilot got impaled in his cockpit, then he managed to land on one engine. They wrapped him and flew him straight here.'

She leaned back against him, smiling up at his sharp cheekbones and long nose. 'Tell me about the surgery.'

35

PRESENT DAY, 10 AUGUST

Six weeks later, Eleanor was working at Sally's kitchen table, putting the final polish on a couple of press releases and planning interviews with bands booked to play the best slots.

Ruby, newly released from school, was helping Sally in the garden. She came in and walked over to the sink.

'Can I get you a drink?' she asked Eleanor over her shoulder.

'There's homemade lemonade in the fridge,' she answered, looking back at the pile of papers and envelopes she still had to deal with. 'I'd love some. With ice would be great.'

'It's so hot outside,' Ruby said, filling up two tall glasses for them. 'What are you doing?'

'Just checking out last bits and bobs. Like set lists. The lighting and sound people need to know what order the bands will play their songs in.' She waved a couple of sample CDs at Ruby. 'These are from new bands who need to know they have to stick to the timings they promise. It's probably their first big outing.'

Ruby looked at the covers of the CDs, then sorted through

some of the others. 'I love these guys,' she said. 'Ooh, Alicia Hart, I *love* her!'

'You can have them, if you like,' Eleanor said. 'I've got all the information I need.'

Ruby squealed with excitement and rounded up the discs. 'It will almost be like hearing them at the festival.' A shadow passed over her face. 'At least I get to hear them first,' she said, smiling back at Eleanor.

'Just don't tell your dad,' Eleanor said to Ruby's back as she ran through the door to tell Sally. 'In case he gets the wrong end of the stick and thinks I'm encouraging you.' She didn't want to rock the boat with Bruno. Since the kiss, since he'd relaxed and become this happy, funny friend, she couldn't stop thinking about him. But she knew that his Achilles heel was Ruby.

She put her pen down and stretched back. She was just sipping her cold drink when Sally came in.

'You sent Ruby off very happy,' Sally said, with a slight frown. 'Are you sure it's wise to wind her up even more? She tells me she and Bruno have been having some big arguments. Shouting matches, she calls them.'

'Well, he should get over it. She's a very sensible fourteen-year-old and it's literally happening in her back garden.'

Sally sat down next to her. 'Yes, but neither of us knows what it's like to be a single parent. She's grown up in a very sheltered environment on the island, and she is *just* fourteen. There are going to be thousands of strangers crammed into her little world. I can see why he's concerned.'

'There are so many people watching over everyone, especially the younger ones.' Sally was looking at her when she glanced up. 'What?'

'I couldn't help noticing that you've been a bit... distracted.'

Eleanor managed a small smile. 'What do you think is going on?'

Sally looked down at her hands, still green from gardening.

'I think you're interested in our grumpy farmer. And I think he likes you so much he's stopped being grumpy a lot of the time.'

'Except about Ruby.'

Sally sighed. 'He's had his problems with her, things he hasn't told you about. Perhaps he ought to – but there are reasons he babies her.'

'Why don't I know all about it already? Isn't that what the island gossip is all about?'

Sally shook her head. 'The island keeps the big secrets for the islanders. They wouldn't have told you, but Ruby was ill when she was little.'

'What do you mean, ill?'

'That's not my story to tell. Ask Bruno, or Ruby. But if he's a little overprotective, you have to make allowances.'

Eleanor started to tidy her notes into rough piles. She could still bring to mind the feeling of his lips on hers. She almost lifted her fingers there. 'I'll talk to Bruno, if you really can't tell me. Would that help?'

'That's a good idea. He's probably back at the farm by now.'

Eleanor pushed the piles of papers away; she'd almost gone word blind over her lists.

'I'll go now, then. I knew there was something he wasn't telling me.'

As Eleanor walked down the road to the farm, she wondered what Sally meant. She was partly anxious that there was something wrong with Ruby, and partly excited to see Bruno.

She met him outside, where he was tinkering with a quad bike he used to carry bales of hay out to his sheep.

'Hi there!' he said. He already had smudges of oil on his forehead. He seemed to get dirty no matter what he did. 'Everything OK?'

'I wanted to talk to you about Ruby.'

He wiped his hands on a rag, looking as if he was resisting saying the first things that came into his mind.

'Not you, too. There isn't much to say. She's too young to go to a festival and it's my decision.'

'I know it's your decision. But her friends are going, and I'll be there. There will be stewards all over, they always look out for the children. Mostly, I suspect she would be dancing on the beach, or giggling with her friends.'

'Maybe next year,' he said, returning to the exposed engine of his bike. 'It's not up to you. I'm her father.'

'Of course.' Eleanor bit her lip, struggling not to start an argument. 'You're protective of her—'

'I am,' he snapped. 'She's my child.'

'But what happened to make you so overprotective, Bruno?' she asked. 'Sally said Ruby was ill when she was little but—'

He walked towards her, dropping the rag. 'She got leukaemia when she was four, that's what. A year of chemo, a remission, a relapse and then another remission.'

She was shocked, upset. 'That must have been awful for you. But she got better,' she said. 'She beat it. She's not fragile, she's strong.'

He shrugged, looming close to her, scowling. 'You don't know that. You weren't there. Every time she throws a temperature or gets a sore throat, I think it's come back. And she has to have blood tests regularly and I don't sleep until they come back clear.'

'I'm sorry you had to go through all that.' She wondered if that really was the stressor that broke his marriage up. 'But other kids her age... her whole class is coming. She'll miss out.'

'It won't kill her.' His jaw was tense in profile. 'Let it go, Eleanor. Just because we kissed...'

'Yes,' she snapped, finally losing her temper. 'What about that? You kissed me and then never mentioned it again.'

'One kiss doesn't make you Ruby's mother, Eleanor.'

She stepped back as if she'd been slapped. 'Ruby is my *friend*. She's an intelligent and mature young woman and she deserves to be treated as such.'

'Well, she's *my* daughter and I decide what's safe for her and what isn't!' he growled.

'Are you sure you're not so caught up in winning this battle with Ruby – and me, and the whole island – that you haven't really looked at her argument to go to the festival?'

'I think you should go,' Bruno said, putting his hands on the gate that she was standing behind. 'I don't think we have anything else to say to each other. It's not your business. Have your festival, but leave Ruby to me.'

Eleanor pulled away, turned and walked towards the town, hands shaking. It wasn't until she got all the way to the harbour that she felt the tears wetting her face, and the ache of loss in her chest.

36

AUGUST 1943

I'm engaged.

It was the strangest feeling for Dorothy. Hector wanted to buy a ring, although what jewellery would be available in the middle of the Atlantic during a war was debatable. She was quite enjoying hugging the news to herself for a little longer, and hadn't told her family yet.

She didn't really have time to mark the engagement, anyway. She not only had regular clinics now, but also had to take on the patients from the other islands as Dr Penrose was close to death. She decided to do a clinic at the St Petroc's Island practice once a week, although times were tide dependent. Nurse Penhaligon there was a brilliant organiser, and had insisted on taking on the off-island district nurse visits with Nurse Harper doing St Brannock's. She had met the no-nonsense midwife, another Ellis. With Jeannie looking after the house and a sensible woman doing administration, Dorothy now had a team of five.

Beryl Livingstone must be halfway through her pregnancy, but hadn't attended the clinic, so Dorothy decided to offer her support with a home visit.

When she got there, Beryl was outside, rinsing washing in a tub. The water supply at this end of the island was fitful at best; a bomb had damaged the pipes and a temporary repair had yet to be replaced. A barrel attached to a downpipe provided water.

'Morning, Doctor,' Beryl said, continuing to rinse and wring.

'I haven't seen you at the clinic. You are entitled to free pregnancy care, you know.'

'Never had that before,' Beryl said, her face set in a grim line.

'Anyway, I just thought I would pop in, perhaps examine you. See how things are going.'

'No need,' Beryl said, putting a cigarette in her mouth and lighting it by scraping a match up the wall. She puffed a cloud of smoke out with relief. 'Miscarried,' she said, staring directly at Dorothy. 'Tripped on the step, just after my husband was called up for the navy.'

'You didn't ask me to visit... you could have bled to death.'

'I was all right.'

Dorothy was sick to her stomach at the thought of what might have really happened. 'You have broken the law, Beryl' – she tried to moderate her tone – 'if you have done anything to promote the loss of that baby.'

'You don't *care* about the mothers, do you?' she spat. 'Trying to feed and clean and keep children safe in the middle of a war with no money and no work. Are you going to buy them clothes and put food in their bellies, *Doctor*?'

'There is poor relief,' Dorothy said. She knew what Beryl was saying, she understood the argument, always had. But this barbarism was no way to solve the problem.

'How are you preventing future pregnancies?' she asked, outright.

'I've got ways,' she said.

'Where would I find Mrs Oppy?' Dorothy asked.

'Nurse Oppy won't want to talk to you,' Beryl said, but with less confidence. Suddenly she looked much younger, more like the uneducated and inexperienced girl who had married at sixteen.

'I might have some work for her,' Dorothy lied. 'And if you come to the surgery, I'll talk to you about the Dutch cap. It's very effective at preventing pregnancy, and I think I can get you one for free.'

If I buy it out of my own pocket.

'She's over on Morwen, with her sister,' Beryl said. 'But I don't want to get her into trouble.'

'It's too late for that now, isn't it?' When she saw the fear in her face, Dorothy softened her tone. 'What's done is done. But let's make sure it never happens again.'

After her clinic she made a visit to old Mrs Ellis, whose infected knee was healing up well despite the various folk cures she occasionally used.

Mrs Ellis was as chatty as ever. 'That nice American doctor,' she said, smiling at Dorothy teasingly. 'He's sweet on *you*.'

As always, Dorothy's face got hot and she knew she was bright red. 'He's a very good doctor.'

'Only, my little Michael, you know, Sukie's son – Sukie's my eldest's daughter – he said he saw you kissing. Up on the moor there, right behind the farm.'

'Well, that's the sort of story children tell,' Dorothy said, packing her bag as fast as she could. 'I really must be going.'

'So can we expect a wedding?' Mrs Ellis persisted. 'Oh, you mustn't mind me, dear, I'm just an old woman. I can't do much else but think about the lives of the young people around me.'

Dorothy opened her mouth to – what? Lie? 'Actually,' she

confided, 'we're not making it public yet. If you could keep our secret a bit longer.'

'Better stop kissing him in public, then.' Mrs Ellis laughed. 'You're a kind woman, I'll say that. You'll make a good wife.'

'I'm not so sure,' Dorothy said, closing her bag. 'I'm a bit old for all this romance.'

'Nonsense,' Mrs Ellis said, folding her hands across her stomach. 'I married my fifth at seventy-one. It was nice not to worry about babies, I can tell you.'

Dorothy shut her eyes at the vision of a seventy-one-year-old amorous Mrs Ellis. 'I think of it as a sensible plan, two doctors working together, no other distractions.'

Mrs Ellis chuckled in a lascivious way. 'Well, I hope you'll both be *very* distracted, my dear. And that you'll find happiness.'

37

PRESENT DAY, 11 AUGUST

Eleanor was in the middle of a long list of phone calls ahead of the first day of the festival when Bruno stormed into Sally's kitchen without even a knock.

'Is Ruby here?'

'No.' She was still smarting after their argument the day before. Eleanor glanced at the clock and noticed it was barely ten o'clock. She folded her arms. 'Isn't she down at the Carlin Centre?'

'I've just spoken to Kayleigh. Ruby's swapped her shifts, and she won't be back until after the festival.' He looked wild, his hair standing on end, some of his shirt buttons undone. 'I don't think she slept at home last night. You've wound her up about the festival and now she's run off.'

'Oh, don't be ridiculous. *You* were the one who was shouting at *her*.' She sat upright anyway, worried. 'Can I help call her friends or something?'

He shook his head. 'I don't know. Is she here? In the garden?' Without asking, he strode through the garden shouting her name, a note of panic in his voice. 'We had a row,' he said, as he walked back through. 'After she showed me those CDs of bands she's not going to see.'

'I thought she could at least enjoy listening to their music,' Eleanor answered.

'I've booked her on the ferry tomorrow. Her mother's meeting her on the mainland to drive her to theirs.'

'So you *were* getting her off the island.' Eleanor tried to speak neutrally. 'I didn't think you actually would.'

'Why not?' he said. 'I told you, I don't want her to have anything to do with the festival.' He bit his lip for a moment before snapping, 'But you would keep encouraging her.'

'You can't blame me,' she said. 'I suggested there were ways she could help with cleaning up the land – which you agreed with – *before* the event. And she helped with the website and programme. It gave her a way of enjoying the festival even though she was going to miss it.'

'Which made her want to go even more!'

'I have never said she could defy you. I told her she had to persuade you, or do as you said.'

'But now she's gone.' Under the anger was fear, raw and visceral. It made Eleanor's heart race, too.

'She's the most sensible teenager I've ever met,' she said, keeping her voice level. 'Why don't we go back and see what she's taken from the farm? That would say a lot about where she was going.'

For a moment she thought he would shout again, but he turned on his heel and headed back to the hallway. 'Come on, then.'

'Sally?' Eleanor said, finding her peering in through the garden door. 'Hold the fort, would you? Ruby's giving Bruno a bit of a scare. Has she said anything to you?'

'No, not really. Go and find her.'

But as she grabbed her phone and followed Bruno, Eleanor sensed that Sally might be holding something back.

He stormed into the farm after a jog all the way down the high street. He ran upstairs, Eleanor following. 'She's taken some stuff from under her bed,' Bruno said, emerging from Ruby's cluttered bedroom floor with dust in his hair. 'She's emptied this one at the back.' He dumped the empty box on the unmade bed.

'What did she store up here?'

'I don't know. Old toys, a few teddy bears, a few favourite mementoes. Her wool – she started doing crochet over Christmas.' He stopped, sat next to the box, which was empty.

She could see a few strands of dried grass. 'Did she have any camping equipment?'

'Just a pup tent and a sleeping bag – is that what she thinks she's going to do? Sneak into the festival?'

'A few thousand people isn't really very many. We'd spot her within an hour. No, this is about the last hours we have left before the festival. Maybe she's trying to change your mind.'

'I can't think straight. And Michelle is meeting her tomorrow. I'll have to tell her Ruby is... *missing*. It took me several calls even to get her to take Ruby for one week. One week, for goodness' sake. Her own child.'

'Does Ruby know that?' Eleanor looked around for a phone or charger. Both missing. 'Can we have a look around the kitchen?'

'It's a mess,' he said, brooding, head in his hands.

'Come and tell me if anything is amiss,' she called out, heading back downstairs.

A few grocery items were missing: bread, butter, a bottle of cola. Also a mug, sharp knife, tin opener and a few cans.

'She's taken the biscuits,' he said. 'I had about half a pack of digestives. Apples, too.'

'And her phone and charger,' Eleanor said. 'She's probably holed up with a friend at the moment, and then hoped to sneak into the festival once it started.'

'Her friends wouldn't hide her overnight,' he said, with certainty. 'Their parents are all friends of mine. I went to school with half of them.'

'How much have you talked to them, recently?' Eleanor asked gently.

'Not much over the last few years,' he admitted. 'I'm going to have to speak to them all now.'

'Half of them,' she said, waving her phone. 'Let me call some of them, too. The school will know who her friends are.'

'The school is shut.'

'I'll call the headteacher. I'm working with her on the summer school.'

Finally, he looked up at her. 'Thank you,' he said. 'I just can't think straight where Ruby is concerned. She did this before, you know. We had a county-wide police search, helicopters, the army, hundreds of volunteers, after she tried to run away from Michelle back to the ferry.'

'Sally told me,' Eleanor said. 'Find me a pen and paper and I'll get the details from the school.'

The list was long. They split the calls but it still took two hours, and a couple of her friends were out themselves and wouldn't get straight back to them. Several parents expressed to Eleanor that they knew how unhappy Ruby would be to miss the whole festival when the rest of her year group were going.

'What do you want to do next?' Eleanor said, seeing Bruno, head in hands, leaning over in his armchair.

'Should we go to the police?' he said. 'She can get into the house if she comes back. I'll put a note on the table for her.'

'They will probably have lots of ideas,' Eleanor said, waiting while he scribbled a note. 'Are the sheep all right?'

'I'll check on them later. Come on, Haze,' he called to the dog. She was unusually subdued, as if she didn't like seeing Bruno so upset. She stayed by his knee as he paced down the high street towards the police station.

Eleanor snatched up her bag to follow him, heart bumping uncomfortably at the thought of Ruby missing, maybe in trouble. She had grown to care about the teenager, and for her father.

Speaking to the police was helpful because they calmed Bruno down. After all, where could Ruby realistically go? The ferry company was adamant that she hadn't left the island because the boat had CCTV for all passengers getting onto the ferry. They were now doing an enhanced search while at sea in case she'd sneaked on, and the Penzance police would check again when everyone disembarked.

But most people thought she was still on the islands. Bruno called Ruby again, but her phone was switched off, and the local police were reluctant to do a house-to-house search while she was essentially just a stroppy teenager staying away to annoy her father.

Once Bruno returned to the farm, Eleanor went for an early evening walk to clear her head, her bare feet in the sand. There was a knot of anxiety about Ruby, but it was balanced with a huge feeling that she knew what she was doing and wouldn't make herself unsafe. *But how much does a fourteen-year-old know about the world?*

She got a text just as she turned back towards home.

Are you alone? I don't want to talk to Dad.

Ruby! We've been so worried. Where are you?

No Dad.

She must have turned her mobile off then, because she didn't respond to any more messages or calls. Eleanor didn't know whether to rush back to Bruno or tell the police or... Ruby needed someone to talk to. That person seemed to be Eleanor. She couldn't ignore that, so she wrote a careful message back.

I'm alone on the beach. I'm here if you want to talk. As long as you're safe, I won't tell Bruno, or anyone.

A few minutes later, her phone started ringing. Ruby.

'Hi there,' she said.

'Dad's really not there?'

'I sent him home to wait for your call. *Please* let him know you're OK.'

'They aren't tracking my calls or anything?'

'I don't think so,' Eleanor said. 'The police have told him you're not a missing person, just a stroppy teenager.'

'It's not just the festival,' Ruby said, and Eleanor thought there was a wobble in her voice. 'It's my mum. I don't want to be shoved over there as if I was in mortal danger. And she doesn't want me, really. She's so busy with her new kids.'

'She's coming over now. You've really worried her as well. They're going to squeeze her on the ferry as an emergency.'

There was a long silence and Eleanor wondered if Ruby would hang up.

'It's not easy having your parents split up,' Ruby said eventually.

'It must be hard.'

She waited another long time.

'Better than having your mum die, though,' Ruby said sadly.

Eleanor felt tears prickling in her eyes. 'Well, yes.'

'Dad really likes you,' Ruby said. 'But he's blaming you for the whole festival thing.'

'I know,' Eleanor said. 'He's still mixed up about your mother.'

'Can you be there? When they meet? The boat will be in

tomorrow,' Ruby said. 'Stick up for me before they put my story on the news and call in the army?'

Eleanor took a deep breath. 'I will. If you promise me you are completely safe. One hundred per cent. And tell me where you are.'

'I can't. You'll tell Dad.'

'I *so* won't,' Eleanor said. 'The police are right, you're not a baby. As long as you don't spend too much time away and are safe.'

Ruby took her time thinking that over. 'I won't tell you until you've seen me. Then you won't have to lie to him about where I am. You can even come and stay with me.'

Eleanor was so uncomfortable with this, her mind turning over all the possibilities. 'At least tell me if you're safe and on the islands. I assume you're camping somewhere?'

'I am, but don't tell him, he might work out where. It's just one night, then Mum and Dad will listen to me.'

'OK, but he knows you've taken a sleeping bag. I want you to send messages to your dad tonight and first thing tomorrow morning, to let him know you're all right. And I'll let the police know you've been in contact.'

Ruby chuckled down the phone. 'You're the best, Eleanor.'

'So are you. Just don't make me call out the army.'

Ruby laughed.

Eleanor dawdled up to the farm, not sure of the response she would get.

Bruno opened the door before she had even got there, his eyes red. 'You've heard from her?' he said, his voice breaking.

'She's fine, she's all right,' she said quickly, and he lurched forward and swept her into a hug. 'She's going to message you,' she mumbled into his collar.

'She just did, to say I had to be nice to you,' he murmured into the side of her head.

'Well, ease up on my ribs, then.' Eleanor laughed, pulling away. 'She's such a star. She's amazing.'

'She's killing me,' he said, stepping back, hands on Eleanor's shoulders.

'She just wants me to be around when you talk to Michelle. Which is a huge intrusion. I totally understand if you want that meeting to be private...'

'On the quay, as she gets off the ferry tomorrow morning?' He shook his head. 'It won't be private, half the island will be listening. And I think I'd like you to be there. Michelle wants to meet you, anyway.'

'She does? Why?'

'Ruby told her I like you.'

She smiled. 'This isn't the time for this, really.' She looked up at him. 'Oh, in for a penny...' she said, reaching up to hold him, kiss him back, feeling the tension in his body easing.

'You're the Ruby whisperer,' he said, starting to smile.

'I think of myself as more of a Bruno whisperer,' she murmured, feeling tension drain from her as well. 'I like you too. Let's get through tonight and get Ruby sorted out. Then we can talk about who likes who.'

'You sound as if you have a plan,' he said, putting his arm around her waist.

'I'm working on one...' she said, stroking Haze's silky head butting against her hand.

38

SEPTEMBER 1943

Dorothy climbed the hill on Morwen, the 'rocky isle' in the archipelago. The stone quay led up a number of narrow streets, the colourful houses leaning towards each other at the top. It felt quite closed-in compared to the big island, with its stone and whitewashed houses. Hector had offered to accompany her but she didn't feel she needed to hide behind anyone else. She knew what she knew.

She had heard Mrs Oppy was staying with a relative up one of the small lanes, a narrow house with an alley down the side with a handful of scraggy chickens pecking behind a wire gate. Dorothy tapped sharply on the front door, even though it was open to let light and air in through the cottage.

A woman came to the door, a baby balanced on her hip. 'Are you here for my sister, Mrs Oppy?' she said wearily.

'I am,' Dorothy said. 'Dr Harding-Rowe.'

'You won't get any money out of her,' the woman said, rolling her eyes. 'She owes me three weeks' rent, her and her layabout son. They are living in my loft room.'

'Well, if you could just ask her to come down and talk to me, that would be very helpful.'

Dorothy perched on the low wall in front of the adjoining building, which looked like some kind of shed. She glanced at her watch. A few minutes later, she heard the familiar clomp of Mrs Oppy's boots on the cobbles beside her.

'What do you want?' Mrs Oppy said, pulling herself up to her full height. She was angular and tall, almost masculine, Dorothy noted.

'I think you and I got off on the wrong foot,' Dorothy said, swallowing her anger and standing up. 'But you should not have been prescribing medicines.' *No, nor helping women lose their babies*, she thought darkly.

Mrs Oppy walked off ahead, down towards the stone quay. Dorothy followed her as she turned along the seafront and sat on an old bench.

'Who was going to help people if I didn't?' Mrs Oppy snapped, looking away and spreading her black dress over her legs. The fabric had faded to the darkest green and the hem was ragged. 'I read the old doctor's notes, to see what he would do when people came to the surgery.'

Dorothy sat beside her, looking at her angular profile. 'I know you were trying to help, but you took their money—'

'A lot less than *you* would charge. The old doctor wasn't paying my wages or his bills at the end, he was too ill to go to the bank. I had to buy him food. And the locums were paid by the board, they didn't have any money spare for me.' She snorted. 'Useless boys, most of them. They had no idea.'

Dorothy sat next to her, looking out over the fishing boats sat on the mud at low tide, two or three deep. They seemed to have a spider's web of rigging, almost overlapping each other.

'Mrs Oppy,' Dorothy began. 'What really happened with Beryl Livingstone? To make her... miscarry?'

'I didn't do nothing in the end,' she said, staring out to sea. 'She must have listened to you. She was keeping the baby. Her waters went when she was in her house. I just helped deliver the poor little scrap, her afraid of being accused of a crime.'

Dorothy took a couple of deep breaths, trying not to think about Beryl delivering a dead baby in the care of this ignorant woman. 'What did you do with the child?' she asked, her voice as calm as she could make it.

'It was long dead. Her husband wrapped it in newspaper and dropped it overboard somewhere in the Sound,' she answered. There was a pause. 'Did you know I was sixteen when I fell pregnant with my son?'

'I didn't,' Dorothy said, glancing sideways at Mrs Oppy's set face staring out to sea.

'Sixteen. And not married, not likely to be either, as the scoundrel who seduced me already had a family.' She laughed. 'Seduced. More like, filled with strong wine and taken advantage of... But I didn't hide the babe, nor get rid of it.'

'How did you cope?'

'I went to Cornwall, worked until the babe dropped and then came back, saying I was married.'

'Mrs Oppy.'

She laughed, the sound grating and harsh. 'My third cousin in Penzance married an Oppy. We had the same maiden name, she had a copy of her marriage certificate made for me, although it barely covered the date of the baby's birth. So, my boy was registered all right. Mind you, he's as useless as his father.'

'I'm sorry.' It was a sad story, but Mrs Oppy had found a way through.

'I started working as an 'ousekeeper for the old doctor. Just cleaning and cooking at first. But then I learned how to get rid of babies.' She looked out over the water again, the first bubble-edged waves slapping the ships, lolling on their muddy bed, her profile sharp and heavy. 'Safely, like. My great-aunt showed me. I taught her how to properly clean the instruments. And I read the doctor's books.'

'Babies *died*,' Dorothy said, shuddering at the cruelty of the trade. 'And mothers were harmed, too.'

'I always used herbs if they would come early,' she said. 'This is just your word against mine,' she added, turning to stare Dorothy down.

'There are better, safer ways. Isn't it better to prevent a baby, rather than kill it?'

Mrs Oppy looked away. 'You think women around here can afford all that? Or that the husbands would respect them if they did?'

Dorothy looked down at her white hands, so clean next to the brown, ingrained dirt of Mrs Oppy's.

'I am bringing birth control to married women on the islands,' she said carefully. 'I am also offering affordable care in pregnancy and birth. I have found a charity which can offer some funding, and the panel will help with the baby clinics.' She huffed out a breath, her shoulders tense. 'I'm not talking about the past, Mrs Oppy. I'm asking you to be part of the future.'

The woman turned her shoulder to face her. 'To do what?'

'I need someone who can help me reach the kind of people who come to you, but won't come to me.'

She scoffed. 'What do you know about the people at the bottom of the heap? Some islanders can barely find enough food. Rationing is pointless if you can't afford to pay for them or there's nothing in the shops. People here are hungry, children are sick and weak. Why would they even talk to you when you charge them just to put their heads around your door?'

'They will talk to me if you tell them they can,' she explained. 'There will be money for their care, free vaccinations, extra milk and vitamins for the youngest. The National Insurance scheme can be accessed by many more people, and the board is covering more care. One day, all medical care will be free for everyone.'

'I don't believe that.'

'I didn't come into medicine to make myself rich off poor people,' Dorothy said. 'To be honest, I was born rich, by your standards. My family paid thousands for me to complete my medical training, and I have lived on a tiny stipend since developing my knowledge and skills.' She smiled down at her hands. 'I still have an allowance from my father. I only need the practice to support itself.'

Mrs Oppy waved a hand in the direction of Dorothy's engagement ring, which she had finally started wearing when not at work. Hector had chosen a large sapphire surrounded by a circle of smaller diamonds. 'I wouldn't have thought you'd be getting married,' she said, frowning.

'Well, there's a lot of things about me that you got wrong,' Dorothy said, standing up and stretching her back. The quay stank of rotten fish, a layer of fish scales sparkling along the quay like a million stars. 'Will you come to the surgery tomorrow, around twelve, and we'll talk?'

Mrs Oppy took a long time to answer, her nostrils flared, her eyes down. 'Can I have my cottage back?'

'No.' Dorothy couldn't bear the thought of her on the property. 'But you would have a small salary.'

Goodness knows how I am to afford all these new wages, with a new nurse joining and a secretary.

'It's about time my son made his own way,' Mrs Oppy said, after a long pause. 'I might be able to lodge with my cousin, if I could afford some rent.'

'Then I will see you tomorrow,' Dorothy said, holding out a hand.

Mrs Oppy stared at it for a long time, as she stood and faced her. Finally, she put her own hand in Dorothy's.

39

PRESENT DAY, 11 AUGUST

'Apparently,' Eleanor said to Sally, 'I'm going to see Ruby and staying the night. Do you think that's a good idea?'

'If that's what she wants, I would go with it,' Sally said. 'What does Michelle think?'

'She told Bruno I should,' Eleanor said, rolling a pair of jeans and pushing them into her bag. 'But she'll be staying at the farm with him.'

'That makes you uncomfortable.' Sally's eyes seemed to see right into her insecurity.

'I know, daft, isn't it? He can barely speak to her. But Ruby did have a little chat with Michelle, and the police think she's on one of the islands.'

'Ah,' Sally said, glancing up at the clock and the timetable stuck next to it. 'You might need wellies. Let me pack some cake for you both, for a midnight feast. And a big bottle of water.'

'Where do you think she is?'

Sally smiled. 'I think the mystery will last a little longer. I'm sure she will either meet you, or give you instructions.'

'She must be running out of charge on her phone, though. I'll take a power bank with me.' Eleanor zipped up the bag and dragged it to the door. 'I have to be back by tomorrow,' she warned. 'Last-minute checks, and then my team will come over with the first of the campers.'

'And you'll be all set?'

Eleanor rolled her eyes. 'No, then the *real* work begins. Are you ready for them to arrive?' Sally had agreed to house the Sunshine Festivals group during the festival. She and Eleanor had tidied two more rooms at the bed and breakfast and got them ready for guests. They would have to share a bathroom but otherwise would be very comfortable. 'We normally get an old caravan or tent to stay in,' she had explained. 'They will love it, this will be luxury.'

Sally squeezed her forearm. 'You'll be back in time to greet them.'

'I hope so. How can you be so sure?'

'Tides,' Sally said enigmatically. 'Speaking of which, you'd better go or you'll miss Tink on the quay.'

The Ellis water taxi was pulled up at the quay, the young man running it pacing a bit. He introduced himself as Tink and grabbed her luggage.

'We'll ground in a few minutes if we don't get a move on,' he warned, carrying her bag. 'What have you got in here?'

'Three litres of water, as Sally suggested,' she said, stepping in and feeling the boat touch the bottom as she did so. He waved her to the middle of the boat and pushed an oar against the side, guiding them into darker, deeper water, making her heart judder uncomfortably.

'You're off to Morvoren then,' he said, turning the boat into the waves and gunning the motor on the back. 'You'll get there on time.'

'Morvoren? Not Morwen, then?'

'No. It's an islet off St Petroc's. I can just about get into the jetty. It used to have a few farms and cottages but now it's mostly left to the birds and rabbits, and the odd archaeologist and the last tenant farmer. It's attached by a sandy bar, but you might have to wade a bit.'

'So, there's water.' Eleanor started to worry. 'And – we'd be camping?'

'Sounds like.' He looked at her. He drove the boat out into the rougher water, out of the lee of St Brannock's Island. 'I'm guessing this is about Ruby Roskelly? Sally told me not to tell Bruno.'

She sighed. 'Does *everyone* know *everything* on the islands?'

Tink grinned at her, the wind whipping his light brown hair around. 'Pretty well. And I hear you're spending time with Grumpy Bruno.' He curved the boat around some submerged rocks that were just breaking the water with dark teeth and swirling foam. She clung a little harder to the edge of the boat.

'I should mention I can't swim,' she said.

'That's why we brought the boat,' he said, easing the vessel into a long stretch of calmer water. 'But if you're staying on the islands, you ought to learn.'

'How far is it?' She hunkered down in the boat as the wind hit the tips of the waves, splashing her with a little spray.

He pointed ahead. 'It's just the other side of that island, St Petroc's,' he said, expertly piloting through more rough water. 'Nearly there.'

It was a few more minutes, during which she closed her eyes, before he pulled up to a jetty at the back of the island. Ahead the sea rolled in, in white stripes, the horizon uninterrupted.

She stared. 'Wow.'

'I love this long view,' he said. 'We get the same on Morwen. Just the Atlantic, then – America.'

A slim figure ran down the beach to meet them. She held a hand out to steady Eleanor as Tink lifted the case up. 'Gotta go,' he said, pushing the jetty away with his foot. 'Losing the tide. See you tomorrow, Ruby?'

'Yes please!' she called back, as the boat took off. 'First tide. Eleanor has to get back before the festival starts. Come on, we haven't got long,' she said to Eleanor, who stared at Ruby's flyaway hair, her blue eyes ringed with dark lashes.

'I've been so worried,' she ended up saying, lamely, unable to put her fears into words as she looked across the water towards a low island maybe a hundred yards away.

'You can shout at me in a minute.' Ruby dragged the wonky bag along a path. 'But come on. This is the causeway.'

She stopped at a shingle-and-sand path leading towards a broken stretch of green sea, then re-emerging on to another bank leading up to a substantial island.

'No,' Eleanor said, stopping dead. 'No, Ruby.'

'It's just a few inches deep,' Ruby said. 'Honestly. A toddler could walk it. And I'll be with you. The tide's almost out.'

'I can't.' The water was a glorious, rich emerald as the light started to fade. It looked a thousand feet deep.

'I'll go first. And I'll carry the bag. Please, Eleanor. I really *need* to talk to you.'

It was the way she said 'need' that clinched it. She sighed. 'Let me put the wellies on. Sally made me bring them.'

Ruby laughed. 'She worked out where I was? Brilliant.'

After they disgorged the boots from the bag and Eleanor gingerly stepped onto the stone path, Ruby hefted the suitcase and strode ahead in beach shoes. 'It's not too bad,' she said, as she reached the edge of the crystal water. 'Just go slow. It's just paddling, I promise. The water's still dropping, so it's fine.'

Eleanor carefully put one foot in front of the other, her hands sweaty and her heart racing. The lighter water in the middle was narrow in places, the water falling off each side and swirling around her boots, tugging. She counted one hundred and sixty-eight steps before she reached the sand on the other side and blew out a breath of relief.

'Well done,' Ruby said.

'Oh, shut up,' Eleanor snapped. 'Do you know how worried we've all been about you?'

'I hope so,' Ruby said. 'So maybe some of you will start being on *my* side for a change.'

'You can't hold us all to ransom over your *safety*, Ruby!' Eleanor scolded, as sternly as she could.

Ruby was leading her up the gentle slope to a flattish area of short grass on the top of the hill. A couple of large stones lay on the ground, and a few outcrops of rock stuck up above the sandy soil. One large standing stone dominated, and Ruby's camp had been set up beside it. Around them, the islet looked like a huge field, with a few tumbled walls on the other edge.

The view from the standing stone took Eleanor's breath away, and tears filled her eyes. The other islands looked as if they were floating above the water. St Petroc's, that they had just left behind, looked uninhabited – she knew the tiny village was all on the east side. The grass was spotted with flowers, in pinks and purples and yellows, none of which she could identify. She turned to the standing stone, ran her hands over the sculpted surface, feeling gouges that might have been made by the people who brought it here.

'This is amazing...'

'It's been here thousands of years,' Ruby explained. 'There are some old fields and a couple of derelict ruins. Dad says it's about ninety acres, there's even an old farmhouse. No one lives here full-time any more.' Ruby dragged Eleanor's bag over to the stone. 'I hope you brought some water. I'm running out. I don't want to go over to the farm – I'm sure the old lady that lives here in the summer would call the police.'

'I brought lots of water. And Sally packed cake, too. Ruby –

what's all this about? You've had half the islands and the police looking for you.'

'You know why,' Ruby said, sitting on a blanket she had brought.

'It can't be all about the festival,' Eleanor said. 'Was that just the last straw?'

Ruby looked out to sea. 'I'm afraid my dad is going to make me leave the islands over the most exciting week we've ever had,' she said. 'But I belong here. With him or without. He thinks I'm ten years old.'

'You might like to travel some time. Go and see other places that you could fall in love with.'

'Like London?'

Eleanor laughed, opened her bag looking for the treats Sally had packed. 'London, Paris – oh, my, Paris! New York, too. But there are all these other lovely places, besides. Castles and stately homes, cliffs hundreds of feet high, mountains covered in snow. You're not being disloyal, going to meet new people. It might even make home seem that much more precious.'

Ruby curled up next to her, their arms just touching. 'Do you feel like that about London?' Her voice sounded younger now.

Eleanor let her mind wander over the last few months. She had missed a lot of sleep thinking about Bruno, and how it couldn't possibly work... But she hadn't factored in Ruby. What would it be like to never see either of them – or Sally – ever again?

'London is a fabulous place to work,' she said slowly. 'And I have close friends there. But living in a city is tiring. Since my mother died, I've found it – a bit too *fast*. Everyone's in a hurry. If you meet for lunch, they only have an hour. If you want to go out, you have to find a rare evening when you're both free. Everyone is so *busy*.'

'Here, if someone turns up randomly for a chat, they might

stay for the whole weekend,' Ruby said, grinning. Then her face fell. 'Or they used to. Dad's not that sociable any more.'

Eleanor pulled out small bottles of the local apple juice. 'Not quite wine, but perfect for the sunset.' She looked up at the sky, already flushed with pinks and peaches, the clouds dipping towards the sea in shades of lavender. 'It's so beautiful here.' She tugged her fleece around her ears. 'If a bit chilly in the wind.'

'Could you move somewhere like here?' Ruby said, concentrating on opening one of the bottles. 'I mean, full-time, forever?'

The very question that she had been wrestling with. 'I don't know,' Eleanor said, slowly. 'Define full-time.'

'I don't know – buy a house here, spend most of your time on the islands?'

'With time off for good behaviour?' She smiled and took a sip of juice. 'My job is in London, but I could do a lot from home. But I love to travel. Maybe I'd get bored if it was just the islands.' She thought about it. 'It's harder when you live on your own.'

'You might not be on your own,' Ruby said, leaning closer to Eleanor.

'It might feel a bit claustrophobic here,' Eleanor said softly. 'Don't you think that's how Michelle might have felt, coming here to live?'

'But she ran away from her husband and baby. How could she leave us?'

Ignoring the fact that Michelle had definitely not left her baby, Eleanor tried to explain. 'I think, ultimately, we should live for ourselves. If our lives parallel people's that we love, great. But if that love fades, it's OK to move on.' She nudged Ruby, who was staring out to sea, eyes wide, sparks of the sunshine reflecting in them. 'It will happen to you, too. What happens if the great love of your life wants to live in France, say, or America?' The wind was cooling fast, and lifting Ruby's hair up.

'Dad says things like that,' Ruby said, moving away and wrapping herself in a blanket. 'And Mum.' Her face was bleak.

'He's afraid of losing you, or of something bad happening to you,' Eleanor said, pulling up her knees and resting her chin on them, the grass jutting through sandy soil prickly against her feet. 'I get that. But the best way to keep you safe is to teach you how to look after yourself. That's what I think, but with absolutely no experience at all. I'm not a parent. I haven't even got a cat.'

'So why do you get it right so much?'

Eleanor thought about it. The tips of the waves were reflecting back the reddening sky. 'I suppose I remember being your age. My mother did let me try things. I went to my first festival without her at about your age, with two sixteen-year-old friends and my bestie from school.'

'And did you get drunk, try drugs and get into trouble?'

Eleanor laughed. 'We shared a sweet cider, I believe that was it. I did snog a couple of boys, though. But we were drunk on the music, the dancing, the lovely atmosphere that you get in a good festival. That's what made me want to run them.'

Ruby sighed, her body curving forward. 'Dad would never let me do that.'

Eleanor finished her apple juice and looked around the islet. 'I hope there's excellent bathrooms and beds at this resort.' She looked back at what was left of the sandbar that had allowed them on. The tide seemed to be creeping back already.

'I have a trowel, a roll of toilet paper and a tent,' Ruby said, managing a little smile. 'Sorry, that's it.'

'I'm a festival expert,' Eleanor said, wishing the eco-loos were hidden just behind the standing stone. 'I'll be OK. But that sky is amazing, and I wouldn't have seen it if you hadn't asked me over, so thank you.'

'I know I'll have to go home tomorrow, and Dad will ship me off to the mainland anyway as punishment,' Ruby said, huddled up in her blanket. 'I will *hate* missing the festival. All my friends are going.'

'Well, I have an idea about that,' Eleanor said. 'Although my job literally starts at seven tomorrow morning. What time is the tide right to go back?'

'About then should be fine,' Ruby said, her eyes closed, a tear dribbling down her cheek. 'They'll never trust me now.'

'How about you apologise to both your parents like a grown-up – say what you just said to me? That you don't deserve that they trust you right now.'

Ruby opened her eyes. 'I didn't say that.'

'Well, I suggest you *do*. Because what you have done has caused them a lot of pain, and terrible anxiety. Bruno was so upset. Imagine how you would feel if one of them just went missing?'

Ruby was crying now, wiping her face on her sleeve. 'I know,' she sobbed. 'I do love them, but I was just so *angry*.'

'Well, if you've *really* learned your lesson, *really*, then I will propose a suggestion to Bruno and Michelle that might at least get you into the festival.'

Ruby looked up. 'What do you mean?'

Eleanor stretched out her legs again. The sky was more purple and blood reds now, the clouds filling up more of the sky. 'It had better not rain,' she warned Ruby. 'And I need my sleep. Let me see what I can sort out with Bruno. I will suggest – as a penance for frightening everyone who loves you half to death – that you *work* the festival with me. You would be my gofer. My dogsbody.'

'He'd never agree,' Ruby said, jumping up to her knees, her eyes glowing, hugging the blanket.

'I will speak to him now. So you'd better get that tent up, and then I'm having a cup of tea. Sally gave me a flask.'

She left the standing stone and walked closer to the beach, to the sand spit, holding her phone up to get a signal.

The light had almost gone, but she could see a shadowy figure on the beach on St Petroc's, and a flash of white on the dark shape of a dog.

Bruno.

When she dialled his number, a screen lit a face up on the island side.

'Eleanor.' His voice was strained. 'Is she there?'

'How did you know? She's here and she's fine. And very, very sorry. I think she finally gets how worried everyone has been.'

'She can't possibly know,' he said, and the dark stick figure on the island slumped onto a bench. 'I am literally torn between shouting at her and hugging her.'

'She knows that.' She could hear the terrible hurt in his voice. 'How are you?'

'I couldn't stand the idea of waiting for you to call,' he said finally. 'I worked out where she went – we used to camp there when she was little.'

'It's funny that you're just over there, a hundred yards or so away. I could just shout to you.' Eleanor said, turning over some shells with her bare toes.

'Hello!' he shouted, the sound thin over the water. She waved back.

'Well, the phone is easier.' She tucked it under her ear to pick up a cockle in the last of the light. 'It looks like you could almost swim over the causeway.'

'It's pretty dangerous to try,' he replied. 'The water runs over the bank, very fast, and the tide is turning. It's not a causeway, technically – it's a bar.'

'I don't want you to try,' she said, sitting on a heap of sand, the waves just reaching for her toes.

He chuckled, and her heart flip-flopped. 'I'm just so

relieved.'

'We need to talk,' she said, letting the bubbles on the edge brush her feet. 'Ouch, that's cold.'

'Tell me straight, because it's been driving me crazy. After this blasted festival is over – will I ever see you again?' She could hear his breathing, irregular.

'I hope so,' she said, her words coming out softer than she'd expected. 'If you want to.'

'I might have to swim over anyway,' he said, and she saw him stand up.

'Don't you dare,' she snapped back, jumping to her feet. 'You might reconsider talking to me when I tell you my plan for Ruby.'

'Go on, then. Does it include grounding her until she's eighteen?'

'Not exactly.' She outlined the idea, that Ruby would be at her side or with one of the staff or stewards at all times. She would be working, unpaid, very hard but at least she would experience the festival.

'And she can come back and sleep at the farm each night,' she finished. 'Which is punishment enough.'

'What sort of things would she be doing?' he asked, his voice suspicious.

'Mostly cleaning toilets,' she said, knowing that was a big part of the work behind the scenes. 'Handing out water and sun cream to idiots who stay out in the sun too long; getting help for people who are drunk or have fallen over. Checking everything all the time. Washing up at the café and helping kids charge their phones. Working at the first-aid station. Supporting teenagers who have broken up with their partners or argued with their best friends. Fetching and carrying things for me.'

'Sounds like hard work,' he said. 'Tell me again. How many toilets will she be cleaning? She never cleans our bathroom at home.'

'*All* of them.' She laughed. 'And if she has a few minutes left over she can help out in the Carlin Centre. They are hosting all the acts during the day and all the technicians. More tea-making and washing-up.'

There was a long silence. 'I should ask Michelle. But she seems to think you're the Ruby expert already.'

Eleanor was surprised. She let the water run over her toes and gasped at the cold.

'Are you OK?' He sounded concerned.

'The water is freezing. But you're right, I do need to learn to swim, if I'm going to be around the islands. After the festival.'

'So, there will be an "after the festival",' he said, his voice lighter.

She'd found it difficult to make any decisions about her future since her mother died, since she met Sally and Bruno and Ruby. 'There will be. Part-time, at least.'

'Then let's cut Ruby a break,' he said, sighing as if it was hard to say. 'But if she does this again, she's going into a convent.'

Eleanor laughed, punching the air. 'I'd take her myself! I'll tell her. I think by the third day, the loos will have been punishment enough.'

She could hear Ruby's footsteps pattering down to join her. 'Do you want a word with her?'

'No. I'm still furious. I imagined the worst. You tell her. One more thing...'

'Yes?' she said, hugging Ruby, who could tell she was pleased about something.

'After the festival, would you like to go out to dinner? Like – a date?'

She let go of Ruby to point out the small figure in the dark opposite. 'Wave to your dad, Ruby.' She stepped away as the two exchanged waves, and spoke softly. 'And yes, Bruno, I would love that.'

40

OCTOBER 1943

Jeannie, the housemaid and general assistant, had organised her own mother and both the nurses to help sew a gown for Dorothy's wedding. Mrs Oppy, no help with sewing, presided over the task in the kitchen with occasional criticisms.

Dorothy's mother had donated her own, slightly faded and yellowed wedding dress, a Victorian monster made of many yards of silk. Any attempt to say 'I would be happy in a day gown' was overruled. The status of the general practitioner required her to make a statement, and the idea of just a few guests in a small ceremony was also scoffed at. The governor of the islands and the commander of the airbase would be guests of honour, and even Dorothy didn't want their wives' outfits to eclipse her own. She gave in to a barrage of comments on her advanced age, figure, deportment and taste.

'It's a pity you're not taller...' Nurse Harper mused.

The whole thing reminded Dorothy of her own mother's comments when she was struggling at school, a regime that was more about grace, deportment, eating delicately and making conversation than about academic achievement.

'The fabric at the front is more yellowed,' Sister Penhaligon said. 'Is there enough in the back for a whole dress?'

'There's a train,' Jeannie said. 'But then the dress won't *have* a train.'

'I don't need a train,' Dorothy said, looking back over her shoulder to see bits of stiff silk pinned to the cut-off bodice. 'I want to be able to walk.'

'But your bridesmaids will carry it for you,' Nurse Harper mumbled through a mouthful of pins.

'I don't have any bridesmaids,' Dorothy said.

There was a little whispering and muttering behind her.

Mrs Oppy broke the quiet. 'What about the Allen girls? You saved their lives.'

'Would they even want to?' Dorothy said. 'I mean, it should be my sister's girls, but my own family can't get here. And where would we get dresses for them?'

'If you don't mind losing some of the silk on the front, we could dye it and run up something very pretty,' Jeannie said, pinching the waist in at the back. 'If Polly is well enough. Ma has some pink dye, and I think there's a bit of blue left, too.'

'They should be all right to walk down the aisle and have a few pictures taken,' Dorothy said. The silence had a different quality now. 'Did I say something wrong?'

'I doubt the Allens have any pictures of the children. That will be something to treasure,' Mrs Oppy said. 'It's a shame they didn't get a picture of Bathsheba.'

'Hector – Dr McBride – has organised two rolls of film,' Dorothy said. 'I hope you will all be happy to be in the photographs?'

More pulling and pinning ensued. 'I suppose so,' Mrs Oppy said. 'The photographer in the town is away at war and film is hard to come by.'

'There,' Jeannie's mother, Myrtle, said. 'You can step out now, but mind the pins. Do you have a good corset, Doctor?'

'I have one upstairs,' Dorothy said, turning to look at the creation. It surprised her even in its unfinished form. 'I don't wear them any more. You're a marvel, Jeannie. All of you are.'

Jeannie pointed to the hall. 'You and I will go upstairs and try the corset on.'

Dorothy's heart sank. She had never spent a private hour with a dressmaker without adverse comments on her short figure. 'Do I have to?'

'Your mother's waist must have been nipped in like a trussed chicken,' Jeannie said. 'The bodice won't fit otherwise. Let's have a look.'

The old-fashioned garment – made for her sister's coming-out ball – not only still fitted but was a bit loose. 'It does look nice pulling my waist in. It's all that running about seeing patients,' Dorothy said, turning this way and that to admire her shape in the spotty mirror. 'And that blasted bicycle on the hills.'

'You will look lovely, before you get back into that dreadful tweed,' Jeannie said, suddenly misty-eyed.

'I was thinking about getting some trousers made,' Dorothy said, provocatively. 'For the cycling.'

'Don't you dare!' Jeannie laughed. 'You'll look like a land girl. Keep the corset on, put your dressing gown on to go downstairs. We'll see if the bodice fits better now.'

'Suppose a patient turns up?' Dorothy said, stalling at the doorway.

'We'll put them straight in the consulting room. It will be fine,' Jeannie said, shooing her downstairs and carrying the best of Dorothy's shoes, which had a small heel.

'My mother would have sent me to Madame Isobel's for a whole trousseau,' she said on the stairs.

'There is a war on, you know,' Jeannie said.

The other women fussed and squeezed and tied her tighter than Jeannie had dared until everything fitted. And looked very flattering and pleasant, Dorothy decided, smoothing her waist lightly over the pins. 'Well, it's just for a few hours,' she said.

'We'll need to fancy up that corset,' Mrs Oppy said. 'For the wedding night.'

The women giggled a bit, but Myrtle leaned forward. 'Since your own mother isn't here' – she lowered her voice – 'if you have any questions...'

'I am a *doctor*!' Dorothy said, certain her face was bright red to match the heat she was feeling.

'Well, of course,' Myrtle said. 'But if you have any questions about how to *please* your husband... Jeannie, maybe you should sit in the garden with that hem.'

Dorothy found herself stammering. 'I'm sure... I'm sure I will be guided by my husband.'

'Well,' Myrtle said, 'he has been married before. But you can always have a private word with me if you have any concerns. And you can't get that corset off easily by yourself, so it would be worth tidying it up. Jeannie, maybe that blue dye would be useful if we do the girls' dresses pink?'

'I have some baby-blue ribbons,' one of the nurses offered. 'Something borrowed, something blue...'

The acute embarrassment of talking about her underwear and the necessity of Hector seeing it was all too much. 'Can't I change into a going away outfit?' she said weakly.

'But you're not going away,' Mrs Oppy said. 'You're having a reception at the dance hall in the town.' She seemed to be enjoying Dorothy's embarrassment. 'And then back to the Doctor's House, unless you find a hotel for a honeymoon. And God forbid there is a call-out on your wedding night,' she added with amused relish.

41

PRESENT DAY, 12 AUGUST

Very early the next morning, Eleanor met Bruno in the middle of the sandbar. She clung to Ruby's hand and listened to her encouragement as she paddled over. Somehow it had been easier in the half-gloom of the evening before and in her keenness to get to the teenager. He reached out to her to guide her the rest of the way. The warmth of his fingers distracted her from the panic, her heart racing for a different reason.

He only let go when she reached the beach on St Petroc's and turned to stare down at his daughter. 'Do we have an agreement?' Bruno asked, looking sternly at Ruby.

'I am officially Eleanor's unpaid dogsbody, helper and toilet cleaner for the whole festival,' Ruby said promptly. 'And I'll come home at a time you decide, to sleep at the farm.'

'Well, your mother has suggested you stay with Lissy and Cait, in their tent—' He didn't get any further before Ruby launched herself at him, squeezing his midriff until Haze barked and he started laughing, and hugged her back. 'No drinking, though,' he said. 'And you're on a very strict curfew.'

'Teddy bears and stories no later than ten,' Eleanor said, changing out of her boots into sandals. 'I'll keep an eye on them, too. When's the next ferry? I have to get there before my crew arrives.'

'I brought Jory's motorboat over,' he said. 'He's a friend of mine, has a boat design business. He's been staying over on the big island with his girlfriend.'

'Are they coming to the festival?' Ruby was bouncing around Haze but stopped to look up at Bruno. The girl and the dog had the same hopeful expression, which made Eleanor laugh as she walked towards the jetty.

'Libby has taken time off especially, so she will be there the whole time. Jory's going to come when he can, and I expect they'll camp.'

'You'll like Libby,' Ruby said. 'She's a famous costume designer for films and that *Polzeath Manor*. I'm in love with Callum Michaels.'

'Sounds great,' Eleanor said, glancing at Bruno as, without being asked, or asking permission, he grabbed her bag.

'You ought to get this wheel fixed,' he said.

'Does this Libby work away, or is she here full-time?'

Ruby threw a piece of driftwood for the dog, who raced away in a flurry of sand. 'I believe she travels back and forth,' Bruno said, catching her gaze and making her heart speed up. 'Jory is based here; they make it work. Here's the boat.'

The sleek open boat was just bumping onto the sand, beside the jetty. 'We'll have to wait a few minutes for the tide to lift it, with all three of us, but I did bring some coffee from the café in the town. Well, I had to persuade them to open early but – voila!' He pulled a cardboard holder from the seat of the boat with three large cups. 'Hot chocolate for Ruby, black decaf for me and just a black regular for you. But she did let me have milk and sugar if you need them...?'

'Old school,' Eleanor said, her mouth twitching. 'Just milk for me. Ruby looks like she'll have the extra sugar. We ran out of cake about two thirty this morning, between shivering and laughing at silly jokes.'

'Well, she chose to go there and you chose to follow her. I'm not that sympathetic,' he said, putting his foot on the edge of the boat and rocking it. 'I had to bunk in with a friend in the town. The tide's coming in fast, we'll be off in a moment. When are your colleagues getting here?'

'First helicopter.' She sipped the hot brew. 'This caffeine may have saved my life.'

'Good,' he said, and she met his gaze. Both smiled, while Ruby had her back turned. 'Oh, sorry to throw a spanner in the works but Michelle – Mum – is staying for the festival.'

'What? No!' Ruby looked from one to the other. 'Don't you think that's a terrible idea?'

'If she gets drunk and meets someone, it's not my problem,' he said breezily. 'Not any more.'

'If I said that, you'd have a go at me,' Ruby said, watching him warily. 'What's happened to you?'

'I've decided to let your mother go. I kept the best bit of our marriage,' he said, smiling down at her.

Eleanor interjected 'Not to mention there's not going to be a drink or drugs problem at *my* festival.'

'There's going to be beer,' he said, looking at her over his cup. 'These islanders consume a lot of beer.'

'They will be disappointed to know that most of the beer on sale is fairly low-alcohol,' she said. 'And we've banned people bringing in large cases.'

'Good luck with that,' he said, but his mood seemed to have dipped.

'Festivals vary enormously,' she explained gently. 'Seriously, this one we have a lot of control over, and people are paying a premium for that. This will be very teen-friendly.'

'You're right,' he said, stepping into the boat. He held out a hand. 'Step onto the gunwale and then onto the seat. That should keep you from falling in.'

She looked at the water now rushing around the boat. 'Are you sure?' she said, even as she took his hand – warm, strong fingers – and stepped into the boat.

'Come on, Ruby!' he shouted. 'Haze!'

Ruby clambered easily in, sat at the front, and the collie jumped on as the boat began to drift away from the jetty.

'It's only three foot deep,' he said reassuringly, but then steered the boat in a cloud of blue fumes towards darker water.

She shut her eyes for a moment, feeling the soft movement of the boat as it cut through the calm surface. When she looked up, a bird was flying up ahead, then dipped into the water, disappearing.

'What was that?' Eleanor said. 'Is it all right?'

Bruno cut the engine close to where the bird had disappeared.

'He'll be fine. They stay down for ages.' Ruby trailed her hand over the side, making spiral patterns. 'At least a few minutes.'

'They can dive down to the bottom,' Bruno said. 'It'll be up in a moment.'

Within thirty seconds a small sound made Eleanor spin around, to see a reptilian-looking bird pop up barely thirty feet away. It stared at her, opened a serrated beak, then dived down again without a sound.

'It's a cormorant. We had a talk at school about seabirds,' Ruby said, peering down into the water. 'The wildlife ranger took us on a walk around the edge of one of the seabird colonies. We got dive-bombed by gannets.'

Eleanor smiled. 'That sounds great. My school used to go on visits to museums all the time. We did go to Kew Gardens once. I missed the countryside, and the sea.'

'When did you move to London?' Bruno asked, looking

ahead. She stared at his jawline, slightly bearded, strong and tanned.

'When I was little. Then my mother moved down to the Sussex coast when I left primary school.'

'I don't really know Sussex,' he said, glancing down at her. She smiled as her heartbeat sped up a little, then he smiled back. 'I don't really know anywhere that well except for the islands.'

'Growing up here... I don't know if I would have needed to move either. But I like travelling. I love coming home, too.'

'So where's home?'

Eleanor sighed and gave it some thought. She had begun to feel ambivalent about her beautiful flat, at least partly because she associated her mother's last few months with it.

'I feel at home here with Sally,' she said, surprising herself. 'She reminds me so much of my mother, but also of the bits of me my mother always said were the milkman's. She's got this really quick sense of humour, and quick temper. Like me. Not like Diana at all.'

'Have you got a quick temper?'

She grinned at him. 'Not if I get my own way. But I'm a *monster* if I don't. But I'm quick to recover, too, and I'm always sorry if I've been unfair. My last boyfriend used to hide behind the sofa, which just made me laugh. I never actually threw anything at him.'

'Michelle and I were both sulkers,' he admitted. 'Which was a recipe for disaster. We both sulked until she gave up and left.'

Ruby sat up at that. 'You *never* talk about Mum.'

'Well, I talked to her yesterday, didn't I? She gave me some very good advice.'

'How to make me into an unpaid servant?' Ruby said, but she smiled.

'She said, if I treat you like a woman, you'll behave like one.

If I treat you like a child – well, you'll run off and scare me half to death and camp out on a remote islet.'

Ruby looked chastened. 'I am sorry. I can see it wasn't the best idea.'

'If you hadn't spoken to Eleanor, and she hadn't spoken to me, the police would have traced you to Morvoren and you would have been in big trouble.' His voice got gravelly and deep when he was telling Ruby off; Eleanor rather liked it. 'And if she hadn't spent what I'm sure was a very uncomfortable night on Morvoren, *I* would have had to come and get you.'

'It wasn't that bad,' Ruby said, looking at Eleanor with pleading eyes. 'Was it?'

'It was a bit cold,' she said, smiling, 'and it would have been better if it hadn't rained. Your tent isn't waterproof, you know.'

'I did forget the rain cap,' Ruby admitted.

'And I'm a bit old to sleep on the ground,' Eleanor added. 'And the bathroom facilities left a lot to be desired.'

'Oh.'

Eleanor could see tears building up in Ruby's big eyes. 'But we did see one billion stars,' she said, smiling back, reaching out a hand to pat Ruby's arm. 'And the sunset was amazing and the sunrise was like something from another planet. Even if it was about five o'clock.'

'Your colleagues will be there when you get back,' Bruno said, steering around the rocks at the approach to the big island.

'Well, I need a hot shower and a change of clothes, then we'll walk the ground and go over the plans.'

Ruby yawned. 'I need some sleep.'

Eleanor widened her eyes. 'Well, that *is* unfortunate. Because you need to meet everyone and walk the ground, too. Those loos won't clean themselves, and the crew have been setting up for days.'

Bruno laughed at his daughter's expression, and after a moment, Eleanor joined in.

42

OCTOBER 1943

The church was packed for Dorothy and Hector's wedding.

She'd had butterflies whenever she'd thought about the ceremony, the three-night honeymoon with Hector, and Dr Peaty covering her clinic. She and Hector had found a small hotel on St Piran's, closed for the war, that was willing to open just for them.

The brief but intense courtship had been conducted under the eye of the whole population, who seemed to report back to old Mrs Ellis, seated in pride of place next to the governor of the island and his wife. The commander of the airbase and a few senior officers represented the groom. Packed in like sardines were her patients. Young Bobby Moyle, now back fishing, his wound healed. Mrs Livingstone had picked up a little colour as she wasn't pregnant. Mrs Oppy in the middle of a pew. The Allen parents, waiting for their younger girls' entrance as bridesmaids. Other children, too, mercifully vaccinated. Some were either painted purple for the impetigo, which went round and round the school, or close-cropped against nits.

Her most welcome visitor was James, her younger brother,

on special leave from the war and able to escort her down the aisle.

'I like Hector,' he had announced the day before. 'Much more than that pompous banker Valerie married.'

'At least you didn't bring our spoiled nieces,' Dorothy had answered, and they had both laughed.

Now, at the entrance to the church, he seemed as shaky and nervous as her. 'Like facing the guns,' he said, a tremor in his voice. He looked thin in his uniform, Dorothy noticed.

'Are you all right?'

'Just a touch of what they call shell shock,' he said. 'Alongside the shrapnel damage.' He smiled awkwardly at her. 'I don't know why I'm nervous, the guns are all pointed at *you* today.'

Jeannie peeped in the door and then beckoned to them. 'Just remember, Polly, don't drop the train. Branwen, stand up straight. And you, miss, hand me the flowers when you get to the altar.'

Dorothy turned to the little girls, Polly with a clean bandage over her scar, her hair decorated with a few fresh flowers.

'Well done, girls. Now, we won't go too fast.'

Branwen reached for her sister's hand. 'You look beautiful, Dr Dorothy,' she said, smiling with a missing tooth and braids so tight they were pulling her eyebrows up.

'You do,' Polly whispered, still a little breathless.

Dorothy was a bit dizzy herself, perhaps from the tightlacing, or knowing that she was the centre of attention with her beautiful silk gown and handsome bridegroom.

Walking down the aisle past the smiling guests, clinging to James's arm, trying not to outpace the children, she looked down at the uneven flagstones. At the last pew, with Mrs Ellis in the best spot, she dared to look up at the two men in American uniforms by the altar. She registered Irwin Peaty before seeing Hector, beaming at her. He looked younger, delighted;

his hands were warm and held both of hers when James handed
her over.

'I love you,' she murmured.

'I love you too,' he said. 'Let's get married.'

After the exchange of vows, a spontaneous round of applause
broke out, led by Mrs Ellis. The reception was full of delicious
food. Some of it had been scrounged from the American airbase
staff, some contributed by her patients and their families. There
was necessarily a lot of fish, but lobster patties and fresh potted
shrimps were a luxury she hadn't expected. Mrs Keiller had
made the cake, and everyone had a sliver for good luck. It was
rich in prunes and just sprinkled with whisky and sugar, but it
was delicious. After the ceremony, Dorothy had lost her
shyness. Bottles of wine and beer flowed, everyone was in a
good mood and Dr Peaty proved a demanding photographer.
Dorothy wanted to capture the day, and also images of her
brother. Jeannie spent a lot of time flirting with him, even
though he was twice her age.

Dorothy wandered around the loaded tables holding
Hector's hand, so glad she could finally be seen openly with
him. She felt quite light-headed with the pressure of his fingers,
the smile on his face every time she caught his gaze. More than
once he leaned down to kiss her, making her glow with embarrassment. He insisted it was an American custom for good luck.

'I have enough good luck,' Dorothy murmured, staring up
into his eyes. 'Anyway, I'm wearing something old, something
new, something borrowed and something blue. You'll find out
what later,' she said, blushing so warmly she had to fan herself
with a card.

There were telegrams from relatives and her parents, a
couple of her old colleagues and even a school friend she had
rather forgotten about. Hector's mother had sent a letter

through to the airbase, and Dorothy's sister had sent an affectionate message. Today, it was perfect to just be Mrs Hector McBride, newly married, and not care about medicine at all.

Hector leaned down to kiss her again. 'It feels wonderful to be able to do that whenever I please, and you don't mind,' he said, his blue eyes shining.

'I'm never going to mind,' she answered.

43

PRESENT DAY, 12 AUGUST

Later that morning, Eleanor mustered her team as the festival began. Joey, her assistant, immediately gave Ruby a walkie-talkie and conjured a name badge and lanyard for her. Three of the Carlin Centre staff had been recruited for the week; the others were running a summer event for younger children at the school.

There was a gang of regular volunteer stewards and a small medical team of a doctor and two nurses. The biggest risk was heatstroke and sunburn, but the medical room at the centre also had refrigeration for drugs like insulin. Everyone knew what they were doing and sprang into action with trolleys to carry camping equipment, and showed people where to set up tents a safe distance apart. Light rain from a couple of days before had greened up the mown grass, and the view from every part of the site looked down to the sea and the two large tents holding the stages.

Two bands from the islands were already setting up, and people were gathering to relax on the folding chairs Ruby and the others were setting out. The chai tent was already brewing a variety of hot drinks, the smell of hot spiced apple juice and chai mingling at the back of the Carlin Centre. She found Bruno there, chatting to Kayleigh.

'Everything looks good,' she said.

'We're just putting "Please Don't Feed the Sheep" signs on the electric fence,' he said. 'A couple of people already wanted to pet them.'

'Idiots,' Kayleigh said, but she was smiling. 'Oh, and we've had our first medical emergency, too,' she said, laughing.

'Oh?' Eleanor was immediately on alert.

'*Me*,' Bruno said. 'They haven't started making the coffees yet and I need another one.'

'Come into the festival café,' Eleanor said. 'The stewards have been up since six, they'll have something for you.'

As they wandered around, Bruno waved to people he knew and introduced Eleanor to several old friends. They all seemed surprised to see him.

'This is my old rugby mate, Bran,' he said to a tall man, sitting in a circle with a few teenagers. They were moulding clay with their eyes shut. 'He's quite a famous artist now. Is Ellie around?'

'She's looking after the baby,' he answered, looking up and smiling at Eleanor. 'She'll be over tomorrow for the day. Her dad's coming to babysit.' He made a funny face. 'Zillah will have him running around like a sheepdog. Does Ruby want to join in?'

'She's working,' Bruno and Eleanor said at the same time, then laughed.

It felt very natural walking around with Bruno, meeting up with members of the committee who seemed absolutely thrilled with the gentle start. 'Don't forget, we've got two ferries today, one late in the evening,' Eleanor warned. 'It will all be busier and louder tomorrow!'

Liz Retallack hugged her. 'It's *wonderful*! I've joined in the spiritual music event and the choir; we're travelling around singing on the quays and in the churches for five days and I'm bringing my husband with me. Sally is right, he'll love it, and people need to know.' She pulled back to stare at Eleanor. 'Tell me, how are the finances going?'

'You'll make a small profit, I think,' Eleanor said. 'Enough to run a festival next year, anyway. We'll know more later.'

'And how is your family tree coming on?'

Eleanor shook her head. 'It's all loose ends at the moment.'

'Well, I might be able to help. One of our choir – she's singing in the shanty competition too – her mother was born to Branwen Allen. Flora Ellis.'

'Oh, really?'

'She's over there, chatting to Sally.' As Eleanor walked over, something strange struck her about the two older women. Both small, with quick expressions and the same dark eyes.

'Hi, there,' she said. 'I was told you might be a descendant of Branwen Allen?'

'Branwen Monroe was her married name. And I married an Ellis. It's like Smith or Jones on the islands – you don't want to fall into the spiderweb of Ellises. My family tree looks like a cat's cradle.'

Eleanor smiled. 'I did notice the graveyard was full of them,' she said.

'Your mother's name was...?'

'She was born Hecta Allen in 1970,' Eleanor said. 'She was called Diana after she was adopted.'

'And her mother's name?'

'Alys Allen,' Eleanor said, looking at Sally, who seemed very uncomfortable.

'I can't believe we don't remember either of them, but I suppose their names got changed when they were adopted. There was a rumour in our family,' Flora explained as Sally drifted away. 'My mother had diphtheria as a child. She was really ill.'

'I knew one of the children died.'

'The baby. Yes, but Mum's younger sister Polly was desperately ill, she ended up in hospital. They had to put a breathing tube in her throat. It must have been terrible for the family.'

'It must have been,' Eleanor said, watching Sally, who kept glancing over at her. 'What happened to her?'

'I know she went to live with an aunt for a while, so she'd be close to a hospital. They had her doing lots of breathing exercises. And I know she married later in life, had a little boy, my cousin.'

'Was there any rumour about a child she had, a girl?'

Flora hesitated. 'There's this rumour... I just know there was some sort of secret. She might have been sent to the Doctor's House. It wasn't a mother and baby home until later that year. Dr Dorothy had already moved the clinic to the new health centre, and Dr Hector was working up at the hospital.' She shook her head. 'The older generation kept all this stuff very quiet. But I remember them talking, whispering really, about *Polly's baby*. About Easter, 1953.'

'So, she couldn't have been Diana's mother in 1970.' Eleanor glanced over at Sally standing by the stage. She seemed upset and looked away. *She knows something, she's keeping something from me.* 'I see. I'll look into it. I've found a record for a Mary Allen, but it doesn't seem to go anywhere. No marriage or death certificate.' She looked back at Flora. 'But that could have been her. I know Polly was sometimes a nickname for Mary.'

'Well, giving birth up at the Doctor's House, maybe her baby was adopted. Perhaps she was the first baby that gave the doctors the idea to make their house into a maternity home later that year.'

Born March 1953, before the mother and baby home had started. It all started to fall into place. Sally was born in March, according to her own story. But surely she would have told

Eleanor if she was in the Allen family? Perhaps she really didn't know. Could she suspect something? Might she be afraid that she was the product of Polly's mystery pregnancy? In which case, could she be...?

Eleanor walked over to Sally, who looked up at her and swallowed. 'Was speaking to Flora helpful?' Sally asked.

Eleanor looked into her eyes, which were brimming with tears. 'Sally, did you ever suspect who your mother was?'

'I never wanted to know. But now I wonder...'

At that moment, a message came through to her. A volunteer had slipped over and sprained an ankle which might need an X-ray. She tapped a response into her phone, but her mind was full of questions as to what Sally wasn't telling her.

44

OCTOBER 1944

It was Dorothy's first wedding anniversary, a date she had only just registered. As if she had time for all that nonsense.

She had a surgery with more than twenty appointments, there was a baby clinic immediately after that she must make an appearance in, and then she was off to catch the tide for her fortnightly visit to West Island. There was a mother of twins that might even be triplets to keep an eye on, and the possibility of polio in one child – hastily isolated. She was exhausted just thinking of how to manage an outbreak. She also felt ill. Not seriously enough to take time off, but so tired every bone in her body was aching. *I hope this isn't the beginning of the flu...*

Dorothy had read her letters and was putting aside a journal to read when she had time – or to gather dust with the last three months of journals – when Hector clomped down the stairs.

'I'm off to the base,' he said, kissing her quickly. 'Oh,' he said, kissing her again, 'happy anniversary. I might be a bit late – we're taking some poor soul's infected eye out then there's a double amputation.' As he got to the doorway he said, 'We'll do something nice at the weekend,' over his shoulder.

She thought wistfully of the joys of losing her cares and woes in a long surgery. She was just in the mood for a double amputation. The door banged again and she heard Hector cheerily say hello to someone. Probably Beryl Livingstone, who had taken a correspondence course in typing and was now working as receptionist and secretary. The additional income had made a huge difference to Beryl. Now her children were well turned out and healthy, she was successfully avoiding pregnancy and the family had moved to a slightly larger house on the edge of the main town.

'Good morning!' Dorothy shouted while she tried to arrange the envelopes with people's notes in the same order as the appointments. Which was pointless, because the waiting room would arrange itself. Working men always went in first, women with children next. And Mrs Ellis had always come in as soon as she arrived.

Her death, just a week ago, had left Dorothy bereft. She stayed up with her on her last night, listening to her final whispers and wheezes, completely surrounded by the love of the Ellises. In her last few days, Dorothy estimated about seventy people had been to visit, maybe more, and she had been pressed into promising to attend the funeral. In the last year, Mrs Ellis's experience and beliefs had been very helpful through the strangeness of letting Hector share her life and her bed. There had been quite a few questions for Mrs Ellis, about such mundane things as Hector throwing the bedclothes off or snoring, both of which disturbed her sleep. And eating – how can anyone as thin as Hector go to work on porridge and four pieces of toast? If it wasn't for food from his ration at the base, she wouldn't be able to feed him enough.

But her marriage was a success. She could slide her hand into his any time she liked, she would never have to eat alone if she didn't want to, and she had someone to talk to about things that really mattered. They had stayed up late the night before talking about the amazing new drug streptomycin, which might be available after the war. Somehow the possibility of a drug against tuberculosis was more interesting and exciting than their looming anniversary, but she remembered by the time they went to bed. He fell asleep straight away, his ability to sleep anywhere and instantly serving him well as a doctor, but she had lain in bed for an hour knowing the anniversary would pass them by. *It's just a day.*

She stood up to greet Beryl in the waiting room when the room spun around her and she staggered, sat back down, holding her mouth against a wave of nausea.

'Beryl?' she called, when she could. 'I'm a bit wobbly. Could you get me a cup of tea, please?'

Beryl put her head around the door into the doctor's room. 'What you need is a dry biscuit,' she said. 'I'll get tea, but you might be better with water.'

'What? Is there a bug going around?' Dorothy managed to walk to the kitchen and sit at the table. 'I've got a busy day.' *And it's my anniversary*, she thought unreasonably, although infectious organisms didn't care about that.

Beryl put a couple of biscuits on a plate and stood back to watch Dorothy eat them. After a nibble, the nausea did go off a bit.

'Oh, thank you,' she said. The kettle was just beginning to bump on the stove, the new electric cooker. It had been a wedding gift from her parents, and really did help with the early mornings.

'You've been married a year,' she said, still watching Dorothy. 'You haven't worked it out yet, have you?'

'What do you...? Oh.'

She and Hector had hardly talked about children. At their age, pregnancy was less likely but she did feel different, somehow.

Now all she could think about was the tomes and textbooks

of the million things that could go wrong with such an elderly
mother and her fragile infant. She suddenly wanted to speak to
old Mrs Ellis, who had had her last child at forty-eight, a boy
who was now a blacksmith and over six feet tall.

'W-what will I do?' was all she could stammer.

'It's early days,' Beryl said. 'So it might not come to
anything. But I would try and rest a bit more. It helps with the
sickness.'

'Rest how?' Dorothy asked, finishing off the dry biscuits.

'Well, you've got twenty minutes now before the first
patient. Go and rest in the parlour and I'll bring you a bit of
breakfast. Just some toast.'

Beryl's simple wisdom was helpful. Even a few minutes
lying flat and a little food and weak tea restored her immediately.

'Now,' Beryl said, 'I've got Nurse Harper popping into the
clinic for you, she'll help the midwife get through the maternity
patients quicker. You can put your feet up at lunchtime – and
you'll have a sandwich, no arguments – then the tide will be
ready to go to West Island. I've checked, there are just eleven
patients over there this week, and maybe a couple of walk-ins.
You'll be back in time for supper.'

'Thank you,' Dorothy said meekly, getting up slowly so the
world didn't whirl around her head. 'You've been very kind.
Don't tell anyone else, though, will you? It's very early.'

'You've been very kind to me,' Beryl replied. 'I won't tell
anyone, but people will guess.'

Which, as Dorothy went through her day slightly more
gently than usual, left her trapped between nervous and
excited. How was she going to tell Hector?

When she got back from West Island, the house was full of
savoury smells. Jeannie had put a pot in the oven with a note of
what vegetables needed steaming with the Irish stew. She'd also
left a little note about pudding, an apple tart made with their

own jars of apples from the autumn, and a PS: 'Happy anniversary!'

Jeannie, engaged to be married and working as a telegraphist most of the week, still had time to help the domestically challenged Dorothy most days.

When Hector came home, she was on the sofa in the parlour, having just put her feet up for a moment and drifted into blissful sleep. He was looking down at her from the fireside chair when she woke.

'Long day?' he asked, lifting her hand and kissing it.

'No more than usual,' she said, scooting up the settee and running a hand through her wild hair. 'What time is it?'

'Six thirty. Peaty is finishing up, he sent me home for our first anniversary. I turned the stove off.'

'Oh, goodness, dinner must be burnt!'

His hand stayed her. 'It's fine. Are *you* all right?' he asked. 'You just seem a bit pale and tired these days.'

'Yes, I'm all right,' She gazed into his beautiful blue eyes. 'But we mustn't get our hopes up too soon.'

His expression changed from confusion to a huge grin, and he kissed her, what she thought of as a proper bedroom kiss. 'Let's enjoy the idea while we may,' he said. 'Our dinner will be lovely, Jeannie left it on low. Come and eat, and tell me all about it.'

She stopped in the hallway, suddenly shy. 'Happy anniversary.'

'Thank you for the best year of my life,' he replied, and she walked into his arms. 'With or without a baby.'

45

PRESENT DAY, 15 AUGUST

The festival marched on, and most practical problems were resolved with duct tape or cable ties, and the kindness of stewards defusing arguments and problems. A few intoxicated people were laid down in the shade and watched over, but most people were high on the music, dancing and good company.

Complete strangers became friends, the fields became a loose community and everyone seemed to be having a brilliant time. Eleanor made sure that two people trading suspicious packages were discreetly removed by local plainclothes police officers. A few locals were asked not to bring cases of beer onto the grounds to resell, which would undermine partner companies who were doing a roaring trade in local ales. The food outlets sold out every day and had to call on their reserves; the dancing and singing had made people hungrier and thirstier than usual.

The rain held off, and the sky was mostly cloudless. The committee were thrilled and relieved that their big venture had paid off. There were two reporters from national papers sending in positive reviews.

Ruby surprised everyone, and possibly even herself. She

coped with cleaning loos in an hourly rotation, doing fire checks on the tents with fire marshal Tink, and answering festivalgoers' endless questions. She had accumulated a small gang of admirers who chatted to her all day. A couple even helped her top up toilet rolls and hand sanitiser, and one unblocked one of the sinks that had been a problem.

Lifeguards stationed on the beach had to work around the clock, and Eleanor had to recruit several more to cover the night shift when a surprising number of people wanted to swim by moonlight, clothed or otherwise. Bruno decided to water the strip of grass between the campground and the sheep, and ended up spraying many hot and tired dancers who were thrilled to cool down. He didn't seem to worry about Ruby at all, and a few times, she saw him wandering about chatting and laughing with Michelle. Sometimes she saw him deep in conversation with Tink and his partner Corinne, a tall black woman who looked like a model, carrying a toddler wearing noise-reducing headphones.

Everyone seemed so close, like a big family. Her job had been a refuge from her grief but had now created a conundrum about Bruno. She answered queries, ensured that everyone including the musicians had had a good time, and barely got four hours in her own bed each night. But not to sleep, at least not for an hour or two, as she lay awake in tangled sheets in the dark, speculating on everything Bruno had said and done – and that kiss. He could have kissed her again, if he'd wanted to. Or was it just a silly impulse that he regretted? He wanted a date, she knew, but did he want any more?

She was also worried about Sally. She was camping with friends about the same age on the fields, talking so seriously and looking tearful every time Eleanor saw her. But she would smile through her tears and say she was having a great time whenever Eleanor checked on her. She had so many questions for Sally, but was worried she would upset her again.

It was on the final morning of the festival, with the vintage star headliner, a friend of Elk's coming from the mainland by helicopter, that the postman dropped some letters for Sally on the mat of the Doctor's House. Instead of leaving them on the table with the others, Eleanor decided to take the post down to the camping field, as an excuse to have a conversation with Sally.

She walked across the orchard and climbed over the fence, knowing that Bruno wouldn't mind. Past the tent village, through the water points and past the loos, she stopped at a large bell tent. Sally was watching a kettle on a tiny gas stove, her eyes red and puffy. *Maybe it's hayfever*, Eleanor thought, until Sally looked up. She looked devastated.

'Please tell me what's wrong,' Eleanor said, dropping down onto the rug next to Sally. 'You know you can talk to me about anything. Is it this family tree thing?'

'I got pregnant, too, you know,' Sally blurted out. 'In 1970, but I was so ill afterwards – I never wanted to know what happened to the baby. Just that she was happy. But there were so many babies that year...'

Eleanor's mind skittered over the idea that Sally could be her grandmother.

'My mother arranged the adoption because I begged her to,' Sally wailed. 'I was so ill. The birth brought on my epilepsy so badly I was taken to the mainland. I was there for two weeks. I never even saw the baby until I got back.'

Eleanor took her shaking hands. 'And that was my mother?' A bubble of joy was growing inside her chest.

'I *think* so. I only saw her once. Mum just named her when she registered the birth, she didn't even tell me she'd called her Hecta. She did hope maybe one day she would find her way back, so she named her after my dad...' She pulled away and put her head in her hands. 'Then I found out my baby – your mother – grew up to die of *cancer*.'

Eleanor's tears welled up too. 'She did,' she said, her voice breaking. 'It was terrible. She would have loved you so much, you know.'

'But I gave her *away!*' Sally cried. 'I was so young, and Dad had just died, none of us could cope. Mum was too old... I just signed the papers because I had to.'

'She went to the very best family,' Eleanor explained. 'It was the right thing. Like it was the right thing that the doctors adopted *you.*'

'Yes, but now I feel like you need to know who *my* mother was. If it was Polly.'

Eleanor squeezed her hands. 'I don't need to know anything more.' She started crying too, and Sally hugged her. 'I don't care. I have *you.*'

It was strange to have Sally in her arms. It felt familiar, like hugging Diana. Sally's voice was more like her own, she thought, or as it would be when she was older.

The sound of their voices had brought out Andrea and Liz, who were staying with Sally in the bell tent.

'What on earth's the matter?' said Liz, squinting at the sky.

'I've just found my granddaughter,' Sally managed to choke out through her sobs. 'Eleanor is my grandchild.'

Andrea and Liz exchanged looks. 'Well, we did suspect,' Liz said.

Eleanor gasped. 'You suspected? Why?'

'All that gossip about Polly Allen. And then Dr Dorothy mysteriously adopted a baby girl. Then the talk about *you* disappearing for a few months back in 1970. Nine months after we went camping, as I recall. And all those stories about you being so *ill.*'

'I *was* ill,' Sally said. 'After I gave birth to a perfect baby girl, and Dr Dorothy called her Hecta so she could find her way back to me.'

'Well, this doesn't sound like terrible news,' Andrea said

briskly, taking the kettle off the heat and filling up mugs. 'It seems like *wonderful* news to me.'

'Do you still want to find out who my mother was for certain?' Sally said, staring deeply into Eleanor's eyes, her image wavering in the tears.

'Yes,' Eleanor said baldly. 'But I won't look into it if you don't want me to.'

'I've sent off for my birth certificate,' Sally said. 'I had to fill in loads of forms and speak to a social worker in London, but they are sending it over. I thought it would come before the festival. I needed to know if Mum – Dr Dorothy – registered my baby with my *original* name as the mother, or my adoptive name.'

Eleanor looked around for the pile of post she had dropped. 'Is it one of these?'

Sally sorted through them until she came to an innocuous-looking brown envelope. She stared at it, before sliding a finger under the flap and peeking in the top. 'It is a certificate,' she said, looking at Eleanor. 'Suppose we're not related? I mean, suppose we have this wrong? Wouldn't that be awful?'

Eleanor had to bite her lip, but Andrea snapped, 'Oh, for goodness' sake, you won't know if you don't look!'

'I love you like a granddaughter anyway,' Sally said.

'I love you like a grandmother, too,' Eleanor said. She took Sally's hand in hers. 'Do it.'

Sally laid the envelope on the rug and all four leaned in as she opened it.

46

MAY 1945

Hector Junior was a month old, and one of the best things that had ever happened to Dorothy. The birth had been a revelation, so intense and terrifying and wonderful, all rolled up in one explosive day.

Now Junior was smiling and gurgling, so pleased to see her at two in the morning, and three and four. They had engaged a nanny, but she couldn't feed the baby, so the night-time feeds were just for him, snuggled in the bed with his parents then slid into his cot when he dozed off.

His father was just as besotted. He was torn between his work at the base, intensifying as the wounded came back from operations in Europe, and taking time to play with the baby. He took Junior out in his pram every afternoon he was free – the only time the baby slept for a long time.

Dorothy was just coming down from the nursery where the nanny was putting him down for a nap when she saw Mrs Oppy standing in the hall.

'I need to see the doctor,' she said, folding her hands over her large handbag. 'The *other* doctor.'

'Well, he's busy at the base,' Dorothy said, 'and I'm only doing a few hours a week.'

Mrs Oppy stared at her until Dorothy sighed. 'Come and talk to me while I eat my sandwich,' she suggested. She hadn't seen the woman in several months, now that the surgery was well accepted and the patients very happy with her. Except Mrs Oppy, apparently.

Mrs Oppy just inclined her head in a stately way and walked into the consulting room. Dorothy fetched her own lunch and a cup of tea, and sat at the desk.

'What can I do for you?' she asked, as Mrs Oppy sat down, looking around.

'It 'ent changed much,' she announced.

'You haven't registered as a patient since I got here,' Dorothy said. 'It must be a big problem or you wouldn't consult with me.'

'Yes, well. Beggars can't be choosers,' she said, looking at Dorothy with disdain. 'I hoped to see Dr Hector because I want an operation.'

'I see. Well, the first step to having an operation is to see me, then be referred to the hospital. Our *local* hospital, unless you need to be referred to the mainland. So, tell me the problem.'

'My mother 'ad it,' Mrs Oppy said, looking around the walls. 'And my grandmother. You haven't changed it much. They is the same pictures.

'Indeed. People don't like everything changing at once. What is this problem that runs in your family?'

'I 'as a lump,' Mrs Oppy said, her gaze swivelling around. Like a lizard, Dorothy thought. She patted her chest lightly. 'My mam had one taken out. She lived until she was seventy-seven.'

'That sounds hopeful,' Dorothy said, pushing her plate away and unscrewing her fountain pen to make notes. 'When did you first notice it?'

'Just before the war.'

'Oh.' Dorothy couldn't think of a single reassuring thing to say about a breast lump ignored for six years.

There was a loud and urgent knock at the door and the post boy burst into the room. 'It's happened, missus! I mean, Doctor! The war's over! In Europe, anyway.'

'My goodness,' Dorothy said, unable to take her eyes off Mrs Oppy. 'Thank you for telling us, but I'm consulting with a patient just now.'

As he scampered off, Mrs Oppy looked her squarely in the face. 'I know it's bad. I know the surgeon will have to take the whole thing off, scrape the bones, they said to my mother. She was in so much pain. The ache never really went.'

'*Please* let me examine you,' Dorothy said. 'Possibly the lump is harmless by itself. But we don't "scrape the bones" at all. In fact, now some hospitals use radium needles to treat some tumours. There is hope.'

But when she looked at the exposed skin, broken through by the angry cancerous tissue, stinking already of necrosis, the hope faded. She tried.

'That must be so painful. Just taking away the tumour would leave you so much more comfortable.'

'And that will cure it?'

Dorothy caught her breath. Her first day in this room, the beginning of the best years of her life, had started with the two of them. 'I don't know,' she said, looking down at Mrs Oppy as she started to button her bodice. 'Wait, don't do that. At least let me put a dressing on for you.'

'I don't need that. I just wanted to know. I thought Dr Hector would know what to do.'

'*I* know what to do,' Dorothy said. 'And that is to go into hospital this week and have it completely removed. And a thorough examination of the other side, too. Sometimes it is present on both sides.' She should be thrilled at the news that the war had ended; she should be out in the town where distant cheering and the foghorns of many vessels were sounding. 'Please. My dear Mrs Oppy, let me help.'

'You don't think it will save me, though. I can see it in your face.'

'Maybe. But there's always a chance.'

Mrs Oppy shrugged on her coat and picked up her bag. 'I'm staying at the Seamen's Mission. I'm housekeeper there. Get word to me what time I should come to the hospital.'

'I will,' was all Dorothy could say. For a long time after Mrs Oppy left, she sat thinking, lost in the sad stupidity of a woman who came for help too late. Her pride – or her fear – had probably cost her her life.

Then Hector burst into the room and shouted loud enough to wake Hector Junior.

'It's over! In Europe, anyway. *They did it!*'

PRESENT DAY, 18 AUGUST

The festival was almost over. A few hundred campers still had a ferry to catch, although the last of the local ticket holders had gone home on the tide in small boats. The final bands had been helicoptered off, food vendors were packing up or serving their last meals, even the big tent had come down already. Swarms of technicians were packing up the electrics, the lights, the stages… It was always amazing how quickly everything went away. Eleanor wandered around the island in a bit of a daze, wondering if she could leave this place she had grown to love.

She had recently discovered Sally was her mother's mother. Confirmed by the birth certificate. Alys Allen – adopted as Sally – had given birth to Diana, registered as Hecta. And Alys was the child of Polly, little Polly Allen who had almost died of diphtheria, who had her sisters' and brothers' descendants all over the islands.

After the news, the two had become shy around each other, Eleanor suddenly awkward about asking Sally about her pregnancy with Diana. She was also hiding from Bruno, who had been busy with Ruby and Michelle and seemed to be avoiding her, too. A grey feeling of uncertainty settled in her when she caught sight of him. How could a relationship work between London and the islands?

Ruby was still bouncing but had shadows under her eyes and was lugging bags of recycling to the edge of the ground, ready to be transported off the island. She waved when she saw Eleanor then carried on pulling. A couple of her young friends were helping, laughing and joking as they sorted plastic or paper or glass.

Eleanor walked down to the Carlin Centre, itself under-going a transformation ready for summer school to restart next week. Kayleigh, who didn't appear to have slept either, was directing people from a position behind a large coffee pot.

She held up a cup and Eleanor nodded, as she sat down in a chair in Kayleigh's office.

'And you do this for a living?' Kayleigh asked, putting a large mug of black coffee in front of her. 'It's like organising a storm.'

'I do,' Eleanor said, closing her eyes. 'I have such a headache. The last band were amazing, though. I saw you up the front dancing with that nice-looking man.'

'Ah, my husband. I think that's the only time we had together all week,' Kayleigh said, laughing. 'I just rolled into bed at two and left at seven each day. But it went really well, no real damage, and we've made a useful bit of revenue to repair the climbing wall.' She sipped her coffee. 'It's been out of commission this season. Your money will help us extend it, too.'

'I'm glad.' When Eleanor opened her eyes, Kayleigh was watching her. 'What?'

'You seem a bit blue... Liz told me you've been on a bit of a journey.'

Eleanor groaned but couldn't help smiling. 'Does *everyone* on the islands know?'

'Well, half the people on the islands got together for the whole week, so probably. You found your mother's family?'

'And we found Sally's as well. She's my grandmother.'

Kayleigh beamed at her. 'That's just a lovely story. It must have come as a shock to Sally, though. She's been struggling a bit since she lost Nessa.' She lowered her voice. 'I think it would have been better if she could have had Nessa nearby, on the islands. Maybe if they'd got married...'

'She still would have died, though,' Eleanor said. 'It's hard. Losing someone. My mum...' Her voice failed her.

'I'm so sorry she didn't meet Sally,' Kayleigh said.

'Me too. The funny thing is, *I* don't look anything like my mother,' Eleanor said. 'And I didn't see how much she looked like Sally. I just felt this lovely warm feeling when I met her, like being back at home again.'

'That's a result, then,' Kayleigh said, and finished her cup. 'More coffee?'

'No, thanks. I need to organise my team – a couple of them are going back today, the rest will go back tomorrow. I'll fly back, too, do all the paperwork. Maybe do some prep for next year, if they want to repeat the experience.'

Kayleigh laughed. 'You are joking, aren't you? They will *definitely* want to do next year!'

Eleanor walked along the suddenly quiet beach, just a lot of footprints marking the festival, soon to be wiped out by the next tide. She was lost in her own confused thoughts when she looked up to see Bruno paddling along the shoreline towards her.

'Ruby said I'd find you here.'

'I think it's my new favourite place on the island,' she said, smiling at him. 'Is everything all right with Ruby now?'

'Michelle has had a great time with her, the two of them were dancing down on the shore together last night. It's really healed some old wounds, I think.'

She smiled at that, and let her toes wander in and out of the lapping edge of the sea. It tickled, and the cold burned.

'Come and swim with me,' he said, turning to her.

'You know I can't swim...' she muttered.

'Come anyway. I won't let anything happen to you.'

She looked out towards the sea, her nerves making her freeze. 'I can't.'

When he held out both hands, she reluctantly put hers into his warm grasp.

'What's bothering you?'

She shook her head, not sure which thread in the tangled mess of her feelings was making her sad.

'I'm not going back to Michelle,' he said, 'if that was worrying you.'

It was like one of those jumbled strands was yanked out and left on the sand. She smiled wryly. He really could read her like a book.

'It was... a bit,' she admitted. 'It would have been a big complication to all your lives.'

'No, she's happy where she is. It was just good for her to let her hair down in a safe place, with friends, and leave her bloke with the kids.'

She smiled but didn't answer. She looked down at his brown hands, thick, stubby fingers, the hands of a farmer. 'I have to go back to my real world, soon,' she said. 'Back to London.'

'But this is the real world for you, now,' he said softly. 'It never was for Michelle, but it's always been more vivid for me than any holiday destination, any job on the mainland. This is your place, too.'

She stared at his dark eyes, arched eyebrows, curls tangled over his forehead. How could she ever have thought of him as grumpy and difficult? He just wore his heart on his sleeve, which she had never learned to do. Tears gathered in her eyes, making his image blur out of focus. 'Is it?'

'You're island stock, through and through. No wonder you love it here.'

'I do.' Her tears were falling freely now. He hugged her fiercely, and she couldn't stop crying. She tried to apologise, but he soothed her with words as she imagined he would gentle an injured animal. 'But I'm not sure if I just love you, and you're stuck here,' she blurted, immediately embarrassed as she pulled back.

He lifted her chin, and patted at her face with some cloth that smelled like sheep. 'I love you too,' he said. 'If that helps. But I'm not *stuck* here. I just love it here.'

She looked at the rag he was wiping her face with and managed a tearful chuckle. 'What was that used for last?'

'I don't know. I just leave it in my pocket and it goes through the wash.' He grasped her hands again. 'Please, come swimming with me. I promise it will relieve all your troubles.'

'I can't. I'm not dressed for it.'

The tide was creeping up, and he had taken a step out into the water. Lapping her ankles, it made her feet tingle and sting. 'Neither am I,' he said. He let go, stripped off his T-shirt and took out his phone. He held his hand out for hers and her sandals, then jogged up the beach to deposit them on the dry sand. 'Come on,' he said, holding out one hand and walking into the deeper water. Her hem rippled and floated in the water as it reached above her knees, but she wasn't scared, just mesmerised by his absolute confidence that it would be all right.

'Just a paddle, right?' She gripped his hands and stared into his eyes.

'When I was a little boy, my mum used to pick me up from the school,' he said as he inched further into the shallow water. 'A few of the mothers would walk down here and we'd strip off to our underwear and go in. I just recall being so hot and bored and sleepy at school, then, bam! Down to the sea.'

'What... what else do you remember?' She was shivering now, as the water reached her waist and her dress billowed around them like a jellyfish.

'We would always come out of the water thirsty and hungry, and the mums would distribute apples and crisps and sometimes strawberries, and they were always covered in salty sand.'

Her feet wouldn't move forward into the darker, deeper water. 'But you could all swim like fish from birth.' Her teeth were chattering. 'Why didn't you die of the cold?'

He placed her hands on his shoulders, then held her waist and drew her close. 'We had the metabolic rate of dolphins,' he said. He was looking at her hair, her eyes, her mouth, smiling at her in a sort of possessive way. 'I still do. I'm warm as toast,' he said, as he moved in for the kiss.

She met him, and his body *was* warm, and somehow she was pulling him in and the gulls were wheeling overhead with that mocking cry and... She broke the kiss, glanced over her shoulder. People waiting for the next helicopter were sat along the wall, watching. One waved.

'We've become the entertainment!' She laughed.

'I think Kayleigh and Ruby are watching us, too,' he said, his lips nibbling at her neck.

'Ruby will be appalled,' Eleanor said, taking a small step back.

'Ruby will be impressed that her antiquated, heartless dad can use hypothermia to get a beautiful girl to kiss him.'

'I'm not really beautiful,' she said, grabbing his hand again. 'Come on, then, let's really put on a show.'

'You are beautiful to me. Even though you are terrified of water.'

'No, I'm terrified of *drowning*.' She slid down a small ridge and suddenly she was chest-deep in water and her breath was gone. 'Cold,' she gasped.

He waited until she got her breath back and started laughing. 'What's your game plan here? Are you going to test my life-saving skills?'

'Ruby said you used to get her to dive under the water for a kiss,' she said, holding her arms above the water, her fingers clawed on one of his hands. He seemed anchored to the seabed, but she felt like she could float away at any moment.

He laughed again, relaxed and amused, a sound she hadn't heard before. He was usually holding something back. 'All right. But we do this safely. I hold you all the way down and back up. And a quick peck, before you panic.'

The water was calmer away from the beach, almost oily and flat. She put her hands on his shoulders, gripped him tight.

'Keep your eyes open underwater,' he said. 'It will only sting for a second.'

He dipped, her heart galloping when he pulled her down, his arms tight around her waist. Then she was under, breath held, staring into his underwater grin, and then a kiss, the only warm thing in the sea. Then he rocketed them out of the water, and she screamed, a release of all that terror and relief.

'Can all our other kisses take place on dry land?' she asked, desperately holding onto him as he carried her towards the beach. When the water drained from her ears she could hear cheering.

'Where will we have those kisses?' he asked as he set her on her feet in the shallows.

'I don't know, in the field, under the moon, in Sally's garden, in my bed...' She smiled as his eyebrows rose. 'Is that too forward, Mr Old-Fashioned Island Farmer?'

They were in waist-high water, walking hand in hand. 'Not forward enough,' he said, laughing. 'My grandmother would have put you down as a hussy, though.'

By the time she had waded out of the water, the dress tugging at her legs, the little group on the wall had come down to applaud her. Joey was there, ready to return to their office, and he reached forward to kiss her wet cheek.

'Well, you had a good festival,' he said, laughing.

'I really did,' she said, trying to drape the dress around her so it didn't show her black underwear. Kayleigh walked along the beach with a brightly coloured towel. 'Here you go,' she said, her face straight but her eyes completely understanding. 'Good swimming lesson?' she asked, innocently.

'The best,' Eleanor answered with a smile.

48

MAY 1969

When Hector Junior was eight, Dorothy and Hector adopted baby Sally. She was the blessing that completed their family. Born too early and small to a weak Polly Allen, at first she had needed both doctors' commitment and knowledge to save her. She was nursed in an incubator in the hospital, with nurses working around the clock to help. Her first few fits had been tiny quivers, and her face would go blank. When Dorothy realised her condition would put her beyond a normal adoption, she was ashamed that she felt relieved. The baby would be theirs. She and Hector would be allowed to adopt her, despite their relatively advanced ages.

Hector was an engaged father. He had worked long hours at the hospital when Junior was a baby, but with Sally it was different. He was semi-retired by then. He put her in a home-made sling and carried her around, even when doing his paperwork.

Joy had been in the little things. Sally walking everywhere, hands held by her big brother in his school uniform. She giggled as Junior splashed her face in the bath, chased her as she crawled all over the ground floor and eventually clambered up the stairs. There was hardly a day when Dorothy or Hector didn't stop and say how lovely their life was. There were sad times, too, like when Mrs Oppy died of her cancer eight years after her surgery.

Hector took them travelling. The children loved going to London or flying – what a novelty – to America to see his mother.

Sixteen years later, Sally was about to finish school and Hector was finally retiring.

One afternoon, Dorothy had just taken a cup of tea into the garden for Hector when she realised he was down in the orchard. She saw him lying, draped half on, half off the fence. She screamed for Sally to call 999, dropped the cup and ran to him.

'Is the sheep all right?' Hector kept saying as he lay tangled in the wires, and Dorothy didn't know how to help him. His gaze was unfocused, wobbling to see her, then to the upside-down sheep that had fallen on its back.

'I'll get someone to turn her over,' she said, unable to stop the tears streaming down her face. 'Sally has gone for an ambulance.'

'Oh, good girl,' he said, closing his eyes, clutching his left arm. 'They can help with the sheep.'

'No, you idiot.' She tried to untangle his ankle from the wire that had tripped him up in his effort to help the bleating animal. 'They need to get you out of this fence first.'

'It's my heart,' he said clearly. 'Not a stroke or anything nasty.'

'I know. You need another one of your nitro tablets.' She rummaged in his breast pocket, fumbled for the pillbox and slipped one under his tongue. There was something faraway about him. 'Don't leave me, my darling,' she begged. 'Stay focused on me. You can do this, Hector...'

He turned his face towards her, and she cradled it on her lap, stroking his tears away. 'I've been so happy with you,' he said, his voice soft now, his Boston accent more pronounced. 'You saved me from a life of mediocrity and boredom. You gave me two wonderful children, and I have loved my life here.'

'When you get over this, we'll send for Junior to come back for a month. Like we did last year.' Hector Junior, the son she adored, was finishing medical school in Massachusetts. She had always hoped he would come back and live on the island, but he had flown the nest to go to medical school and met and married an American girl during his studies.

'Don't make him come back,' Hector murmured, his face white and shiny with perspiration and twisted in pain. 'Just for a funeral.'

She couldn't answer, the tears coming faster now, sobs crowding her throat. 'Don't leave me,' she managed to sob, knowing the words were useless. Either his heart would survive or it wouldn't. 'I love you so much.'

He closed his eyes. 'I love you too,' he breathed.

'*Mum!*' Sally, still in school uniform, raced over the last of the grass and hopped over the fence. '*Daddy!*'

'He's here. He was trying to help that stupid sheep,' Dorothy said, reaching out for Sally. She looked down at Hector, seeing the slackness around his mouth, his eyes almost closed, his head suddenly heavier. 'Oh, no,' she whispered as Sally screamed.

'*Do* something!' she shouted, pulling out of Dorothy's arms. 'Mummy, do *something*!'

Dorothy checked the pulse at Hector's throat, bent her head to kiss his forehead, closed his eyes. They had known for some years that his heart was diseased, but she had never thought it would happen yet – that she would have to live without him.

'There isn't anything I can do,' she whispered. 'He's gone, darling.' Her mind raced over what she could have done – adrenaline, morphine. None of it would have helped. He went so quickly.

'Don't just leave him!' Sally cried, staring at them. 'Try artificial respiration, won't that work?'

'It's his heart. It just gave up,' Dorothy sobbed, seeing his beautiful long hands, so skilled at helping people. His hair was snow white now; she brushed it off his forehead. 'He is seventy-three...' she began, her words jumbling up with her tears. 'He *was* seventy-three.' *And I can't imagine life without him.* The future looked as grey as a winter sky, even as the spring sunshine filtered down on them.

The ambulance came, the men respectful and kind, but they made only the most rudimentary checks on him before carefully loading Hector onto a stretcher.

'Can you help the sheep?' she managed weakly. 'He was trying to save it.'

'Of course,' one of the men said. Reg Ellis, one of the boys she remembered looking after through measles, rolled it over. Jim Trethewey, who broke two fingers playing rugby just two years ago, covered Hector gently with a blanket.

The animal had been at risk of suffocating, but once it was righted it trotted off to its fellows. Sally crouched by the fence, distraught, but she wouldn't let Dorothy hold her. Yet.

'Come on, maid,' Reg said kindly. 'Help us carry your dad down to the ambulance.'

'I don't want this!' Sally wailed. 'I want him back!'

'We all do,' Reg said, looking at Dorothy, still standing by Hector's peaceful body. 'Now you need to look after your ma, because she's got a lot to do.'

Dorothy looked around the peaceful orchard, the laden trees. Sally came over and curled against her. 'I wish we could bury him there, under a tree.' She startled herself as the idea was spoken aloud. 'We could have him close, then, looking out for us.'

49

PRESENT DAY, 21 AUGUST

Eleanor wandered around her room, packing a few things, trying to decide what she could leave on the island for her next visit. Sally had been adamant that she couldn't talk about things yet, and she'd respected that. Sally was turning her emotions into baking, and there was another cake cooling in the kitchen while she was wandering the garden in bare feet, muttering to herself. It was a surprise when she turned up at the open French doors to Eleanor's room.

'Can I come in?' Sally asked. It seemed like a redundant question in her own house.

'Of course! Talk to me,' Eleanor prompted, sitting on the bed. 'Tell me how you are. I don't want to leave if you're not one hundred per cent.'

Sally sat next to her. 'Am I anything like your mum? I mean, Diana?'

'Very like her,' Eleanor said, smiling. 'Are you ready to see a picture?'

Sally took a deep, hissing breath. 'Go on.'

Eleanor pulled up a few pictures on her phone; the last one

was when Diana was staying at the flat, still smiling but thinner, paler.

'I can't believe my mother chose her birth name so she would be able to find me. Or that you would.' Sally shook her head. 'I can't say I recognised you instantly or anything, you're so different to me, but I liked you *so much*.'

'Me too,' Eleanor said. 'I felt immediately at home.' She looked down at her hands, roughened by the work around the festival. Putting up tents, taking them down, moving the recycling, arranging transport for a few young people... At the back of her mind, like a warm cat, the certainty over Bruno was curled. 'People here are very *real*,' she said, laughing. 'They are unguarded. They can be themselves.'

'I never thought that,' Sally said. 'It was me who wouldn't get married to Nessa, even after she was diagnosed. I would have had more rights to decide for her. I felt the whole island was watching and judging.'

'They weren't,' Eleanor said. 'I mean, they were probably intrusively *nosy*...'

'I have a lot of regrets at the moment. Grief that I missed Diana by what? A year.'

Eleanor used the argument Sally always used with her. 'The past is done. Let's write the future.'

Sally swatted her. 'Where do you get all your wisdom from?' she said, laughing.

Eleanor hugged her. 'My wise grandmother.'

'The whole island is buzzing about you and Bruno going in the sea the other day. What's going on?'

'He's on the mainland with Michelle and Ruby. They are sorting out some issues. I think Ruby saw another side of both of her parents during the festival.' She still had lots of questions, but a hundred texts a day from Bruno kept her entertained. He was funny online. Less intense.

'And you're going back to London,' Sally said, turning over a cardigan that had got unrolled. 'Are you taking this?'

'I think I'll leave it here,' she said, 'for when I get back.' *I'm back to London and then Bruno is coming to stay and we'll have the time and privacy to work out what we're doing.*

'Bruno's asked me to have Ruby come to stay, while he's away,' Sally said, innocently. 'And Tink will be over to look after the sheep and lambs. Although the lambs are so big and fat they're almost ready for slaughter.'

Eleanor finished packing, leaned on the case to zip it up. 'I shall be very sorry to leave. I'm lucky to get a seat on the helicopter, though. I mustn't be late.'

'Months ago, when you showed me that birth certificate, I sent off a DNA test from one of these genealogy sites. Liz suggested it. I thought you might like to do one, too.'

For a moment, Eleanor had a horrible thought. *Perhaps we're not related, perhaps I've been deluding us both because I was so missing my mother...* She looked back at Sally, who had her head cocked and looked like a robin, just like Diana had done.

'Of course,' she answered. 'I haven't because... I don't know if I'm ready to find out too much about my father. Mum never told me much about him.'

Sally reached out to hold one of Eleanor's hands. 'You see, I've *always* known who the father of my baby was. It's funny, isn't it? The only man I ever slept with, and the only time, and I conceived a daughter who gave me a granddaughter.'

Eleanor swung around to face her. 'Is he still alive?'

'He is.' Her eyes were flooded with tears. 'His name's Davy Ellis. He lives on West Island now. He has kids and grandchildren. I didn't want to tell you or anyone, because he doesn't know I got pregnant.'

'What happened?'

'It was the late sixties, we were all restless and sick of the islands and my dad had just died. A group of us, Liz, Andrea, me, Davy, Jimmy Roskelly – that's Bruno's father – and a couple of others went over to the mainland to wild camp on Dartmoor.'

'You hadn't come out as gay, back then?'

'I didn't do that for years.' Sally smiled. 'I went along because I was secretly in love with Liz. She was so beautiful back then. But somehow, with too much beer and weed, everyone started to look irresistible. We were the last two around the campfire, so we ended up together.' She started to laugh. 'It could have been Jimmy Roskelly. That would have been awkward!'

Eleanor smiled. '*Very*. And my mother was conceived? It feels nice that it was an Ellis.'

'You know what they say, if you throw a stone on the islands, you'll hit an Ellis two times out of three,' Sally said, then her smile faded. 'Are you disappointed? It's hardly a romantic story.' She squeezed Eleanor's fingers.

'I think it's a very romantic story,' Eleanor said. 'Did you remain friends?'

'Not at all!' Sally said. 'He was a bit older than me and, in the morning, sober and hungover, I didn't fancy him at all. I didn't realise I was pregnant until I started having fits for the first time in years.' She looked down at her hands. 'I was working in a supermarket in Truro, sharing a flat with a couple of girls. They couldn't handle it. They called my mother to come and get me. Then I had to explain.'

'Was she upset?'

Sally shook her head. 'She was lovely, even though she must have been worried for me. My dad had died the year before. That's why I wanted to get off the island so badly. Mum was throwing herself into work, distracted all the time. She was horrified at first, that I hadn't learned the lesson from all those unmarried mothers coming to the home.' She smiled through her tears. 'She didn't warn me about *that* moment, when it seems like the most natural thing in the world and you don't consider the consequences. And I think she would have preferred us to keep the baby. Diana.'

Eleanor knew just what she meant. 'I'm going to meet up with Bruno while he's on the mainland. But don't tell anyone.'

'Well, I'm sure you know how to look after yourself. No surprise babies.'

'I promise,' Eleanor said. 'But Diana's unplanned baby was a wonderful gift for my adoptive grandparents, too.'

'Do you still see them?'

'Regularly. They live in West Sussex. Grandpa is a retired potter, he teaches at the local college sometimes. Grandma is a fundraiser for Save the Children. You'll like them.'

'How appropriate,' Sally said, trapping Eleanor's hand between her own. 'They sort of saved both of us, sixteen-year-old me, and your mother. Dorothy chose them specially.'

'Where were you?'

'I was in hospital, for two weeks. I had a lot of fits around the birth. So I never got a chance to bond with the baby and I didn't want to. But my mother spent every moment looking after the baby, although she never told me what she'd named her. If I had died, I think she would have wanted to bring her up, but she was nearing retirement and still broken by Dad's death.'

'Well, Diana went to a very happy home. But when she grew up she wanted a baby of her own, a biological family. She got pregnant at twenty by a boyfriend. Her parents supported her in keeping me. They helped bring me up, too.'

Sally hugged her again. 'Look at us, crying over a happy ending! You need to go or you'll miss your helicopter. They say they're all booked up for days.'

Eleanor threw her last toiletries in the bag.

'Last hug,' said Eleanor. 'We'll do the DNA thing. And if we're wrong, we'll just ignore it. You can adopt me. Or I'll adopt you. That's what this family does.'

50

JANUARY 1970

Dorothy held Sally's hand as they sat on the couch. 'And you're quite sure you're pregnant?'

After Hector – dear, darling Hector – had gone, Sally had gone off the rails and left school. She went off the islands with a group of visiting gig racers over the summer and came back thin, tired, penniless and pregnant, eight months later. Dorothy knew it was her way of flailing about to find anything that could ease the pain of Hector's death.

'I know I can't do as good a job as you and Daddy did,' Sally said, her eyes running. 'I can't look after a baby.'

'Even with my help?' Dorothy asked, but part of her knew the answer anyway. Hector's death had put years on her. She had a persistent cough, she ached in the mornings, she was starting to lose her energy. Age was catching up with her.

'You always said adoption was a wonderful choice for the babies and the new parents,' Sally said, settling against Dorothy on the sofa. 'Please help me. I'm no different from those other girls.'

The mother and baby home was winding down since

Hector had died, but there were a few girls still to deliver. Hopefully, they would be allowed to keep their babies – many did now.

'We can talk to the agency,' she soothed. 'But you have time to think about it. Do we need to – can I ask who the father is?'

'I don't want to talk about it,' Sally said, closing her eyes.

'He's not the man for you, then,' Dorothy said. 'Don't worry, the right one will come along for you too, like Daddy did for me.'

Sally shook her head. 'I don't think so,' she said sadly. 'I don't think… That's not going to happen for me.'

Dorothy tilted Sally's chin to look into her eyes. 'Are you trying to tell me you don't like men?'

Sally shut her eyes.

Dorothy hugged Sally harder. 'Well, that's all right. Whoever you fall in love with will be fine with me.'

'Daddy wouldn't have approved,' Sally said, her voice muffled in the cardigan she had knitted Dorothy for Christmas one year.

'Oh, you'd be surprised,' Dorothy said, starting to chuckle. 'Aunt Lena – his favourite sister – never married. But she did have rather a lot of lovely *lady assistants*, if you remember.'

'Her secretaries!' Sally said, fumbling in her sleeve for a handkerchief and blowing her nose. 'But he never said anything.'

'You are barely seventeen,' Dorothy reminded her. 'We should have had this talk a lot sooner.'

'I knew I *could* get pregnant,' Sally said. 'But it was only once. I mean, it wasn't horrible, but I don't want to do it again.'

'So why did you wait so long to come home?'

Sally's face was blotched and swollen. 'I didn't know about the baby at first. Then I had two fits on consecutive days, and went to the GP in Truro. They did a load of tests.'

Dorothy's heart had sped up when she heard about the seizures. Sally only had a couple a year on medication. 'Your blood volume has gone up, it dilutes the medication.'

'He said that. He also said there might be a chance something is wrong with the baby because of the medication. It's not the best in pregnancy. He started me on another one.' She rummaged in her patchwork bag and pulled out a pill bottle. 'These.'

'Well,' Dorothy said, slightly relieved. 'That's probably what I would have done.' She put her hands either side of Sally's face. 'I'm only part-time now. I just cover for doctors on holiday. If you want to raise this baby, we can do it together. But if you want him or her adopted, we'll find the best, kindest parents in the whole world.'

Sally managed a sad smile. 'Will the baby be all right? I've had lots of fits since.'

Dorothy grasped her shoulders and shook her gently. 'We'll look after you so well, he or she will be fat and healthy. I promise we'll do our best.'

'And you'll be there? When the baby is born?'

Dorothy nodded. 'As your *mother*, not your doctor. Dr McDonald will be there for that. I just want to be holding your hand and cheering you on.'

Sally lay back against the sofa cushions.

'Are you tired?' Dorothy asked.

'No. Just relieved,' Sally said. 'I didn't know if I could walk back into the house with Daddy gone. Let alone pregnant.'

'I would have thought this was the one house where you *could* walk through the door, pregnant,' Dorothy said wryly. 'I just hoped you knew enough not to get caught the same way the girls here had.'

'Apparently not,' she said, closing her eyes.

'Is this a good time to discuss your... biological mother?'

Sally rolled her head on the cushion to look at her. 'No. In fact, if you have any paperwork on her, get rid of it. I'll never want to see it. The same as I don't think this little scrap deserves to be saddled with *me*.'

51

PRESENT DAY, 11 NOVEMBER

Eleanor waved furiously at the welcoming party at the airport. It had been nearly three months since she'd been on the islands. She was coming *home*.

Bruno was quick to lift the bag off its stupid wheel, and Ruby flew into her arms. Sally was wrapped up in a purple velvet coat, smiling and looking relaxed. She looked better, as if she had emerged from a heap of worries and grief.

'Hello, sweet girl,' Sally said, when it was her turn. 'I see you cut your hair again.' She ruffled it. 'I know, it's such a grandma thing to say.'

'More like a mum thing,' Eleanor said, waving goodbye to the other passengers, all locals. 'I'm here for six weeks, it will grow again.'

Bruno leaned in for a quick hug, a kiss and a glance that promised more. Much more. Their few days alone at the London flat had been a revelation to both of them. He'd loved meeting her friends and colleagues, and she enjoyed showing him her favourite places. But every return to the flat was coming home to his arms, another night together. The flat had seemed so echoey and sad when he left that she had almost put it on the market. But Ruby was going to stay in the flat after Christmas with Michelle and her family, and she and Bruno would have two weeks alone in the farmhouse.

They hadn't talked about moving in together, but the possibility was there. She didn't really want to move into the seventeenth-century farmhouse with low ceilings and deep, stone windows. Bruno had stayed in London and absolutely loved it; the views, the museums, the bustle. They didn't have to choose one or the other. Ruby had chosen, though. She said she wanted Bruno to live with Eleanor so she could grow up, move out and travel the world. 'He'd be useless on his own,' she had said, rolling her eyes, but Eleanor wasn't so sure.

'Careful with that new bag! I don't want to break another wheel,' she said to Ruby, and laughed. As the plane was only half full, she'd been able to bring an extra bag of presents.

Ruby placed it in the back of Bruno's car with exaggerated care. 'Is my present breakable, then?' she asked, as Haze jumped up at Eleanor, demanding her strokes and hugs, too. She settled on Eleanor's lap in the back of the car while Sally sat in the front.

'Tell her, Sally,' Ruby urged. 'About Marina.'

'Oh, shush, you dreadful child. There's nothing to tell.'

'Sally has been internet dating!' Ruby almost shouted.

'I was thinking about boarding school,' Bruno said, looking back at Eleanor. 'Surely there's a nice Victorian one with gruel and stone cells we could look at?'

Sally laughed. 'I don't mind, really. I met a nice person, that's all. She's an actor, about my age. She's very good company. I might go and visit her. She lives in London, too.'

'Oh, where?' When Sally told her, she smiled. 'That's about a mile from my flat. You could stay at mine and still meet up. I'm determined to get you to stay with me.'

'That's what she said when I told her where *you* lived.'

'We'll look at dates, then.'

Sally's ears went pink.

'Sally?'

Bruno started laughing.

'She's booked a room at the bed and breakfast to visit for Christmas, too,' Sally said. 'She's flying in on the nineteenth after she's recorded a radio play.' She turned to Eleanor, still a bit flushed. 'I'd been listening to her for years on the radio, and never knew. I recognised her voice instantly, just couldn't be sure where from.'

'So *you'd* better come and stay with *us*,' Ruby said. 'Who knows what will be going on at the Doctor's House with Sally's new girlfriend.'

'Board games and jigsaw puzzles, mostly,' Sally said. 'All sorts of walks and possibly fireside reading. We're not children, we're just becoming friends.'

Eleanor understood instantly. They didn't have a biological imperative to form a family at seventy; they could allow their friendship to go wherever it wanted. They didn't have that pull that she had had to Bruno.

'Well, I look forward to meeting her.'

'If Dad and Eleanor are together,' Ruby said, a small crease between her brows. 'Does that make Sally my new grandma?'

Sally caught Eleanor's eye. 'If you become Eleanor's daughter, that makes me a *great*-grandma and I'm not sure how happy I am about *that*.'

Eleanor started to laugh. '*Great*-grandma? I hadn't thought of that.' She looked over at Bruno. 'I know it's too early to tell people—'

'They aren't just *any* people,' he replied, grinning back.

'I'm pregnant,' Eleanor blurted out. 'And no, it wasn't really an accident, more of an – impulse.'

Ruby shrieked with excitement and hugged Eleanor.

'So you're going to be a great-grandma anyway,' Eleanor said to Sally over the excitement. 'But it's early days.'

'So this baby would be related to me *and* you,' Sally said softly, 'and to Bruno *and* Ruby.'

'I only did a test a few days ago,' Eleanor said. 'It's miles too early for it to be a baby, really.'

'But it would tie all of us together,' Ruby said, leaning in to hug a stunned Sally.

Bruno looked at Eleanor. 'I have an announcement of my own to make,' he said. 'Not as groundbreaking and stellar as a baby, and yes, Sally, we did talk about a baby before. Not exactly planning it, just not caring if it happened. But I have been working with Tink on something.'

'We're not having sheep next year?' Ruby said, stroking Haze and pulling her ears through her fingers gently.

'No, we are – well, there will be sheep at the farm, anyway. Tink and his partner Corinne have a third of my flock on Morwen already, and they really want to get into microgreens and even dairy. They can rent the farmhouse and develop their business.'

Eleanor caught her breath. 'Is this why the two of you have been walking the land over the last few weeks?'

Bruno pulled his car up outside the Doctor's House.

'I didn't choose to be a farmer,' he said to them all. 'I came home from college to help my dad when he got ill, and took over when he died. But I was always going to be an engineer.' He looked at Eleanor. 'You love your job, your colleagues, the life. At least, at the moment you do. I don't want to make you choose to live on a rock in the Atlantic, flying back and forth every time you want to see us.'

'But I love it here,' she said, tearing up. A few extra hormones and she cried at everything. 'I really do.'

Sally put both hands over their clasped fingers. 'Well, I have an easy solution. You know I can't really cope with the Doctor's House indefinitely. How about you do up the old cottage in the garden for me, then you can start to move in here while you work out what you want to do. Tink and Corinne will be right next door, I'll never really be alone.'

Eleanor turned to Ruby. 'Could you move out of your child-hood home?'

Ruby scoffed at the idea. 'In a heartbeat,' she said. '*They* can have that ratty old kitchen. We get Sally's gorgeous house to stay in. Anyway,' she said, adding her hands to the pile for a moment. 'Soon I'll be off to college and then university and you can have the place to yourselves. Come on, let's go indoors, it's getting cold.'

Sally nodded as she got out of the car and walked up the path. 'And Ruby can finish school while staying here with me, if you're in London.'

Eleanor followed her in, emotions bubbling up. She covered her face when she walked into the kitchen. 'I don't know why I cry when I'm happy,' she wailed.

'You'll inherit the house anyway,' Sally said. 'You may as well make your home here before you move in long-term. Maybe when the baby has to start school.'

Bruno wrapped his big, warm arms around her. When she could finally look up, he was holding out a tissue, and Sally and Ruby were singing by the kettle.

'I know this is all going very fast,' he said, as she mopped her face. 'You can take as long as you like to decide.' She followed him into the living room.

'Are you mad? It's a brilliant idea,' she said, smiling with a wobbly lip. 'This baby may not come to anything, but...'

'There will be another baby.' He smiled. 'I can't believe I'm going to do it all again.'

'I hope she's like Ruby. Or he's like his dad.'

'I expect he'll be tall, like his mum,' he said, kissing her. 'And super smart.'

She stepped back, put her hand on his cheek. 'I'm going to have a real, biological relation again.'

'Along with Sally, and me and Ruby, related through our children,' he answered. He gave her another quick kiss. 'All ten of them,' he said, laughing, as he escaped back into the kitchen.

She sat down and leaned back against the cushions. She was so tired, so relieved that everyone had taken the news well. She looked around the south-facing living room, through the bay windows and the sparkling water beyond. She could just hear the sound of the sea curling up the sand, opposite the entrance to Springfield Lane.

'One at a time,' she told herself, smiling at the thought of her new family. Of a little bit of Diana and Sally and Bruno and Ruby tucked up inside her.

EPILOGUE

SEVEN MONTHS LATER

Eleanor traced the tiny face with one gentle finger. Snub nose, fat cheeks, rosebud lips pursed in her sleep. 'She's amazing.'

Bruno leaned over to kiss the baby's head, then Eleanor. 'We can't keep calling her Pixie now she's here.'

'She's too little to have a proper name,' Eleanor said, still unable to take her eyes off the face so close to hers. 'Hello, Pixie.'

'Ruby says we should call her that officially,' Bruno said, slumping into the chair beside her hospital bed. 'How are you feeling?'

'Tired, but OK. That epidural was brilliant. I'm glad she wasn't ten pounds, though.' She brushed her lips over the furrowed little forehead as the baby dreamed. 'I still like Ivy,' she said, looking over at him. 'Ivy Markham sounds OK.'

'Or Ivy Roskelly. It's your call, you did all the pushing,' he said, closing his eyes. 'What about a middle name? Sally, Diana?'

'How about your family?'

'My mum was called Jackie,' he said. 'My gran was Hilda.'

Eleanor made a face. As the baby made a little sound,

Eleanor held her breath to see what she would do next. She sneezed, making them both laugh.

'I know,' she said, stroking the dark hair on *Ivy*'s head. 'We only got together because one person found the best adoptive parents for my mum, and a way to find Sally. And that led me to you.'

'OK,' he said, smiling crookedly at them. 'Ivy Dorothy it is. Ivy Dorothy Markham.'

She rolled her head on the pillow to look at him, and smiled back. 'Ivy Dorothy *Roskelly*.'

A LETTER FROM REBECCA

Dear Reader,

I'm so glad you found *Second Chances at the Cottage by the Sea*. I hope you enjoyed meeting Eleanor and following her journey towards finding her family and future on the islands. I loved writing Dorothy's journey to becoming loved and respected as a doctor on the islands. If you enjoyed their stories, too, you can keep in touch with other Island Cottage stories by following the link below. Your email will never be shared and you can unsubscribe at any time.

www.bookouture.com/rebecca-alexander

I have spent many years living on islands and visiting them. I love a trip on a ferry; it seems like a new story is being written. My imaginary island of Morwen is based on the village where I live, and many wonderful islands all around the south-west of England, like Lundy, Guernsey, St George's and St Agnes. The cobbled alleys, narrow streets and tiny cottages all seemed to have their own stories – and histories. I encourage you to find a favourite island of your own!

If you want to support me and the Island Cottage books, it's always helpful to write a review. This also helps me develop and polish future stories! You can contact me directly via my website or X (Twitter).

Thank you, and happy reading,

Rebecca

www.rebecca-alexander.co.uk

 x.com/RebAlexander1

ACKNOWLEDGEMENTS

This book wouldn't be in your hands without a great deal of guidance and support from my editors, Jess Whitlum-Cooper and Rhianna Louise. When I agreed to write books for Bookouture, I found it a bit intimidating, but Jess was full of confidence and advice, and it has been a great learning curve. I enjoyed writing *Second Chances at the Cottage by the Sea*, my expert editors helping me make it into a coherent book.

Thank you also to the wonderful team at Bookouture, for continuing the process of presenting the novel by copy editing and proofreading. They also produce the lovely covers and understand all the marketing business. I am truly grateful.

Thank you to Kayleigh Parkhouse for being so inspiring and generous a person that she agreed to be in the book!

Much gratitude goes to my son Carey Bave, my first reader, who knows all my books. He keeps me writing, asks important questions and advocates for the characters all the way.

As always, much love goes to my patient husband, Russell, who also loves island living and gives me space and solitude to write.

PUBLISHING TEAM

Turning a manuscript into a book requires the efforts of many people. The publishing team at Bookouture would like to acknowledge everyone who contributed to this publication.

Commercial
Lauren Morrissette
Jil Thielen
Imogen Allport

Data and analysis
Mark Alder
Mohamed Bussuri

Cover design
Debbie Clement

Editorial
Rhianna Louise
Nadia Michael

Copyeditor
Angela Snowden

Proofreader
Jenny Page

Marketing
Alex Crow
Melanie Price
Occy Carr
Cíara Rosney

Operations and distribution
Marina Valles
Stephanie Straub

Production
Hannah Snetsinger
Mandy Kullar
Jen Shannon

Publicity
Kim Nash
Noelle Holten
Myrto Kalavrezou
Jess Readett
Sarah Hardy

Rights and contracts
Peta Nightingale
Richard King
Saidah Graham

Printed in Great Britain
by Amazon